DEZI GOLDEN

Soul of a Tantric

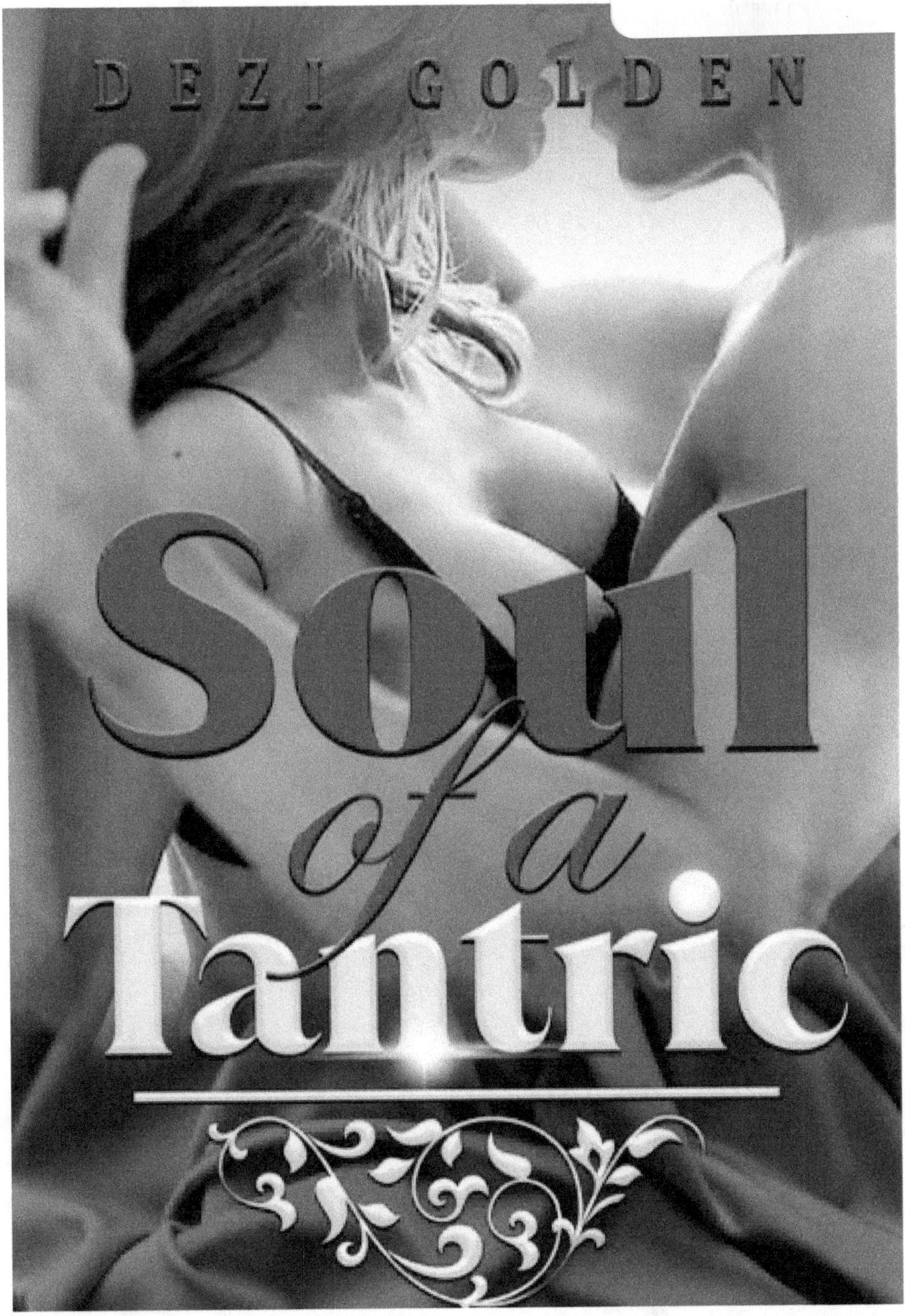

Soul of a Tantric

Dezi Golden

1st Edition

SOUL of a TANTRIC

Dezi Golden is an author, intuitive healer, wife, mother, and grandmother retired in the United States. At the age of ten, on long school bus rides to and from school in New Jersey, she began writing stories. Years went by. Careers in law enforcement, martial arts, massage therapy instruction, and relationship coaching put writing last. Dezi still made her books a reality for all to enjoy. This novel is the story the body wants to tell.

Other Books by Dezi Golden

BreathHealer Book I

BreathHealer Book II

The Kris

Guide to Living with CPTSD

Soul of a Tantric

Soul of a

Tantric

Dezi Golden

1st Edition

Soul of a Tantric

First edition 2021
Cover and book design by Dezi Golden
Printed in the United States of America.

ISBN: 978-1-7370464-5-5 (Paperback)
ISBN: 978-0-578-82353-9 (Ebook)
ISBN: 978-1-7370464-4-8 (Hardcover)

Contact the author at dezigolden@gmail.com

Table of Contents

Soul of a

Tantric

To All the Women and Men

*Brave enough to allow a **"Soul Love"** on this journey,*
I hope your flame reaches those who've been pushed out in the cold-

1

The Last Job
Riordan

Riordan Tate sits facing the mirrored bar, peering at his own reflection, from in between what seems like three hundred bottles of alcohol on the back display. He makes a mental note that he needs a haircut, before departing on *The Passionista* in the morning, for his last undercover job. He'll be posing as the yacht's most senior officer, and captain, to a crew of eighteen. He's not entirely sure how long this job will take. The cruise is a ninety-day tantric immersion retreat, but if his undercover team cannot recover the stolen items from the AdlerGetics scientific-engineer-turned-thief, Lubna Nathan, the job could take longer than three months. As the fake captain of such a luxurious super-yacht, his grooming is essential. As a real-life undercover security expert at the top of his game, he knows the job won't last two weeks.

Grant Aptone, Riordan's best friend and now former brother-in-law, turned security team member, returns from the bathroom and takes his seat again on the barstool to the left of Riordan.

"Everything all right?" Riordan asks, picking up his Guinness glass, staring into the bottom at the last remnants of the brown and cream beer.

Grant huffs, "Everything came out just fine, brotha! Wanna smell my hand?" Stretching his long arm out and in the direction of Riordan's jaw, careful not to actually touch him.

Riordan smirks, shaking his head, "No, fuck you very much. You took a while, thought I'd have to send in a search party."

"Ah, you know I like to finish what I start." Grant retracts his hand and uses his bar napkin to pat at the last water drops on his skin left by the energy-saving bathroom hand dryer.

"Right."

"What? I'm serious. Shitting is a masterpiece, man, master-pieces take time."

Riordan cracks a smile, "Sure, Grant. Tell that to the umpteen relationships you started and finished."

Grant laughs, "What? A shit-show, you think?"

"Certainly not a masterpiece, my man." Riordan chortles. Grant follows, shaking his head in agreement.

Rita, their busty bartender with a name far older than her twenty-two years, appears unexpectedly in front of them. Grant's eyes widen, his beer bottle almost to his mouth. He's astonished, yet again, at her perky promptness. She just appears, sometimes from below the counter. He wonders if she heard their odd exchange about his bathroom trip. As with most women, Rita's got it bad for Riordan, and Grant knows Riordan never sees it.

"Get'cha another, Tate?" Her voice, high-pitched and eager. She lingers with soft, puppy-dog eyes until he nods. Her body pivots, and she's at the tap with a freshly cleaned glass pouring Riordan's beer, her butt slightly tilted out. Grant's eyes pan from her butt to Riordan, back to her butt, back to Riordan…the man could care less! Grant huffs and shakes his head. Rita turns and places the beer down in front of Riordan, with a perfect head foaming at the rim of the glass.

"Thanks, kiddo." Riordan glances at his watch, noticing nothing about how much Rita tries to work her sex magic.

Rita turns and disappears before Grant can show her his beer bottle is almost empty, his smile moving to a lost-chance frown. "Shit. Could be a half-hour before she comes back around this side of the bar." Grant mumbles, not realizing Riordan is listening.

"Good." Riordan exhales.

"You know Tate, if you said more than just one word to her here and there, she might stick around longer."

"That's precisely the point."

Grant leans in, "Come on, man, she's been throwing herself at you for months. What's a girl gotta do?"

"Not throw herself at me."

"Oh, is that it? You'd prefer they act disinterested? You want the chase?"

"Not interested."

"Dude, it's been nine years, man. NINE…years, I miss her too but-"

"I'm aware of how long it's been, Grant. We don't need to go over this every time a young lady makes her presence known to me in a bar." Riordan's voice is low but calm.

Grant leans back and elects to ease up. At least Riordan speaks of Evelyn now. The first three years after her death, he only spoke in grunts, yes's, and no's. Grant misses his sister terribly, but he misses Riordan's vibrant personality more now. As the years have gone by, he's opened up here and there, but the fun, carefree best friend from childhood and college has yet to fully resurface. Grant can't think of a smarter guy or anyone with better character, and it's been that way since they were six-years-old yet, he's somehow quieter now…reserved. His light has dimmed.

"Feeling better about the job now?" He changes the subject, hoping it will ease the tension in the air.

"Oh, you mean about Adler? Nah, Adler's a hot-head poe-hunk, spoiled rotten cowboy, and this job could seriously tank if he has his hands too deep in it. I've got to keep ahead of him…and whatever sociopathic behaviors he'll throw at us this time. Luckily, I've arranged for the real captain and crew to be on a lower deck, operating from a control center I had Adler install. I'm hoping that will keep Adler busy. He's better when distracted by his latest spending spree."

Grant reiterates, "And how about you? Feeling confidant we'll get the microchip and vials fairly quickly?"

"I'm hoping, yes. We just have to look the part in the mean-time. At the moment, I'm feeling prepared with the plan. It's been a decade since I've run a ship crew. I'm a bit rusty, but, with you and those you've vetted, I'm shooting for a closed case between day one to four."

Grant nods, his confidence in Riordan the same. He's a man of very few mistakes. Even when he thinks he's making a mistake, it's usually not him. He still blames himself for Evelyn's death, but that wasn't a mistake. It was revenge. "What's Adler's deal anyway? Why's he always calling you? I thought you set him up with your guy from Belfast?"

Riordan nods, "Yup, did that. He lasted…how long has it been? Seven months? …and here we are again."

"What's his malfunction?"

"The fucker can't get along with anyone. He's a complete borderline personality. That's the fourth agent I put with him in eleven years. He's just a tall, bald, type-A, cowboy-hat-wearing-bil-lionaire with too much mouth and money and not enough brains. If he didn't pay all of us so well, I'd lose his number."

Grant agrees, "Errol Adler does pay well."

"This is it, though, Grant. I'm done after this one. I've got enough money, I need to build with it now. I've grown tired of all the baby-sitting. You ready to take over?"

"Rior, I'll do whatever you need, man, but you know you *are* Tate Inc. Besides, what the hell are you going to do with time off? Do you even know what time-off entails?" Grant feels bad as he says it. He knows Riordan had dreams to retire with Evelyn, and all he's done since her death is work and add to their fortune.

Riordan shifts his eyebrows, "I'll think of something." He sips his beer, contemplating what one should do first with upwards of 27.3 million in off-shore accounts. That island he and Evelyn dreamt of buying is now a dream in the wind. He's not interested in building anything for tourists. A house is easy, but a family with kids didn't happen. He figures he'll create some sort of training site for the Seal or Delta guys…maybe do contracting where he doesn't

have to run all over the world; instead, they come to stay on his island and leave.

"Like what? Playing with the coast guard a few days a week?
Hanging with Delta the other days? It's not good to risk your life
for no cashola, bro. Nobody gets a trophy for dying as a ride-
along."

"I can afford to. Money doesn't bring fulfillment, and tro-
phies aren't my thing. I'll settle for great memories and bonded relationships, thanks." Riordan takes a swig from his beer. He's tiring
of the taste.

Grant knows Riordan can afford it, and moves on to something that will yield more interaction. "Okay, so you only want my
two guys Isaac Owens, Oscar Griffins, and the woman, Constance
Levy? No more? I can bring the Russian as well. He counts for
two."

Riordan's eyebrows raise for a second, and his teeth show
through a quick smile, "He's one big motherfucker, isn't he?"

"He really is." Grant chuckles, "But he isn't as big as you,
man."

Rita appears again, no doubt because she saw Riordan smile,
a rarity, but a panty-dropper-smile nonetheless. He really doesn't see
how he magnetizes women to him. Grant shows her his empty
Heineken bottle, but her eyes aim at Riordan, hopeful, but he gives
her the sign that he's cutting himself off at three. She looks sad and
bounces her twins off to get Grant his beer.

"That's not true. Your boy has at least twenty-five, thirty
pounds on me."

"Yeah, in his fat ass, maybe, but height-wise I know you've
got him by three inches."

"Are you telling me you stare at our employee's asses now?"

Grant laughs out loud, "How the fuck does he put those
glutes in jeans, man? It's like two fuckin' baby hippos wrestling in a

pair of Levi's!" Riordan lets out a short laugh before checking his watch a second time.

"Shit, I really need to get going. Oh, and we got a job tomorrow, so wrap it up. No booty-calling tonight. We board at 0600. Don't be late!"

Grant looks serious, "So no big-booty Russian, boss?"

Riordan smirks, "No, leave your Russian on the wire. We should be okay if this goes the way we plan."

"Fill me in one more time?"

Riordan huffs before lowering his voice, "Errol Adler had a serious theft and security breach at AdlerGetics. He's almost positive it's a female scientific engineer he hired some years back from UCLA. He's got this superyacht he owns and chartered it out for some three month Tantra Toga retreat for couples. He somehow arranged that the scientist, Lubna Nayhan, and her Norwegian wife, Sagrid Hamsum, who is also Adler's contact and *side-piece*, are booked on this couple's cruise. It's going from this New York port to the Caribbean Islands, for some spiritual Tantra life-changing immersion stuff, then back here after the eighty-seven days. Plenty of time for us to work our magic and put this lab rat in her new cage."

"What'd she steal?"

Riordan leans in, "Adler thinks she stole the formulas... well the whole program from the computers, err...copies of them on a jump drive, little by little, over time, and also two vials of some DNA serum. Says her wife, Segrid, Sagrid, whatever...has been giving him the intel from watching her at home. I don't like the drama of it or that her wife has been fucking Adler, but the money is there, and the job seems a breeze, really."

"Yeah, but for what? Revenge? Money? It's got to be big if a billionaire is going through all this to catch her."

"It's DNA genetics stuff." Riordan smirks, "It really can't get into the hands of another country, if you get my drift."

"Oh shit! That's true."

"Yeah, we have to find both parts on this yacht; the jump drive, as well as the two vials of serum so they can't be tested and replicated by another party."

Grant closes his eyes as he sips his beer. He realizes how serious this job is. The last time they had a human genetics job like this, three agents got killed, and the collateral damage was horrendous, leaving Riordan and Tate Inc. in an almost precarious financial situation. Luckily, Riordan's reputation in the world of undercover operations is pristine, and the fault was not that of Tate, Inc. "That's a big fuckin' yacht, dude."

"It's large, yes. We have two weeks to find what we need and put her in jail. The sticky part is Adler is sleeping with our suspect's wife making this job uncomfortable. I've got to be clear on things before we turn her in. So far, my gut is telling me something is up. I'll need you four to stand in as top crew while I fill in as Captain but use Adler's go-to captain as a crew member and let him do all the shit that actually runs the boat and his people. I understand all the ins-and-outs of sailing this thing, but I can't do both jobs and properly focus on our mission. Besides, the learning curve of this superyacht could take two weeks, and I'd really like to wrap this up within a few days."

Grant frowns, "Wait, what about the rest of the crew and this captain guy?"

"They know the vague details about our mission…well, they know they have to follow the orders of their Captain, Nero Ufla, who'll appear as my co-captain. They know there's a confidential case. Adler lied and briefed them on us being security for one of the other couples who'll be joining. Apparently, his son and daughter-in-law are one of the pairs wanting the Tantra experience as well, so the crew thinks they're in danger, and we're investigating an abduction threat on Adler's son. Their names are Chance and Natalia Rubins."

"Wow, there are way too many elements already to this for my comfort Rior. But we've been in worse drama. Wait, Adler's son is Chance Rubins? The *surgeon?*"

"Yeah. Took his Mom's name or something, or Adler found out about him later in life, I think. Adler has eighteen crew on board. We need to focus more on our goal of finding what we need to find before we reach any of the island destinations. If not, this Lubna asshole can hand over the serums to the highest bidder, or worse, the fucking formulas to the science behind the serums and how they were invented. I don't want this to go any further because Adler has tense relationships with the government. I really don't need any involvement with them."

Grant sips the last drop in his bottle, realizing that Rita is not returning to him with a beer any time soon. "Listen, we could make this super easy. Let me visit this Luby whatever, and I'll get all the info and items needed. We can return them to Adler, get paid the rest of what he owes, and call it a day. Doesn't that sound better? We don't have to share the money with our employees...not even put them in danger. I'll take care of it all. You know I love a good two-week fling!"

"Well, Casanova, we *are* talking about Errol Adler here. His money, his way. Second, she's married...to a *woman*, Grant. I know you think you can turn any lesbian with your ways, but you haven't been completely successful at that...ever, bro." Riordan smiles.

"There was that Vicky chic, though."

"Noooo Grant, no. You, stepping in as a lab rat to an already established relationship at a seven-year downswing...that eventually crashed and burned, is not a success."

Grant laughs hard, his eyes squinting. He loves the memory.

Riordan smiles and shakes his head, "You were their experiment, man, an *ex-per-i-ment*..."

"Oh, man, was I! I was their very willing participant."

"Participant? Yeah, I'll say."

Grant sticks his tongue out and down to his chin like Gene Simmons and laughs. Rita returns with his new beer, pops the top, pushes it to him, grabs his empty bottle, and storms off, all in what seems like one motion. He raises his eyebrows in surprise and blinks a few times, watching her disappear down the bar to a few other patrons. He wonders if that was her "attitude" he'd heard so much about. He doesn't mind much. He's happy she didn't cut him off.

"Uh, ok, well, what about this tantra yoga stuff? What do I need to tell Oscar, Constance, and Isaac about it all when I brief them?"

"Actually, it's a Tantra Toga thing, not a Yoga thing."

"Yoga-schmoga, whatever. It's some weird fucking orgy boat shit, right?

"Wrong, Grant."

"Is tantra, just sex and uh, what the fuck is it, karma sutra or something?"

Riordan rolls his eyes, "See, there you go with your strange societal views, instead of doing your research, ginger snap! Just what I need in this line of work."

"In all fairness, Rior, you just told me the nature of this job five minutes ago. And what does *that* mean? You know I research shit!"

"True, but KAMA SUTRA and TANTRA should not be new to you. We learned about this in Bali, man. And what does WHAT *mean?*"

"Okay, okay, back up, man. What does *"just what you need in this line of work"* mean?"

"Well, we need to be pretty open-minded to things, for instance, *and as we learned on that job in Bali,* Tantra is not mostly about sex. The word alone means *inter-weaving,* actually. An interweaving of energy, mostly between souls, for a life bond. Sadly, we still live in a country with prudish Queen Victoria era thinking that rots minds into believing tantric energy as inappropriate. As if only cults, secret societies, or sex-crazed guru orgy types use tantra. Nothing could be further from the truth. He speaks low and smooth.

Grant inhales before responding, "Tate, I believe those are about the most interesting words I've ever heard you put into a paragraph." Grant tries to remember. "We learned this? In Bali?'

"Grant, you were there."

"I know, I know…it was a really long time ago, Tate. Like nine fucking years back, dude. We lost three guys on that mission. It seriously was a long mission too."

Riordan checks the door, he wants to head over to *The Passionista* yacht and get his office and living quarters situated to look as if he's been on the boat for a few years. He's got fake files and used office decor for his captain's office. He had Rupert deliver his belongings from storage and a few personal-looking trinkets with his name on awards from the naval academy to appear as if he was a graduate. Since his office quarters are huge and have a large closet, bathroom, and bedroom connected, he wants to complete the final installation of the hydraulic hidden door under the closet floor…for his and his team's weapons. He has too much to do before meeting with Errol Adler in the morning and wonders if all the conversation with Grant is purposeful or going to need to be repeated since he is on his fourth beer. "True, it was a long mission, one of our worst, so I'd think it'd be something you remember."

"I do remember it, man, even though I'd like to forget. That was the first mission we lost men on." He takes a long pause, as well as a long sip of beer. Riordan gives him a moment before continuing.

"Grant, the job was a cluster-fuck of a lesson. We've had a few. You did the best you could, brother."

"*We* did the best we could. We lost three, but we fuckin' saved many."

Riordan is pleased to see Grant isn't getting sloppy drunk and still has enough wits about him to recognize the positives. "Well, look, man, I've got to go tie up some loose ends before we depart. You alright here?"

"Wait, Rior, help me out with this Bali Tantra stuff."

"It doesn't matter; you're gonna be busy searching for a hard drive and serum vials. This mission is about retrieval, not *your* tantric bonding energy."

"No, seriously, I'm curious now. Did I learn this before and just blew it off?"

Riordan smiles, "You watch porn?"

"Watch what?"

"Porn."

"Not as much as I'd like." Grant smiles wide, raising an eyebrow. He's pleased with his own humor.

"Then you didn't learn much. If I recall correctly, you were more *sleeping* in Guru Pashna's meditation class, then absorbing her tantric lessons."

"Oh shit, Guru Kura Pashna! Wait, was she teaching all that?"

Riordan stands up from his barstool, stretching his six-foot-seven frame, towering at full height. He smiles, "Yeah, shit-brick. It was part of our mission to be in the class with Baresh's wife so we could tail her remember? We were supposed to be the gay American couple looking for enlightenment."

Grant, beer in hand, gently touches the bottle to his forehead, as if suddenly remembering, "Oh yeah! That was so much fun!"

"Loads." Riordan smirks, remembering Grant's eagerness to put on an overly affectionate performance for the other couples. Riordan pulls his keys out of his front pocket, scanning the bar, as he'd done all night, then rests on Grant's face.

Grant smiles, "Okay, man, I'll see you in the morning. We gotta go over this tantra-porn-yogi stuff. I'm confused."

"Yeah, yeah. It's like high school all over again. Me giving you the heads up, so you hand in intelligent-sounding assignments."

"Come on, we're here, aren't we?"

Riordan nods, "We are." Eyebrows raised.

"So why does watching porn mean I didn't learn much?" Grant pivots fully as Riordan moves towards the door and begins to walk with him.

"Think immediate gratification versus long-term soul-satisfying ecstasy."

"What the fuck?" Grant's eyes widen with interest.

"Porn versus Tantra Sex. Like your booty-calls versus Jeanine." Riordan stops and looks at Grant, knowing what her name does to him.

Grants shoulders sink, his eyes softening, "Steamy Jeanine..."

"Yeah." Riordan smiles.

"Aw, man, I can't believe you're bringing up Steamy Jeanine. I can't get that woman out of my fucking DNA, dude. You're killing me, brah." Grant exhales, rolling his eyes while sipping the last of his beer. He puts the bottle on the end bar and waves to Rita. "You know I would have wifed her up in a heartbeat!" Grant continues to follow Riordan.

"I know that, Grant." Riordan turns and gives him a reassuring look. "She's wife material."

Riordan pushes the first door open, holds it for Grant, and exits through the second door. They stop under the bar awning, pretending to be retrieving cell phones and keys, but both are undercover-scanning the area over each other's shoulders. "Oh, how I miss that woman, she's..."

"You cut her loose, Grant, leave her be. She's married now. Got a hubby and a house...all of it."

"I can't believe that fucker gets her arms around him every night." Grant shakes his head in disbelief. "She...ahhhh."

Riordan nods, "I know. That's the difference. You can have booty-calls, hook-ups, porn sex, immediate gratification, detached partners, whatever you want to call it. Or....tantric connection like Steamy Jeanine...the soul-stuff that makes you want to commit!" He walks towards his truck. Grant watches him and walks in the opposite direction.

"Aw, Fuck me..." Grant slumps his shoulders with marred remembrance.

Riordan chuckles, "She could've just fucked you...but she made *love* to your sorry ass instead...tantra style, yes?"

"Every time. You know I saw her a few months back, right?"

Riordan stops and turns, "What do you mean "saw" her?"

Grant smiles, waving his eyebrows, "As in, she "saw" me and I "saw" every inch of her."

"Are you fuckin' serious?"

"Dude, she came to my doorstep at my house. I was minding my own business...and she knocked on my door." Grant shrugs, holding a toothpick in between his fingers.

Riordan squints, "She all right?"

"Not really. Marriage isn't what she thought. Feeling loved, security, all that "American Dream" bullshit turned out to be bullshit for her. I feel bad, man."

"How bad?" Riordan rests his hands across his biceps, body language closing.

Grant lowers his voice, "Tate, I didn't do anything she didn't want."

"She's married G. Like, on paper married."

"Yeah, on paper. But, her body…err her tantra soul or whatever you were telling me, well…she keeps gravitating my way."

Riordan rubs his forehead, trying to think, "Grant, that's a dangerous game. That could come back to bite you…even us, the business. I don't mean to pry but are you at least using birth control?"

"It was only a few times, bro. I don't know what she uses. I can't refuse her. She needs me."

"How much? Like willing to leave her marriage needs you, like you settling down with her needs you?"

Grant steps closer, "When I'm with her, yes, it feels that way. I could take her away from it all I…I, don't pressure her. It's got to be her choice."

Riordan raises his eyebrows, "What about you? What's your choice?"

"Apparently, I'm smitten."

"Really?"

"Rior, I don't even want to look at another woman. I have no desire for anyone else." Grant looks at the ground as if realizing his loyalty to Jeanine for the first time.

"Well, I believe if it's meant to be, it will unfold, brother. I want what's best for you." Riordan reaches out and lightly punches Grant in the arm. "At least you'd stop wasting yourself on those less than Jeanine."

Grant shrugs, "Truth be told, I haven't really been able to be with others… I just don't have it in me."

"Wow, well, she's got you then. I really hope she makes the right choice. I hope it all works out." Riordan back up and starts to leave again. "You might want to wrap it though, brotha. You don't want fucked up little Grant's running around the globe with no daddy around. Or worse, being raised up by someone who isn't their daddy."

Grant exhales with regret, "You're cruel, man, you...are... cruel." He says it jokingly and knows no one looks out for him like Riordan. The guy has the biggest heart. He just keeps it hidden.

"0700, my friend. See you then."

"Roger that."

2

For the Money

Demi

Demi Greer closes the zipper of the second of her two travel suitcases. This one, unlike the first, actually consists of her personal belongings. The first case has all the program items, products, laptop, binders, client files, and props needed to effectively start couples on a ninety-day tantric bonded journey. She's not a high-maintenance gal, so she only packed for herself for three weeks, with the hopes of laundering her items and using them again for the weeks that follow. It's a *superyacht,* after all. It should have a laundry area. Her cell phone rings over on the end-table near her reading chair. She answers it, sinking down into her plush purple chaise lounge. She was adamant about taking the damn couch with her, from her Connecticut ocean-view home, before everything was seized when her *now-ex-husband* was arrested. Teo turned out to be everything a husband shouldn't be.

"Yes, sir."

"Demi darling, I've been calling."

"Yes, I know, Guru Nate, it's been a little chaotic, but I'm set to leave here in just a bit."

Guruji Nateo Amri is as calm and understanding as always. He's aware he did not give her much time to consider his offer. But that was the plan. He and her sister, Deidre Greer-Alva, knew they couldn't give Demi a chance to refuse this trip. She needs to get out of town and quick. The witness protection program would be more appropriate, but that was never offered since Demi wasn't a key player in the case against her husband's cartel crimes. Luckily, she didn't know much about his misdeeds, but that didn't necessarily make her safe. "Yes...yes, okay, so you have the port address, the directions? Thank you, sweetie. I really need you to do this while I heal up. I am happy you can go, and the three months will do you good."

"Well, of course, sir, I'm glad I can help. I'm sure they'll be disappointed to hear you're injured, though. Perhaps you can join us when you're feeling up to it?" Demi reaches for a flip flop with her big toe.

He chuckles softly, "They won't even think about it. You are the BEST instructor. They'll love you as everyone always does, Demi dear."

"Thank you, sir."

"Yes, yes…I've transferred the payment into your account."

Demi frowns, "Oh, I can do this for you, sir, no worries about money."

"No, no, no, my darling. You've started a whole new life. This income will help." He smiles to himself at the shock she'll have when she sees the large amount of money he sent her, and it has absolutely no ties to her ex, Teo Lazcano. He hopes that she'll open her own healing arts school with it, far away from Connecticut, New York, and anything having to do with Teo in the Georgia State Penitentiary. She's too talented to waste time in a tiny Connecticut town, trying to teach spoiled rich wives and husbands how to value energy more than their financial status.

Guru Nate and her sister, Deidre, worked together to help her get on her feet. Now it's time to highlight her talents in a way where she can give her gifts to the world and feel contribution and purpose. Teo was careless and took the life she loved away from her. Demi never deserved any of his antics, and Teo never deserved her.

"Well, this is only twelve weeks. I'm not sure how much more "new life" I can start there, but I'll try." She laughs sweetly. "Any other information you think I need to know?"

"See the Captain when you get there. Inform him of my fall and apologize for my untimely injury. Let him know you're my replacement on this retreat, and Mr. Adler approved of the change.

I've sent the paperwork already, so there shouldn't be a problem." Guru Nate doesn't share with her how he was surprised that Errol Adler called and specifically requested Demi. Although odd, Adler explained she was referred, and since there were couples chartering his yacht, he preferred a female instructor. He took that opportunity to tell her a little white lie about being injured in the hopes that she could immerse herself in her work and stay safe. The money is a ridiculously large amount, which he knows she'll invest and multiply. With his age a factor, he has no need for it and feels good being able to help her. He hopes she's safe and enjoys her three-month sabbatical.

"Yes, sir."

"Demi, have fun. You're a very good teacher, my Shishya. My favorite and the best of all my classes! I want you to enjoy this big boat, the students, the luxury…all of it. You deserve to be happy."

Demi smiles, "Thank you, sir, I'll try."

"Don't forget to journal. I'd love to have your experiences written down."

"I'll do that, sir."

"Thank you, my tantra daughter. I will speak with you when you return."

"You're welcome, sir, talk with you soon. I'll call from the yacht if I can."

Demi hangs up, grabs her charger from the outlet, and decides to get an early start on the road. The yacht isn't set to disembark until tomorrow, but there is so much to prepare for with a three-month tantra immersion. This is not a small group. She's done this many times before, but never on a yacht. She can't help but think how this time away can really help. With losing her marriage, her home, all her fortune, and her future, she hopes she's driving right into a whole new life.

3

The Answer Is No

Riordan

"Errol, it's not going to work. There's not enough time for me to properly vet her. It's unsafe, and with the type of mission we're dealing with here, I can't ensure her safety or that she's not involved with your suspect, Lubna Nayhan." Riordan is trying to calmly disguise his temper. He doesn't like that he's internally gone to anger so quickly. Errol Adler walking into his office, handing him a resume, and telling him the tantric yoga instructor has been replaced only hours prior to departure, would normally just agitate, but, today it's about to send him over the edge. All crew and guests had been properly investigated. The addition of Mrs. Demi Loczano is not all that problematic if the circumstances were normal. For Riordan, she is NOT normal…and he knows he cannot be near her. For mostly, VERY personal reasons.

"Tough shit Tate, it's a clock that can't be unwound now. The guru is injured, and his top instructor is already on her way here. She's the best out there, Tate, and even though this is a mission, I still have to successfully provide this tantra retreat to the couples who paid my hefty fee. You'll do fine. You always do. Now, what else should we clear up? You have everything you need?" Errol dismisses Riordan like he were one of his two-thousand-dollar whores. His big Texas attitude is almost as offensive as his billion-dollar worth.

Riordan stands, running his hand through his hair. He tries to solve the issue the way he always does, in his head, on his own, but he knows he can't get an instructor on such short notice. He just doesn't know of one for such an important subject, and he can't ask one of the agents to even fake it for the next few weeks. Sex can be faked; tantra energy cannot. He has to get out of this. Not only is it a conflict of interest from a previous case, but Riordan knows he should not be near Demi…ever. He was responsible for putting her husband away after an eighteen-month cartel FBI case. He watched her, heard how manipulative her husband was to her, allowed his connection to go too far, and his feelings ignite for her…all while completely ruining the life she knew. He tries every day to forget her, and now she's coming to him!

"No, Errol, I don't have everything I need. I *need* a new instructor."

"The answer is no, Riordan. She's the best and-" Errol Adler quiets, and he never quiets.

Riordan purposely has his back towards Errol. He leans his fists into the file curio and squeezes his eyes shut, trying to erase the vision of running Errol's face and body along the desk knocking all the fake photos and office supplies on the floor with his big, dumb, Texas comb-over balding head. This mission is fast becoming one he wished he'd refused. The only option now is to replace himself. He realizes Errol isn't speaking…and that a soft knock on the door jam had shut the fucker up. *Shit.*

Riordan turns around slowly, his breath pausing…his eyes lock on hers immediately, and he knows there's no way he's getting off this yacht. This is why he didn't want to even see her. Just the sight of her leaves him unhinged. He has no idea how much she's heard, nor does he know how's he's going to survive the coming weeks with her onboard.

"Demi Greer," Demi says softly and steps into the massive captain's office with her hand extended to Errol. He accepts, his face shaped into a slightly stunned expression. Riordan is annoyed yet knows the look. Demi is the most beautiful, sensual-looking blue-eyed woman he's ever seen. She's thin yet voluptuously curvy and looks like a goddess with her long dark hair hanging loosely around her face and torso. She looks every bit her Black-Irish roots, with creamy, porcelain colored skin and long, dark eyelashes engulfing eyes that pierce through the soul. She's absolutely breathtaking.

Errol finds words, "Hello, Ms. Lacz-err, uh Greer?"

"Greer, yes. Demi Greer. No longer a Loczano." Riordan closes his eyes a moment, pained that he caused her divorce, pleased she actually went through with it and ending her link to covert sociopathic narcissist and cartel leader, Teo Loczano.

"Well, my pleasure, darlin'. Errol Adler and this is Riordan Tate, Captain of this here lil' canoe." Errol moves aside, revealing Riordan's massive size.

Her eyes float up to meet his. Instinctively he steps around the desk towards her, offering a beautiful yet exhausted half-smile as her hand perfectly glides into his. He nods, locking eyes, feeling her warmth. The energy she emits hits him in the chest like a brick and travels down, causing a pulse in his body. He'd only ever dreamt of touching her. "Captain Riordan Tate. Pleasure, ma'am."

"Demi Greer. Nice to meet you. I'm a little early."

Riordan knows this…a whole day early, in fact! He just can't seem to be upset at the moment. All anger has dissipated, much to his surprise. "Not a problem. We can get you set up in your VIP quarters just as soon as I finish up here with Mr. Adler."

Errol interrupts, "Now, Ms. Greer, why does this paperwork here say Demi Laczano?" Riordan almost rolls his eyes. Errol's known for his inappropriate interviewing techniques. He steps aside and motions for Demi to sit in one of the empty chairs in front of Riordan's desk. Riordan returns back behind his desk, inhaling deep. Errol takes a seat, completely dismissing Demi's need to sit first, his etiquette as ridiculous as the ten-gallon cowboy hats he wears. Riordan wants to pull her chair out, but she's already beginning to sit.

"I've recently divorced sir, my maiden name is Greer."

"Oh, well, I hope that's an improvement for you." Errol crosses a leg, resting ankle to knee, his potbelly spilling over his large belt buckle.

"It is…very much, thank you. Small detour."

Riordan is pleased but saddened at the thought of destroying her family plans. He did enjoy solving and completing the Laczano case after almost two years of undercover work but absolutely hated hurting her. Before sitting, he clears his throat and points towards her, "Ms. Greer, may I get you a cup of coffee or tea?"

She smiles at him with her eyes, "No, no, thank you. I'll make some when I settle in. Thank you for the kind offer, though."

"Ms. Greer, how is Guru Amri? Is he very ill?" Errol is gentler than normal with his questioning, and Riordan is annoyed. The man treats women as possessions, and he doesn't want him speaking to Demi with any sort of interest. He wonders if he can get him to leave…and why he suddenly feels overprotective of her.

"No, no… he says it's going to take him a bit longer to heal up from an unexpected muscle tear." She smiles apologetically. "I also understand that he does not fare well on ships."

Riordan speaks, so Errol does not. He's sure Errol's eyes affixed to Demi's breasts would offend her. "And how do you fare, Ms. Greer?" He remembers she did very well on her husband's yacht. Days when she was in a safe view on the surveillance cameras were his more favorable days…but he could never share that with anyone.

"I absolutely love anything that floats." She turns her body towards him slightly, giving Riordan a pleasant smile. He stares at her perfectly plump lips and remembers them from all the surveillance recordings he'd studied. She's still perfect in his eyes. More beautiful now that she doesn't have Teo wearing her down. He knows he should put Grant in charge of this mission and excuse himself…but seeing her now, he knows there's no way he can be away from her.

"So no sea-sickness, fatigue, headaches? Anything in the past?"

"No, nothing. I love the ocean…and I am quite impressed with this ship. It's a superyacht, yes?"

Riordan is impressed; marina interests were not brought up during the previous years except when Teo was trying to spend money behind her back. Errol jumps in before Riordan can answer her. He spouts off the make and model, how many guests can be accommodated, and then roughly how much he spent on it. Demi listens but is unimpressed with his answers. Her body language is still turned towards Riordan. She looks at him and directs her next question to him.

"Do you prefer superyachts, Captain Tate?"

He stares into her deep blue eyes, "I prefer anything that floats." He blinks, smiles, his face soft and compassionate. She smiles back. Their eyes linger for a moment. She likes that he has a presence and lets her know he listens. She finds his answer appropriate and humorous. There's odd chemistry she's sensing. Unfamiliar but, stirring. She's noticing her body reacting to him.

Riordan breaks their gaze when he sees Grant appear in the doorway, knuckles up, ready to knock. He hopes Grant is in full work mode because seeing Demi Greer could make his jaw drop if he's not on his game. Grant hasn't been briefed on the abrupt change of old guru to updated gorgeous tantra instructor. It's a mystery what his best friend, and most trusted employee, might do. Riordan is still half-pissed at Errol for the unexpected change, but he knows the dumb bastard doesn't care. In all honesty, he knows she's not a threat to the security aspect of the mission. It's his damn heart he's more worried about.

"Yes, Apton?" Riordan nods to Grant, and when Demi and Errol turn to see him, Riordan gives him their eyebrow signal to "downplay" whatever is transpiring. He receives confirmation that Grant understands by the way he lightly clears his throat.

"Sorry to interrupt, Captain. We're ready for inspection when you are, Sir." Grant tries not to frown, and Riordan can tell that was not the sentence he was originally going to deliver.

"Thank you, Chief Mate Apton. I'll need more time here, and then I'll find you down below." Riordan flicks the corner of the roster he's holding, and Grant knows he is to "move things along". Riordan is pleased Grant's sharp today despite a few too many beers the night before.

Grant steps into the office doorway, "Mr. Adler, sir, can I walk you out? I have a question about the new window seals. Great choice, by the way."

"Well, I guess that'd be fine, son. Ms. Greer, can I interest you in a short tour of *Passionista?*" Errol Adler leans and places his palm on her shoulder.

Riordan inhales deep, calming his unease. He thinks how annoying Errol is today. She smiles, "No, thank you, Sir. I'd like to go over a few things here with Captain Tate regarding the next three months, if that's alright. I'm sure I'll get a tour at some point, or I can just wander around. I'm impressed thus far, great choice... in yacht." Her eyes dance, she gives Riordan a little wink.

"You'll know the *Passionista* by the time your clients arrive tomorrow, I assure you, Ms. Greer. We can't have you getting lost." Riordan keeps his elevating mood from affecting his voice, and smoothly answers. Grant averts his eyes to him, and his eyebrow lifts faintly. He's anxious for questions.

Errol stands, slapping his hand playfully on Riordan's desk, then nodding his hat towards Demi, "Well, that'd be my cue to de-part then. Have a safe cruise all. I hope you enjoy her as much as I have. She's one hell of a boat." He quickly shakes Demi's hand again and salutes Riordan on his way out the door. "Come on, Grant, let's go see those window sills and get your questions answered, then I've got to see a man about a horse." Errol exits, cackling his good ole' boy laugh.

Grant looks at Riordan one last time with his best concealed "what the fuck" look as he follows Errol out. Riordan nods to let Grant know he'll come find him when he can. He looks back towards his guest and is surprised to see Demi staring up at him. She crosses her right leg over her left. His training kicks in, reminding him she's right-handed, left-brain dominant, so her body language indicates closing her vulnerability to him. He finds it interesting how she's now going to her logical side and instead guarding her emotions with him alone in the room. All with a warm, inviting smile on her face.

"Captain Tate, let's have a discussion." Demi pushes her long black locks of hair behind her shoulders and smiles softly.

Riordan wonders if he's prepared for more discussion. This day seems to have a theme of "no" becoming "yes".

4

All Along

Demi

Demi is intrigued at how her body is reacting to Captain Riordan Tate. It could be the saltwater air, being newly divorced, the absolute divine scent of him… It could be the freshly pressed uniform over his incredibly fit physique. Yet, it seems to be more how he handles himself, the calm demeanor, the passion, and intelligence she senses. She doesn't think she's ever seen such a resplendent looking man, with perfect bone structure, evenly sculpted muscle under smooth, evenly tanned skin, perfect teeth, a well-groomed haircut, and faint salt-and-pepper colored beard indicating early forties wisdom and experience. She'd say he's forty-one, forty-two maybe. Although he's over six foot and intimidatingly large, there seems to be no fat on the man. She wonders if he's vegan. His skin reflects so, and his waist is very slim for such broad shoulders. She's been watching him, and he doesn't seem to notice his attractiveness. Crossing her legs, she squeezes her "parts" and inhales deep to draw the energy up and through her body. She wonders if he has this effect on everyone.

"I'm sensing you weren't properly notified of my participation in this retreat. Is it a problem for you or your crew, Sir?"

Riordan senses her body language stiffen a smidge further. He's sure she heard the conversation he and Errol were having as she walked toward the office and knocked. He hates not being able to tell her the truth, especially since he knows how good of a person she is and how she despised her ex-husband's deceptions.

"It shouldn't be a problem, Ms. Greer, I just prefer knowing ahead of time who my crew is, so I can keep everyone safe and trust who will do what, in an emergency. I also hope we can accommodate you and provide for your comfort here on *Passionista*." None of what he says is a lie. Riordan relaxes, taking a seat in his office chair, the large desk between them. He rests his elbows on the arms of his high-back chair, placing his index fingers together on his lips. He looks at her fully, realizing he has no idea how he's going to manage being around her these next few weeks. On the one hand, he knows he'll solve the case with Lubna Nayhan inside of a few days and turn the ship back over to Captain Ulfa; on the other hand, leaving her on the yacht for the three months after, is whats truly weighing on him suddenly.

"I'm flattered to be thought of as one of your crew. What can I tell you that would help you feel more trusting?" She tilts her head slightly to the right, her hands clasped in her lap. She's curious about him…and feels unnaturally relaxed in his presence.

Riordan already knows her, inside and out. She's the *best* kind of person. He knows her body too. He can't unsee her in his mind. She has no idea how beautiful she is. Even in her relaxed gray yoga pants and matching angel-winged shirt that says **Breathe** in big mistral-font letters on the front, she's just radiant. He's seen her at work in her old home studio, helping couples with tantra, assisting women and men in knowing themselves first, so they can grow in relationships. He's watched her sculpt her body, meditate, massage herself with the utmost care. He's even seen her swim nude in her pool. All of it through the lens of surveillance cameras. It means so much more now, meeting her personally and secretly knowing the character she has. Gorgeous on the outside but even more beautifully authentic on the inside. He hates to do it, but he's going to have to piss her off, so she keeps her distance from him for the duration of his time on this case.

He begins, "Do you mind if I ask you about your work?"

"I would expect you to. What can I share?" She straightens her back against the chair.

"Do you ever feel your tantra work should have saved your marriage since it saves so many other relationships?" As the words left his mouth, he wanted to cringe. It sounded better in his head… but again, he has to piss her off.

She narrows her eyes at him. "That's a very interesting and fair question. I'm thinking you may know the answer, Captain Tate."

Her statement startles him. "Oh?"

"Most begin with, 'So you teach that sex and orgy or weird positions stuff?' But you went right to relationship questioning. Have you studied tantra, Captain?"

He's relieved she isn't questioning him about knowing about her relationship. "Briefly, yes."

"And what are your thoughts? Or, better yet, what's your definition of tantra?" She rests her temple on three fingers, head tilted farther, awaiting his opinion. She wonders if he will spew off some definition of intense sex with weird positions as most do because of the stigma.

"Hmmm, well, it's more a personal preference for each, yes? In my understanding of it's Buddhist, Hinduism, and Jainism base...it's texts, rituals, techniques, monastic practices, meditations, yoga healings, and ideologies are freely selected without religion or cultural ties...oh, and no deity is needed, just a strong *personal* balance, or *desire of*, soul-mind-body alignment. Like true freedom, really. The kind that comes from knowing oneself and acquiring self-love."

She blinks and stares at him.

Riordan softly continues, his voice entrancing, "And...when that self-love is balanced, the *wrong* love leaves life, and only love that matches one's healthy vibration comes forward, creating bonds that last lifetimes. I'd say that's why so many life-long marriages come out of tantric commitment. Yes?"

By her stoic expression, he's not sure she understands him. "Or I could be way off base." He huffs in discomfort.

"I don't think you're at all *off* base." Demi continues to stare at him as if she's known him her whole life. He's super smart...and aware! She wonders if climbing across his desk and mounting him would result in being terminated before she's even started her new position. *He's probably taken. He's got to be taken.* If so, she admires the hell out of whoever gets to share his energy...and bed. She's never heard a more profound explanation for Tantra. She wants to know more about him, "And tantric sex?"

He wonders if it's appropriate to answer. He decides to continue to speak in a professional manner, "I feel that comes later...."

"Later?" She quips.

"Yes, and energetically. Like a magnet."

"How so?" She's curious.

"Well, it's been proven psychologically and scientifically, that when one loves him or herself **first**, you know, as in *really* develops their interdependence, it creates a vibration, an energetic attraction that emanates out. Often times, this energy brings a match to another's energy that is the same vibration." He pauses, softly dragging his fingers down his lips. He shifts his weight in the chair, leaning on his left elbow.

She's almost holding her breath, "So you believe in soulmates? Soul sex?"

"Well, that's energy too, yes? Isn't that what tantric sex is about?" His eyebrows raise with his questioning.

She smiles, glancing around at the photos of him with various groups, employees, and his dog. No ring on his finger, no family photos. "Well, I know that, Captain Tate, but I'm pleasantly surprised to hear that you do as well. I can't tell you how refreshing it is to hear something other than the normal taboo bullshit." She raises her eyebrows, bringing her three fingers up and over her lip, playfully, "Oops, can I say bullshit?"

Riordan laughs out loud, briefly showing perfectly straight, white teeth, "Yes, you can say bullshit."

She smiles at him; his face is so jubilant, and his laughter contagious! She loves how his eyes squint as his happiness shows in every feature on his face. She hopes to see him laugh more. "Okay, good."

"After all, it is bullshit. I've been around the world, and I can say with all honesty, the contradiction of lies put forth in *some* countries is tragic *bullshit*."

"Wow, that's something coming from a military, man." She's enjoying their exchange and points towards the photographs showing him in uniform.

He nods, and although pretending to be a captain, is no stranger to high-rank military training, "I love my country Ms. Greer, but only the true parts, the other stuff and the game I've had to play...uh, not so much."

"I can understand that. Well, I thank you for your service, the true parts, especially." She smiles again, glancing at his physique in the chair, admiring his *true* parts.

He wonders if they're flirting and realizes he's been enjoying their conversation way more than he should have allowed. He's trying to figure out how he'll be able to distance from her when it's so enjoyable and easy to be around her. He feels just as drawn to her as years before. He looks around, trying to change the subject.

She senses his regret, "Well, Captain Tate, I'm honored to discuss my work with someone who understands the seriousness of it all, that it's not about immediate gratification, external looks, and temporary relationships. I hope to help as many as I can on this retreat."

"I'm sure you will, Ms. Greer. They're lucky to have you. Anyone that gives tantric energy a chance deserves the amazing life it holds for them." He stands up, towering over her, even across the desk. "I'll take you to your quarters now. We need to get you familiar with *Passionista* and comfortable with your new surroundings." He politely smiles, placing one hand behind his back and motioning with the other towards the office doorway.

She's sad their great conversation is cut short. She stands and walks as he follows, and as he nears her, she purposely slows her stride. His energy is more than she's ever dreamed of, and as she turns, not knowing where to go, she feels peace...a calm she's always wanted, almost as if she's known him all along.

5

It Won't Matter

Riordan

"First Crewman Daemon, you have all surface security and crew reporting? Second Crewman Lee, you're comfortable with the kitchen and housekeeping? Third Crewman Jennings, you've got engine room and surveillance monitors?"

"Yes, Captain...err, Sir." Grant smirks, answering for his new *fake* ship crew comprising of his new field agents.

"That's okay, it's Captain in front of all the guests and staff. Remember, the actual captain and crew are two decks below running things. We shouldn't see them unless on the monitors. They'll move about down in their own areas and exit and enter when at ports, but that will be from their own private door and only when I give orders. They cannot be seen by anyone."

Grant steps forward, "Okay, any questions about who's doing what?"

"No, Sir." They say in unison. Riordan enjoys the employees Grant has working for him. They're very proficient in elite security skills, as well as great actors for the diverse roles they are given. He especially likes the uniforms Grant picked out. They all look like yacht crewman with *Passionista* stitched into their polo shirts, tactical khaki shorts that hide all their weapons, and impressive matching boater shoes.

"Dismissed. Check in with me at your designated times. I'll be in my office or patrolling above. And keep your ear-piece tucked way in, no mouthing or speaking if anyone can see you. Wipe your ear, and we'll all know by the swiping sound that it's not a time where you can answer. Okay, all? Have fun getting acclimated now because we set sail tomorrow at 1600 for a nice evening sunset departure." Grant nods, and the three agent-crewman nod back and exit the small supply room. He closes the door and turns wide-eyed.

"Yes, I know," Riordan answers even before he speaks.

"What THE FUCK Tate! Did you know?" Grant flings his fingers off his forehead, pointing his arm towards the ceiling to indicate Demi two decks up.

"Only about twenty minutes before you. Nice non-reaction, by the way. I know you wanted to shout out loud, and I'm so glad you were on your game."

"I told you, brotha, I only drink between jobs." Grant snickers.

"Yeah, good thing. I wasn't sure if you were still sauced from last night."

Grant leans against the back wall, "Dude, fucking Demi Laczano?"

"Yep."

"How the fuck?"

"I'm still trying to figure it out. I wanted to smash Adler's face on my desk when he showed me the paperwork. The fuckin' Guru guy who runs the Couples Tantra retreat is injured, so he sends his top protege' in his place...Demi Greer!" Riordan's voice is low.

"There's no way to even fix it or replace her?"

"Grant, I've got no time, and who the hell could I vet better on the subject than Demi? And...she is a really decent person so." He leans against the wall and puts his head back. Grant stares across at him.

"True. Wait, Greer? Oh shit, she's divorced? Oh, and that body...aw Rior, *that body.* I can't..."

Riordan points a finger at him, "Stop. She's a former subject." His warning much deeper than her being part of a former job they had.

"No, no, you're right...but dude, Demi Lacz- err Greer. She's...she's just..." Grant sucks air in through his teeth.

"Enough. We've got to get this job done, and the sooner, the better. She's got a job to do, and so do we. She'll just be a subject on a second case." Riordan is speaking not only to Grant but to himself as well. He needs to keep away from her and focus on the real subject of the case, Lubna Nayhan.

Grant smirks, "You're right. It won't even matter. She's going to be doing that tantra stuff anyway. We won't have much contact with her, right? I mean, she's not even going to be around much other than teaching and coaching the couples, yes?"

Riordan gives him a look. He runs his hand through his hair, then down around to his beard. He certainly hopes so.

"Oh shit, dude, did Adler put her in a VIP suite?" Grant half-whispers.

Riordan sticks his bottom jaw out, moving it side to side… thinking. VIP means she's too close to him, on his same deck. He looks at Grant and reluctantly nods.

Grant smiles, "You mean the big ass VIP suite down the hall from yours?"

Riordan nods again, "I just took her there with her bags. She's making herself comfortable." He exhales, "Fucking *Errol.*"

"Oh, wow, good luck, my brotha. He gave her the best room. He must want to impress her."

"She was impressed; hell, *I* was impressed. Have you seen that suite?" Riordan shoves a thumb towards the ceiling.

"It's for the Captain's guests or family. I saw it when we conducted the security sweep this morning. Pretty bad-ass. Living room, office area, wet bar, windows galore, four-post huge bed… and that master bath with the two-person jet tub! Super nice. Definitely more for a woman, with all the flowing cream-colored fabrics across the ceiling and the canopy part of that bed. That's baby-making shit, Tate." Grant has his hands in his front pockets, still leaning against the far wall, nodding convincingly.

Riordan nods, attempting to remove the thought of Demi in the baby-making bed, "Yeah, well, she's a woman, so she'll enjoy it. We've got this Lubna issue to monitor. Has all the crap been removed from her room? There's nothing in the way of the cameras?"

"Yes, we've got everything in place, and she can't change her mind and shit. She may throw a fit if she expects to be on the same deck with the other couples, but I'll tell her there are only so many rooms on each deck, and she and her wife's room is the next one down. I'm hoping it won't matter. From the footage I went over, she seems pretty distracted. She's definitely acting like she's got something else on her mind." Grant stands upright, looking at his watch. "Fuck, I've got to go meet up with the other crew now. Listen, you need me anymore tonight?"

"No, I'm going to go unpack and grab a power nap before dinner. See you then?"

"Oh, you want to do dinner?"

"Well, Ulfa has his cook serving us up on the top deck. He says the guy is a fanatic about the Captain's dinners, and since the cook thinks his boss has gone home for a wedding and I am his temporary replacement, I have to at least be at dinner most nights." Riordan stands to his behemoth height and opens the door for Grant.

"Okay, if you say so. I wouldn't want you to have to eat alone...and we don't want it to look weird." Grant teases, and Riordan grabs the back of his neck playfully.

Through clenched teeth, trying not to smile, "It's not going to look weird, you ass, you're my first mate. It'll be business. We'll talk shop, make this neurotic chef happy, and I'll retire to my quarters most nights so as not to run across the guests too much. You know, be the elusive Captain no one sees."

"Okay, boss, if you say so but, you've always been more hands-on, lingering type...just so ya know. And watch out for that sweet ass- err Ms. Greer there, down the hall."

"Hey! No more of that. It's going to be an easy, smooth case. In less than a week, we'll be sipping crown at some beachfront bar, talking about how we're going to invest the last installment of the remaining obscene amount of money Adler will transfer into the business account. I may need you to sign some papers." He turns to walk a different hallway.

Grant nods, "Got it. Just remind me." He never worries about money with Riordan. The man is more than fair and has made Grant a millionaire a few times over.

"I am reminding you, Grant."

"Right!" Grant fades off down a different hall. Riordan shakes his head. Satisfied that everyone has their assignments, everything they need, and Grant is set, he makes his way to his room to further unpack and try to get some sleep. He hopes to avoid Demi and lock himself in his cabin, then again...deep down, he hopes to catch a glimpse of her too.

6

Appreciation
Demi

Demi lies in the middle of the enormous bed in her VIP suite. She looks up at the sheer fabrics swirling through and around the four pillars of the bed. The entire room is dressed in different shades of creams and whites against masculine dark espresso wood furniture built into the walls. It's truly exquisite, and the contrast between the masculine and feminine energies makes her feel balanced and calm. She could get used to such luxury again. She could get used to seeing Captain Riordan Tate in her suite as well, his dark hair against creamy white sheets. He stirs something inside her, something she's never felt before. He's quite attractive, but what she likes more is his mindfulness. He's so aware of his surroundings yet, able to speak of worldly topics with well, thought-out research. She finds it easier to respect his intelligence and authenticity. With Teo, it was difficult to respect him with so many secrets. She thinks about how lovely life is now that she doesn't have to live in so much uncertainty. It seemed living with less would've been more difficult…but, less is definitely more in her opinion now. She praises herself for the contrast and for recognizing gratitude from the awful situation. Luxury is nice but only when you can appreciate it. She's definitely appreciating this tiny trip so far.

Her mind shifts. She's ready for her new clients to arrive tomorrow; tonight, she decides to treat herself to dinner in New York before departing for the Caribbean tomorrow. She jumps up and skips happily off to the massive jetted tub to relax before putting on her little black *strappy* dress with her favorite black *strappy* heels. A night on the town, with an amazing vegan meal, is just what she needs.

7

Amok

Riordan

Riordan startles awake, eyes wide, looking up at the ceiling. *Bam, Bah, Bam, Bam, Bam.* He hears Grant's signature knock and jumps out of bed to get to the door.

"Cap'n Tate, Sir!" Grant calls him by his title. He flings the door open half-awake, ill-prepared for the sight of her standing next to Grant. Suddenly, he wishes he had thought it through before opening the door, his shirt off, uniform pants on, bare feet protruding out from the bottom of his trousers. *Shit*

"Yes, Apton." His sleepy eyes meet Grant's then down to hers. "Oh, Ms. Greer, my apologies." He uses the door to half-shield his chest, his eyes trying to focus. She looks incredible.

Demi steps back in her heels, unable to unsee the exquisite sight of him shirtless. She doesn't speak. Grant gives him "the look" while maintaining his cover, "Very sorry to disturb you, sir, Ms. Greer was heading into the city, but I mentioned to her that you requested she join *you* for dinner." Grant twitches an eye, and Riordan registers that she was trying to leave the ship, and he stopped her with a bogus invitation to "Dine-in with the Captain".

"Oh, oh yes. One moment please." Riordan closes his cabin door, rushing over to put his bathrobe on so he can invite them into the common area quarters of his suite. He squeezes his eyes shut and takes a deep breath, trying to compose himself. He can't believe how fucking gorgeous she looks in her black dress and matching six-inch heels; her hair half up half down is not lost on him either. She makes his heart race. He opens the door, "Come in, come in. I thought I'd catch a catnap, but I must have been more tired than originally thought. Let's not talk in the hallway." He motions his arm outward guiding them both into the sitting area of his suite.

Grant motions for Demi to enter ahead of him, not quite sure if he's still needed. He's sure Riordan does not want to have dinner with Demi but, it was all he could think of to get her from leaving in the Uber taxi she had waiting on the dock. "I didn't want to disturb Ms. Greer's unpacking, so I didn't extend your invitation in time. I found her getting into a taxi heading to "The Greener Leaf" for dinner."

"Oh, I see." Riordan plays along, "Ms. Greer, it is customary for some guests to have dinner with the Captain the first evening they arrive on *Passionista*. Since you're our first guest, can I interest you in a small feast with me on the top deck, Salon B?"

Her eyes trail up the opening of his navy blue bathrobe and rest on his sleepy gaze, "I was going to spend the evening in the city before we depart tomorrow..."

"Oh, I see."

"But I would love a meal out on the deck with...such a lovely sunset. Thank you for the invite." Her voice is smooth and calming. She wasn't so sure her feet would survive such high heels in the city anyway.

Riordan smiles. He looks to Grant, then back to Demi, "My pleasure, I'll just be a few moments." He points towards his master bath, indicating he'll go shower and be there.

Grant raises his eyebrows, "Sir, shall I show Ms. Greer to Salon B?"

"Mr. Apton, I'll just sit right here if you don't mind. I could use the rest. This yacht is quite large, as my feet are just now telling me so." Demi walks over to the library area and takes a seat facing them. "I'll be fine." She crosses her legs and begins turning through the pages of Riordan's rifle magazine, determined to stay put.

Grant looks at Riordan apologetically, "Okay, well, I'll go notify the chef then." He turns his back to Demi and gives Riordan a "you lucky bastard" look as he says, "will there be anything else, sir?"

"Will you be joining Ms. Greer and myself, Apton?"

Grant squints and smirks, facing Riordan, "I've eaten, sir, but thank you. I have a few more deliveries to clear before my shift ends. Perhaps I can join you for a nightcap."

"That would be great." Riordan watches him depart, realizing he's alone, in his private quarters, with Demi Greer, just on the other side of the room. All to keep her from running amok in New

York City alone. He looks over at her, glowing skin peeking out from everywhere; her tiny dress doesn't cover much. He shakes off the thoughts...knowing *they* can never be. She looks up from the magazine to meet his eyes, the quiet from Grant's exit surrounding them. She thinks he is just divine. He says while backing away from the room, "I'll be back shortly. There's water in the fridge...cocktails over there at the bar. Please help yourself."

"Take your time." Her eyes follow him...*oh my.*

Riordan locks the bathroom door, just in case. The day has gotten stranger as the hours have progressed. This is not going the way he'd planned when he woke up at 0500 this morning. He feels he's getting weaker and more lenient being around her, yet oddly it feels, *right?* He runs his hands through his hair and tells himself *it's just a week. Just get through the week, solve this case, and everything will be fine, Tate.*

8

Horizons

Demi

"Thank you."

"My pleasure." Riordan pushes her chair in for her. She watches him make his way to his seat, admiring how wonderfully snug his dress slacks are. He looks so nice she almost wishes there was somewhere they could dance. She's curious as to how his energy would feel up against her. So far, it's divine from a slight distance…and walking together in the halls. His scent makes her almost weak in the knees.

"I'm really impressed with this yacht. That view is amazing!" Demi points towards the setting sun on the horizon.

Riordan turns to look over his shoulder, "It's really something." He turns back, giving her a small smile and putting his napkin on his leg. "I've never tired of it." He's seen the sun come up and go down all around the world, and he's always grateful to be able to admire it in yet another location.

"Do you find you ever tire of the sea?"

He shakes his head, sipping water. "No."

"Not even a little? Don't you miss your family?" She's curious.

Riordan doesn't want to get personal. He could lie, but he doesn't want to lie to her…ever…again… "Not even a little. And not much family to speak of…an uncle in Seattle, with his son, err, well my cousin, in San Diego."

"Are you close with your cousin?"

"Not really. *He* is now a *she*. I try, but…"

"Oh."

He smiles, "*She* doesn't really approve of military men."

"Oh, I see." Her eyes narrow as she smiles. She's pleasantly surprised he doesn't have a problem being open-minded. "So tell me, what do your days consist of in that huge office over-looking the uh, steering area there?"

He enjoys the way her eyebrows raise slightly as she asks him questions. He remembers watching her on surveillance and thinking she looked like a beautiful little child, inquisitive and seeking answers. "The bridge? That's actually a very important area of the vessel."

"It looks it, but I've only seen the office part."

"Right. Well, the desk is where most of my work is done. I have to be in compliance with immigration and customs regulations, maintain the ship's certificates and documentation, update the vessel's security plan as we move from area to area, as mandated by the International Maritime Organization." Seeing how attentive she is, he continues. "Respond to and report any incidents and accidents, including injuries and illness among the ship's crew and passengers, uh…did you want to know all this?" He checks in, just in case. He's done all of it in the past, but surveillance, security, and solving cases is more his forte' now.

'There's more?" Demi smiles.

"Just personnel and payroll stuff, but I don't want to bore you." He unbuttons his shirt sleeves and rolls them up, exposing defined, muscular forearms with just enough hair. He's a bit warm in black evening attire out in the setting sun. An older short woman appears with a bottle of white wine and a bottle of red. She smiles wide at Riordan, and he addresses her sweetly, "Hola, Gerdie. How are you today?"

She nods to them both and presents both bottles to Riordan, "I'm well, Captain Tate, thank you, red or white this evening?"

Riordan looks at Demi, "Do you have a preference, Ms. Greer?" He knows her answer already and forgets to even ask if she likes wine. *Ahh, Tate! Come on, man, you're slipping.*

"I'd love red, please."

He brushes off his mistake recognizing how she relaxes him a little too much, "I'll do the same, Gerdie, thanks." Gerdie pours him a taste. He checks it, nods, and takes the bottle. Gerdie scurries away in her super clean uniform and apron. Riordan's pleased with the staff that's been provided so far and how easily they've acclimated to a new captain for this trip. He pours Demi's glass first, and then his own.

"So, do you have any time for yourself or just dinners?" She sips her wine and likes the deep oaky taste.

"I have an equal balance. That's the perks of an elite crew. We work as a team and cross-train, so there's often someone to cover someone else's duties." He's talking more of his security team, but it applies to the yacht crew...in theory.

She smiles, "I like that. It sounds like you're a great manager." She watches his face to see how he takes a compliment. He's staring down into her eyes, studying her as well.

"I handpick my crew. I think it's important to match personality, as well as experience, with such a small vessel. Close quarters and all."

"You think this is a small vessel?"

"Compared to a carrier with 5,000 soldiers, yes."

"Oh, yes. You're a navy boy?"

"Something like that."

She tilts her head slightly, "Ah, so you hitched rides." She winks and smiles.

He loves how intelligent she is; it's such a turn on. He changes the subject, "So were you headed to see family before I pressured you into dinner?" He looks down her body at her tastefully provocative yet classy black dress. Her skin is glowing from a glitter moisturizer mixed with the evening sun.

She looks down at herself, "Oh, oh well no...I mean, I was going to take myself out on the town. Dinner...dancing. I don't know. It's been a while since I've been out and enjoyed myself. But this, this is much nicer."

Riordan smiles appreciatively. She's newly unhitched, he knows she's got a seductively slow wild side, boy does he *know*. She's gonna be working for the next twelve weeks straight, helping other couples with their lives...she probably needs a night to just be *Demi*. He wonders if he should have let her go. *No*, he can't. It would have been unsafe, and now that she's near, he doesn't want her away from him...*ever*. He's enjoying their time alone...despite knowing they shouldn't be and that he can never *be* with her. He'll take just conversation then. Being in her presence makes him feel alive but calm and peaceful.

"Thank you for joining me. I do apologize if I've thwarted your plans to go dancing. Dinner I can help with, but dancing is about the only activity we do not provide on *Passionista*. No room for a band." He jokes and sips his wine watching her.

"Oh, I'm pretty sure that big area there inside between the bar and that first living room would do just fine." She points towards the glass sliding doors and the massive deck Salon on the other side of them.

He looks over, seeing a very large amount of floor that could be used for dancing if the stereo or wifi television was put on a proper volume. He's impressed with her creativity. "Well, it's carpeted."

"No problem, mon, deez shoes come off!" Demi's inner child comes out in the form of a Jamaican accent attached to a gorgeous long, porcelain leg she hikes up to display her footwear. Her eyes are wide as she delivers her joke. The wine is working its magic.

Riordan laughs out loud and surprises himself. "Ah yes, bare feet can work well on carpet."

"Captain Tate, do you not dance? I'm sensing some resistance." She puts her leg back down, leans in with her elbow on the table, looking deep into his warm brown eyes as she awaits his answer. It's been years since she's flirted. He makes it feel good.

Riordan loves to dance. It's been years since he's enjoyed it, though. He's had to dance with other women or co-workers while undercover on missions, but to dance with Demi would be heaven…not a *have to*. He quickly erases the visual from his mind. "I dance just fine, Ms. Greer, but it's not something the Captain is always able to do when in charge."

"Oh, I see. Not even if your uh…wife is sailing with you?" She's prying. He has no ring on but wears a beautiful bracelet, watch, and matching necklace. She's aware of no tan line on his left ring finger, but a girl can't be so sure these days.

He smiles at her as he sips his wine, "Wives don't accompany employees. I'm on duty, and I do not *own* this yacht." He's aware he did not give her an answer, and he's trying to remain professional.

"But you may drink?" She teases.

"At dinner, yes, especially when docked." He likes her sass. He fears if she really wants to go dancing after dinner, she'll do so. He can't stop her. He'd have to have Grant tail her, though.

She takes a large sip from her glass, he watches her lips. "I like that." She's aware he's not answered the "married" question. She'll find out.

Gerdie returns with two plates holding large bowls and sets them down. She refreshes their water, nods, and leaves again. Demi grins from ear to ear. She has a titillating bowl of sugar snap pea and carrot soba noodles, topped with plenty of cilantro and a thick lemongrass sauce. She closes her eyes and inhales deeply...taking in the aroma. Her mouth salivates, and she opens her eyes to see Riordan smiling at her food immersion experience. She locks eyes with him and smiles wider. She looks and sees he has the same dish.

"Ms. Greer, that sounded like a universal tantra breath if I ever heard one." He chuckles deep in his throat while reaching for his set of jade chopsticks.

"Oh, it most certainly was! The scent is divine." She loves that he's eating the same meal she is. He hands her a set of chopsticks, and she touches his hand as she receives them. His skin is warm. She feels exhilarated. *He pays attention!* She can't ever remember a man paying attention to how she breathes, let alone know how and why she's doing it. She wants to taste him, even more than the dish before her. "Are you vegan, Captain?"

He's waiting for her to take her first bite, "As much as I can be, yes."

"By choice?"

"Yes."

She finally takes a bite. He does too. She closes her eyes and chews so slowly, he finds it difficult to concentrate on his own bite of food as visually she's so attractive. The chef is five stars all the way, and not just on paper. The joy on Demi's face makes Riordan happy. Just spending these moments with her, he knows he'll never forget this. Her energy is everything he remembers from years prior. *Infectious.* He finds pleasure in knowing he can make her happy for this moment...after knowing how her life was turned upside down. Demi's pain was his greatest regret from Teo Loczano's case. Something in him wants to make that right. She takes a second bite, then remembers their conversation. With a small bit of food in her mouth, she asks, "Oh good, so you're not vegan because of health issues or anything?"

He thinks how cute she looks talking with her cheek slightly full, "No, it feels better really, and I get much better results from my workouts."

"Yes, I can see that." She raises her wine glass to him, then sips from it. She wonders for a moment if he also likes the enhanced circulation a vegan diet affords a man's prostate areas, then tries to erase the vision of his nether region from her mind...unsuccessfully.

Riordan looks down and takes another bite. She sees his reaction and wonders where her filter has gone. She's only sipped her wine a few times...albeit on an empty stomach. She feels he's trying to be very professional for her sake. He looks up, smiles, and then pours her more wine. She realizes he doesn't mind her loose tongue. She makes a mental note not to drink too much. It's been a long time...*for many things.*

"So what does that mean, *as much as I can?*" She continues with the conversation.

"I enjoy clean eating, but if I go to someone's house for a meal, I'm not going to make them uncomfortable by not eating what they've prepared. I'm grateful for food, period. I just prefer a plant-based diet."

"I think that's fair. I'm the same. I'll eat almost everything put in front of me and just leave the meat to the side...or share it with whoever is closest and wants it."

Riordan nods. He's happy to see she's eating and drinking her wine so eagerly. He's hoping she won't want to walk around New York City afterwards, in her sexy heels. As beautiful as she looks, her hair laying softly around her shoulders, her amazing cleavage poking tastefully through her cross-chest mini dress, her open energy...she'd surely be approached by multiple men...and he just can't seem to settle with that. His mind takes him back to the case. She has no idea of how men responded to her, and Teo, without her ever even knowing, would punish even his own staff if they even so much as looked at her too long. In fact, one of the charges he put on Teo during the case was for a homeless man Teo beat severely, for just reaching out to touch Demi's ankle as she walked by. She never knew. Riordan remembers how they saved that man's life by having Teo under surveillance. He surely would have killed the old man. Being in close proximity to Demi now, Riordan understands her energetic magnetism. His teacher in Bali had explained it…the very way tantric energy can be irresistible. Teo never appreciated her authentic gifts. He was protective of his possessions. And Demi…is not to be possessed.

After a more pleasant conversation on the topics of Bermuda's pink sand beaches, Einstein's Princeton, New Jersey years, and the importance of B17 for cancer prevention, Demi is ready for dessert. Riordan pours her more wine and finishes the last of the bottle into his own glass. He notices Demi has developed goosebumps on her upper arms. Their bantering and laughing, back and forth, has distracted them from the setting sun. The large candle in the center of their table is illuminating the entire outside deck but not necessarily warming her.

He points to her arm, "Ms. Greer, shall we have dessert in the salon? A cup of hot tea for you?"

Demi looks around, seeing the time had just flown by, and the sun disappeared. She's chilly, and feeling like a walk in the city is not what she wants anymore. She prefers the company of Captain Riordan Tate. She can't imagine him looking any sexier and smiles at the glass of wine in her hand. "Oh my, yes! That'd be fun. Have you seen the size of that flat screen?" Before he's able to answer, she's up on her heels and sauntering away from the table, through the glass doors, and into the large salon.

Riordan backs his chair out and wipes his mouth one last time before picking up his glass of wine and following her. He looks into the tiny camera mounted at the far corner of the deck, nodding a signal to Grant, who he knows has been watching them. Gerdie appears, "No dessert Captain Tate?"

"In the Salon if you please, Gerdie, and two herbal teas as well…chamomile if you have it."

"Certainly, sir, right away."

"No hurry, please tell the Chef dinner was just divine, a very…*very* good job."

She smiles as she picks up their plates, "Sure thing."

"Thank you." Riordan inhales, gazing at Demi. He walks towards her…*happy*. He realizes it's been quite some time since he's allowed himself to feel this. He's content in knowing he's made this memory with her…even if only for a few hours.

9

Thank You

Riordan

He chuckles watching her fumble with the remote control to the theater-size flat screen, singing along to Jimmy Buffet's "Cheeseburger in Paradise" music video. Demi moans in pleasure as another spoonful of vegan chocolate mousse covers her tongue. She's a vision to behold. Riordan sips his tea, leaning back against the navy blue high back chair he carefully chose so she couldn't sit next to him, although sitting next to her would be his first choice in a different setting. He wonders what's taking Grant so fucking long. He signaled to him on camera over an hour ago. He continues to keep her engaged, "So, after your last tantric couple arrives and gets settled in, you'll begin with ice breaker games Ms. Greer?"

She nods, sliding back against the sofa with both hands around her cup of tea. She crosses her long, perfectly sculpted legs, one over the other, and Riordan catches a quick glance before averting his eyes towards her face. He feels his body react and tries to ignore his feelings. She sips, "Yes, the first day is always about me evaluating the character of each person while they're busy getting to know each other and having fun."

"Do you ever get a real difficult person, maybe one who is contradictory or interrupts you too much? I know not everyone is on board with Tantra being still a 'taboo' topic here in the western world."

"Most are already on board and behaved because the intake and subject matter is intense. They either agree or shouldn't even bother coming. But, every so often, you get a real ball-buster...like a huge prick that makes a joke of very serious explanations or, worse, giggles at the sexual bonding exercises like an immature teenager. I try not to absorb the emotional handicaps of others, but it doesn't mean I don't get frustrated at times. I feel energy is life... and sexual connection very natural, important too. Teaching is not as easy as it appears to be. I decompress on my own, usually after, by myself…if I have particularly difficult coaching sessions or those blocked from their bonding abilities."

Riordan's breath hitches slightly in his throat. His mind seeing her, and what tantric goddesses do to take care of their energy…and bodies. He agrees, "I understand. Well, I do hope you get a good group for this retreat. Twelve weeks can feel like a year if you want it to end quickly because of a rogue student."

"Ha! You ARE right."

He thinks about how much he's enjoying her company. In less than twelve hours, he'll be full force into the reason he's on board and will need to keep his distance from Demi. Lucky for him, she'll be busy, life will move forward, and at the end of this case, he'll reluctantly say farewell, or not, he may just disappear to avoid it. He tries to erase the thought. "Do your clients progress at the same time?" He knows the answer already but loves to hear her talk about her passion to mentor.

"Oh no, I've sent them all itineraries that are different based on their relationship goals. Some of the schedule requires them to all be together for certain activities, but a lot of the work is done on their own or in their cabin." She smiles excitedly and waves her eyebrows up and down.

He nods his chin towards her and titters. She is very, VERY captivating to him. "Well, that sounds well thought out." He wonders if he can get his hands on a schedule for Lubna Nayhan and her wife, so he knows when and where they'll be. He has to put Grant and his team on searching her cabin, her luggage, and anything or any place she may be hiding the stolen items. He could just ask Demi, in a cleverly nonchalant way, yet he doesn't want to involve her or ever make her feel uncomfortable. "What's your favorite part?"

"Right now, I'm favoring our dinner! This whole day has been so much more than I expected. I'm having a grand time!"

He watches her move her shoulders to the music, a little spot of mousse on her face mimicking a Marilyn Monroe mole. She swings her hair slightly. It moves against her bare arms, caressing her smooth skin. He's getting aroused…and pissed at Grant. Demi is obviously a bit tipsy, and he needs her escorted to her cabin. It's best if Grant does so. Riordan smiles at her and touches the underneath of his watch face. He's hoping the signal pings Grant, who must not be watching the cameras as originally thought. "Oh, that's nice to hear. I'm glad you're enjoying the *Passionista*, Ms. Greer."

"Thanks! Oh shit, I better get myself to my cabin. I've got an early start tomorrow." Demi stands abruptly. She points the remote at the screen and pushes three incorrect buttons before finding the OFF button. She leans too much, and Riordan jumps up to cup her elbow to help her keep her balance. As soon as he touches her, they both feel a surge of extreme warmth and connection. Demi turns, a bit wide-eyed, realizing he held her from stumbling.

His eyes soften, unable to believe the feeling of her, "My apologies, I thought you might fall." He pretends to be relaxed about their mutual electricity.

She sobers quick, and a small smile appears, "Thank you. I'm going to…I'm going this way." Demi glides away from him, wanting more-so to move towards him.

"Oh, okay. Well, I'm headed that way as well. I'll escort you." The ship is large, and he knows she would get lost trying to find her cabin…wine or no wine. It takes a day or two to get to know the layout of the yacht. Against his plan, he steps ahead of her and opens the door for her. He feels he may have to help her down the three stairwells to the deck both their VIP rooms are on. He hopes to run into Grant mid-way.

"Oh, Captain, you don't have to do that. I can manage."

"I'm sure, but this yacht can be a bit confusing the first day aboard."

A few bumps into each other, two hand-holds down flights of steps, and one stumble against Riordan's crotch and chest later, they both arrive at the beginning of the VIP hallway. Riordan has a semi and is trying to stay two feet behind Demi to get out of whatever gravitational pull she has with his body. He's beginning to ache for her in new ways, and he's suddenly pissed at himself for letting his guard down.

As they reach his door, Demi slows and turns. He gently touches her elbow to guide her past his "Captain" door and further to the end of the hall where her suite begins. She closes her lips from whatever she was about to say and continues walking with a small "Okay," whispered in the hall. She moves her hands along the walls and railing, Riordan hopes she doesn't stop walking until she reaches the door. She still moves with beauty and grace in her heels, just less confident.

Finally arriving at her door, Riordan reaches in front of her, trying desperately not to rub up against her. It's locked. Demi puts her palms on the door expecting him to open it, and when it doesn't budge, she pushes off and up against his chest…her perfect tush then curling into his lap…*again*. They both feel the connection, and it's fervent! He steps back, hoping she'll ignore his growing erection. He tries to distract her.

"Ms. Greer, I believe you'll need to put your four-digit code in. The door is locked." He knows the code but feels revealing that would be even more inappropriate than what just transpired. He exhales, trying to remain composed.

Demi turns around, unable to concentrate on her locked door, "Fuck the door Captain Tate, and no more of this Ms. Greer nonsense, you need to call me Demi." Before he knows it, she slides her hands alongside his neck, pulling him down to her. Their lips meet, and he feels as if his whole world swirls through his body, intertwining with hers. He feels himself lean down into to her, meeting her breath. She opens to him, and he feels her tongue warm and velvety, slide into his mouth. He pulses beneath the fabric of his slacks as he accepts her in his mouth. She's the most exquisite taste he's ever known, and he knows instantly he wants all of her. She moans into the kiss, and although he could die in her hands right now, he has to break the pull of their energy towards each other. *Fuck*. He places his hands over hers, slowly…reluctantly, gently sliding her hands from his face and placing them back to her sides.

"I- I'm sorry, Ms. Gr-, Demi." He apologizes for more than just the kiss. Taking full responsibility for allowing such pleasure to tarry.

She smiles, looking up with glorious deep blue, bedroom eyes, "Don't be, that was every bit as remarkable as I'd hoped." She reaches to caress his cheek. He closes his eyes to her touch and holds her wrist, slowly lowering it. He cannot let this happen.

"What's the code?" He whispers, he needs to leave. *Now.*

"6969…" Giggling, she steps away and leans against the wall to look at him. She's so attracted to him, she can't remember the last time she got wet just by being in the presence of a man. It isn't his massive size and good looks. It's more his captivating energy. It's as if he possesses her. She could feel it from their very first hand-shake earlier in the day. Her arousal…and emotions have grown over the hours. She thinks about how she just met this alluring soul, and already she wants to breathe as one with him.

He stares down into her eyes. He's tormented. Without looking away or breaking their connection, he pushes her code into the keypad. The door opens, he holds out his hand to lead her. She's never been so sure. She steps in and turns to him, to all she wants to do to him, his spirit, and his glorious body. She wants him to come to her, to submit.

"Thank you for an unforgettable evening, Ms. Greer." He smiles sadly and closes the door, never stepping in. She stands there in silence.

10

Focus

Demi

She stares at the door, not knowing whether to get angry or thank him. Demi reaches to unfasten the clasp of her heel, she stumbles and flops down into one of the reading chairs. She decides drinking is no longer going to be a part of her life. She just completely lost all common sense and discipline…but he feels so damn good.

Rubbing her temples, she exhales and decides she'll deal with the embarrassment of her inhibitions in the morning. She stands, one heel in hand, the other still on…and hobbles across the huge suite to the bedroom. She knows she's not overly drunk because she can still do things she needs to, but she doesn't feel shame yet, so she must be a little sauced. She pulls her cell phone out and sets the alarm. Stretching across the bed on her tummy, she pretends to be laying on his broad chest, hugging the pillows and duvet. She laughs into the fabric at how silly she's being. It's almost as if she fell in love with him at first glance…

Closing the door and walking away from her felt horrible, almost as bad as the last day he was on the case, and saw her eyes as Teo Loczano was arrested in front of her. He hates the thought of hurting Demi…or leaving her. He adjusts his crotch as he walks towards his quarters while giving the finger to the camera hidden in the far corner. He knows Grant has all that recorded. Walking her to her room was supposed to be chivalrous. None of what happened was chivalrous! He keyed in his door code, entered the suite, and pondered over which side of the yacht he was going to throw Grant over when he sees him.

That kiss was indescribable. And he knows he'll never be able to erase it from his mind.

Demi steps out of the closet in yoga pants and a long flowing white shirt with her name and title embroidered on it. She slips on matching white wedge flip flops and walks towards the door. It's time to meet her first couple and begin to assess them. She feels good, nothing like she thought she would. His energy and scent still permeate. She wants to see him. She feels no regret, surprisingly. She wants him.

Walking down the long hallway, she wonders if she should knock on his door. She slows as she nears the handle. Something makes her stop; she can smell his light cologne. Her body responds in ways she doesn't expect, and she speeds up to pass by. She knows she needs to focus now. *Focus Demi!*

11

Diana & Claude

Riordan

Riordan watches on camera as Diana and Claude Turner come aboard the *Passionista,* looking awestruck. He leans back in his captain's chair and studies the couple. He already knows they're both artists. Diana has family money. With it, she's built a large art gallery in Virginia to display not only her victorian era paintings but her husband's welded metal art pieces. There seems to be a lot of hype over his niece's collection, they sell in their gallery as well. With a net worth of $433,000.00 per year, they seem to do all right. Riordan looks down to continue reading the file about the Turners. Grant redeemed himself by providing him with Demi's paperwork he somehow copied while she and Riordan were dining on the top deck. He can't be mad at Grant for doing exactly what he's paid to do.

Demi appears, graciously welcoming the Turners and guiding them to sit on the plush sofas and enjoy mimosas. His chest feels fluttery at the sight of her, his breath tethering a bit. She looks amazing in her yoga attire. Her curves are covered in light pink yoga capris and a flowing white shirt. He remembers the feel of her lips and squirms in his seat as his body reacts…again. He leans and turns on the microphones Grant installed behind the couches. The Turners aren't big targets in this case, but he wants to get as much information on everyone as he can. He's also curious as to how Demi runs her business; he needs a distraction from the memory of what she pulled him into last night.

"So here's your personalized itinerary for the next three months. We'll be working on intimacy between you two and also intimacy with the others in your life." She smiles, watching the couple peruse the packet, leaning in towards each other.

Claude rests on his wife's shoulder and squints at the schedule, "Oh, I like all this water fun. Do we ride the jet skis here or on the islands?" Riordan can tell by Claude's welding abilities and interest in physical outdoor pursuits, he's the reason they're needing intimacy training. Men tend to focus on where they *can* be success-ful instead of where they *feel* inadequate.

Demi smiles, "We provide all the physical fun here on *Passionista*...in between the time *you both* provide your intimate physical fun and healing." Riordan chuckles to himself. She's so cute.

"Yeah, husband, me first, then the rewards." Diana lightly pokes Claude's chest with her index finger.

"While we have our time today, I'd like to get clear on how I can best help you both. Diana, why did you choose this tantra retreat? Claude, I'll ask you the same question." Demi is already writing notes.

Diana removes her hat and glasses, "I'd like Claude and I to explore more of our older age 'selves' now that we've established our home and our business and raised a family. Now that we've got success as a foundation, I'd like less "doing" and more "feeling"."

Demi nods, "Good, Diana. Claude?"

"I feel good when I'm in my shop or at the gallery. I'm happy!" Riordan smiles at Claude's short and sweet explanation of his libido fading. He probably has low testosterone.

"And how do you feel when you two talk about things, Claude?" Demi asks.

Claude looks down and shrugs his shoulders. He's a man of fifty-four, feeling as if he's eighty-four with the understanding of a twenty-four-year-old inside himself. "She's never happy."

"I'm happy, Claude! I love you, darling. I just wish you'd pay attention to me sometimes." Diana touches his face lovingly with the back of her hand. Demi knows their problems are from performance issues. He feels less interested. She's needing more. He needs to feel more successful in their relationship, so he stops seeking it so much in his work.

He rolls his eyes, "Well, I'm here, aren't I?"

Diana quiets from not being validated. Demi answers, "Yes, you are, and thank you for making Diana a priority!" His face brightens. Riordan smiles, sipping coffee and watching through the tinted windows. He knows how sharp Demi is, and she's already sized them up and how to best help them. Okay, you two, let's take you to your cabin and get you settled before lunch. Your luggage has already been delivered to your room.

Demi stands with her clipboard resting on the side of one plump breast. Riordan watches, admiring her as she gives her shoulders a small stretch. She waits for Diana and Claude to collect their belongings and follow her. As she leads the way, she looks up at his windows and gives a small smile. He knows she can't see him, but she's letting him know she's thinking of him. He softens at the sight of her walking away, swinging her long hair back off her shoulders, and disappears down the stairwell. He decided, when he awoke today, to stay clear of her, but that was four hours ago, and before he caught sight of her again…now he feels as if he's changing his mind *again*. He can't ascertain if things were easier when she was a memory he yearned for in his mind. Now that she's so near, he's finding his boundaries difficult to follow.

12
No Rules
Riordan

The side door to the bridge opens swiftly, and Grant comes in whistling. "Hey there, Don Juan, how goes it?"

"That's funny, fucker." Riordan finishes his last sip of coffee.

"Come on, it kinda is."

He clenches his jaw and narrows his eyes at Grant, "No, not really."

"Are you still peeved at me? Look, I got you all this paperwork." Grant flicks the packet of guests' profiles Riordan's holding in his hand. "You're not supposed to be mad. Besides, I saw the footage and that…that was fuckin' hot bro!"

"Apton, you are getting on my last nerve."

Grant steps away and takes a seat in the far chair, "Tate, come on. She's Demi Loczano! What's the problem? She wants you big time, bro. Hell, look at the way she kissed you, man, she wants you like she's never wanted Teo, that's for damn sure."

"She had too much to drink."

"Two glasses of wine is not that much. She really likes you, Taters; listen, you said it yourself years back, ninety-seven percent of marriages begin either because of chemistry or proximity…i.e., workplace, college, same town, etc. Well, there is definitely chemistry, even two years ago when you first saw her."

"She never saw me, not even once during the Loczano case!"

"True, but the chemistry was there. For you, it was there." Grant softens. He knows he's hitting some buttons, but it's time. "Now, I know you believe in tantra, and energy, and all that supersmart shit. Maybe it's time to admit that *shit* is happening, man. Energy begets energy, right?"

"What're you talking about?" Riordan leans back against his chair and swivels to face Grant.

"I'm talking about you, how you really feel. It matters to me, Riordan. I know I was teasing yesterday, talking about Demi and all, but in all honesty, this woman is perfect for you. You learned everything about her. Hell, you saw her every day, feared for her, listened to her, watched her every move...you even saved her pain those few times, sending us in to divert her from finding her asshole husband in bed with whatever woman he was trying to manipulate at the time."

Riordan exhales long and mumbles, "That was just being decent."

"Yeah, it was. You knew she was eventually going to go through the trauma of losing her life and home, so you carved out the bigger traumas and kept them from her."

"She didn't need to feel that, Grant. Do you know what being unfaithful does to a good woman?"

Grant smiles, "See?"

"See what?"

"You care for her, Rior...and it's a good thing. It's been years now, years since Evelyn. You're allowed to care for another woman."

"Don't."

"Don't what? Don't say my sister's name?"

"Don't bring all that up."

Grant sits back, "I'm not bringing it up. I know we've healed it. I know all that's in the past...I'm simply saying you're allowed to feel again. It happens. And, my sister would fucking love this woman!" Riordan looks hard at Grant. "It's true, and you know it. She wouldn't want you suffering, depriving yourself of a chance at something so real."

"Grant, this has nothing to do with deprivation. She's a subject...a victim from a previous case!"

"So-fuckin-what Riordan? You own the goddamn company! You solved and closed that case. It was a great job. You took a scumbag off the street and saved countless lives. Hell, you even saved Demi from what he would have turned her into. Better yet, you kept him from procreating and hurting a family with his lies! It's been long enough. No one's going to tattle!"

Riordan hisses, "I fucking ruined her life!"

Grant slams his palm down on the control counter with a resounding thud, "Then give her a new one!" He stands up, his eyes darkening. "Listen, you know this woman, she's the best kind. Give her a chance to get to know you, you stubborn motherfucker! Because I don't know of too many chances where two people cross each others' paths and are more right for each other than this, after all the shit you've both gone through! I think you're the best kind too, and I'm tired of watching you suffer. I don't like you letting those bastards win for taking Evelyn away from us. To sit here, year after year, and watch you in pain…letting them win!" Grant stops himself mid-rant.

Riordan looks at his best friend, realizing *his* pain affected Grant all these years too. Grant didn't just lose a sibling. He lost parts of his best friend too. He looks back down at the control counter, staring at his coffee mug, his hand wrapped around it.

Grant turns, his voice low, "I deleted the footage and sent it to your secured email. That wasn't an ordinary kiss, that wasn't a drunk kiss. I won't mention this again unless you do. There are no rules when it comes to love Riordan. You told me that back in our college days." He continues to the door and slams it shut behind him.

Riordan runs his fingers through his hair and leans back. *Fuck.*

13

Alan & Roderick

Demi

Alan Hamilton, a forty-eight-year-old dance studio instructor and owner, follows behind his tall, dark, and handsome husband, Roderick. He leans to the right and checks out Demi's perfectly scrumptious tush, leading the way to their cabin in front of Rod. He knows Rod doesn't care in the least, but he certainly wants to know where she got that ass and how he could get his to look that good!

Rod Hamilton, a forty-six-year-old accountant, looks around in awe of the *Passionista*. He's quiet, ready for a nap to erase the drive from their upstate New York home, and wondering if this retreat will finally fix his stale twenty-two-year marriage so Alan will stop asking for their nineteen-year-old daughter's "friend" from college to consider a threesome. He thinks Demi is smart as a whip… and her ass is to die for, but he wants to get back to all the great questions she has so their marriage can make it to twenty-three years.

"Okay, gentlemen, here we are. Your cabin is number nine. I'll have housekeeping come by and show you how to program your door code. Unpack, settle in, and we'll meet for lunch up on the top deck at one o'clock." Demi steps away from their door, so they can get by.

"Oooooooh, my gawd, Rod! Look at this place. Have you ever seen a more stunningly decorated room?" Alan is obviously the more expressive of the two.

"It's nice." Says Rod.

Demi reaches to close the door for them, "Laters, guys!"

"Buh-bye, Dems." Alan waves, scrunching his nose, appearing as if he's known her longer than the twenty-eight minutes the three sat and talked together.

She smiles to herself as she walks the long hallway back to the top deck to greet her next couple. Rod and Alan Hamilton are going to be fun to work with. Alan obviously needs a lot of attention and love, while Rod is laid back and gentle but getting to the end of his rope with having to meet Alan's every low self-esteem idea or maneuver. After twenty-two years of marriage, things can get "boring", and bringing a third party into the union is not ideally the answer. Demi is positive they need tantra training to create an intense, deep bond that neither will ever want anyone else to be a part of. Alan simply needs to get out of his head, away from focusing on external looks, and into his heart…with Rod being his priority. Rod needs to learn how to draw Alan back in. Demi already has a plan in mind!

14

Natalia & Chance
Demi

Natalia and Chance Rubins are a very pretty couple. She, a gorgeous light-skinned black girl of five-nine, curvaceous hips, and long curly brown hair. He, a muscular, six-three blond-haired blue-eyed Texan turned New Yorker hipster. Demi steps forward to greet them, her hand extended.

"Chance...Natalia, it's a pleasure to meet you both. Welcome to the Passionista."

Chance places their bags down, stepping in to shake hands and lock eyes with Demi. "Nice to meet you uh...."

"Demi Greer. I'll be your retreat coordinator." She shakes his hand first, then Natalia, who's a bit reserved and not as welcoming as her husband. "Please, come and sit. Make yourselves comfortable."

Demi notices Chance is gentle with Natalia, picking up her bags then guiding her to sit on the couch. His movements are tender and coordinated, not at all like his father, Errol Adler. Natalia looks Demi up and down, curious and somewhat threatened.

"Demi, are you the relationship coach and also the tantra instructor?" Natalia's voice is smooth and commanding.

"I am, yes. I'll be guiding you through your next three months, but you two, of course, will be going at your own pace. Can you tell me about yourselves and how you've come about booking the Passionista?"

Chance looks at his wife then begins, "We're married almost a year, both thirty-two, first marriage...for both of us. DINKS living in New York." He chortles.

Demi smiles, "Double-income-no-kids. DINKS, love it!" She writes something on her notepad.

"Yes, uh, I mentioned the Passionista to Natalia after my father called me three times about it. I really didn't think she'd want to go, but well...here we are. I'm a pediatric surgeon, Nats a Manager at a prestigious night club in the city." Chance sits back against the couch and places his arm around his wife.

Demi looks to Natalia, "How do you feel about a ninety-day tantric vacation cruise, Natalia? Have you ever been away from work for so long?"

Natalia accepts a mimosa from Maurice's tray, smiling in gratitude towards the tall bartender, "I think we need the break. I'm not sure we'll be able to do the entire ninety days but so far, so good. This gives me time to work on us and let my staff show their skills back at the club. Honestly, if his father weren't footing the bill, we probably would've said no."

Demi looks towards Chance to see his reaction. He smiles admirably at his wife. "Chance, does your father do this often?"

"No, I believe he's trying to make up for not being there for me much as a youngster. I don't really know him all that well." He looks around, eyeing the luxury of the yacht. "We've spent maybe a month together total, in my entire life."

"Oh, I see. That's interesting. We'll talk more about Mr. Adler in session then." Demi wants to keep the focus on the couple. "Well, today is more of a meet-n-greet, get comfortable kind of departure day. No pressure, no big schedule. I'll show you to your cabin, your large luggage has been delivered there so you can settle in. Can I answer any questions for you right now?"

Natalia looks at Chance. He smiles and kisses her hand, allowing her to have the floor. She looks at Demi, "How far does your training go? I mean, how involved are you in our uh…retreat experiences."

"Good question. Well, there are four couples aboard, all going through their own self-paced tantra immersion program. I'm your mentor and coach. I'll tailor your experiences to the outcome and growth you're seeking." Demi searches Natalia's eyes and knows her concern.

"Okay." Natalia smiles small, looking towards her husband and back at Demi.

"I have no sexual contact with my clients. I'm your coach and confidant. I only go at your pace and require homework…not display."

Natalia's shoulders release; she's relieved. "Oh, okay…okay, good. I wasn't sure how to imagine this."

Demi smiles sweetly. She knows when a woman is concerned about how she'll interact with their husband. With as good-looking as Chance is, she knows Natalia is pretty protective over him. "Tantra has more to do with the mind than the body. My main concern is creating intimacy and a stronger bond for you both. Everything else will fall into place as the intimacy grows. You're safe here. I'm very confidential, and I'll require that of you both as well. I believe you two are going to love your experience."

"My wife has concerns about how her...interests may be perceived or discussed?" Chance winks at Natalia. She doesn't smile.

"There's nothing you can tell me I haven't heard before, so that being said, I bet I have solutions to any issues. I certainly have answers to all your questions. You can relax and enjoy the process of growing in your intimacy. I want you to know how admirable it is that you both committed to each other with this type of retreat."

They both look at each other with relief on their faces and smile. Chance answers, "Great. Well, I'm excited." Natalia nods.

"Let me show you to your cabin below. We can dive into this more at your private sessions." Demi stands and waits for them to gather their belongings. She knows this couple has some concerns, but it's nothing she can't help with. It has more to do with their childhood than what they think...and she knows if she starts there, they'll both work through more than just first-year marriage stuff. "Right this way."

15

Lubna & Sagrid

Riordan

Riordan returns to his captain's chair on the bridge, his second cup of coffee in hand, admiring the beautiful Demi Greer. He turns to the next page in the packet; this is the couple he's most interested in. Demi hugs Sagrid Hamsum and her wife Lubna Nayhan, the main target in this case. He eyes Lubna. Like her photos, she's tall and slender, middle-eastern with a quiet, innocence…her face soft but distracted. Her wife is an inch taller, porcelain colored skin and very Swedish-blonde hair, an almost white blonde color. They're not affectionate with each other yet. Both stepped right into connecting with a hug with Demi though. *Interesting.* He'd love to hug her as well.

Demi brings them over to the sofa area for her intake interview. The last two couples seemed tuned in to each other. These two are distant. Lubna stares at Demi like she could lick her, while Sagrid looks around at all the expense and detail of the *Passionista*, her overly dark sunglasses lowered beneath her eyes so she can actually see. He listens in to the conversation.

"How long have you been married, Lubna?" Demi directs her body language and question towards her.

Lubna attempts to answer and Sagrid chimes in, "We've been together seventeen years, married fifteen of them." Lubna looks at her wife, unenthused.

Demi is pleasant, "That's wonderful. It says here that you're looking to re-discover your beginnings and take a step towards a more tantric lifestyle?"

"That's what I'm told." Lubna's slow, monotoned voice glides with a passive sarcasm.

"Oh, so Sagrid, tantra is more your interest?" Demi isn't worried; tantra always changes people for the better. It's just easier to know who's going to be the more difficult transitional partner in a couple.

Sagrid pushes her sunglasses up and swings her long hair off of her shoulder, "I've heard it can really change a marriage. We need a vacation, and we need an exorcism dahling!" She's stern with her accent and outrageous. She laughs, throwing her head back. "Or, some sort of ah *sheeft*, I don't know how you say, what do you think dahling…perhaps a divorce would be best?" She squints and smirks at her wife, bumping shoulders with her.

Lubna exhales, "Whatever, Sagrid."

Demi looks sympathetic, "Aw ladies, no worries, by the end of the twelve weeks, you'll know best as to which way to go. You're not alone. Many couples come to my retreats to find out what the next step is. Either way, what's best for both of you will be revealed in the energy."

"Oh, you're so precious, love. I trust you, I trust you!" Sagrid reaches across and cups Demi's face with one hand. She mother's her a moment, and Riordan leans forward towards the windows. He's decided he already doesn't like Lubna but, Sagrid is now on thin ice too. He thinks she may actually be the bigger problem.

"Oh good, I'm glad. Well, let's get you to your stateroom so you can rest before lunch. We'll be getting to know each other, all of us, over delicious food, drinks, and of course some relaxing hot tub fun as we depart to deep seas today." Demi stands and waits for them to follow her.

Lubna speaks low but seems concerned, "Will our luggage be at our cabin?"

"Oh, yes, it should be there already. You'll be able to unpack and change if you'd like." Demi walks towards the stairwell, and they follow.

Riordan knows Grant may still be pissed at him, but work is work. He beeps him through his watch and switches his earpiece so he can hear him.

Grant comes through a moment later, "Ap-"

"Those items delivered?" Riordan speaks low so as not to buzz Grant's earpiece.

"All but one."

"Anything?"

"Negative."

"Securing?" Riordan can't understand why Grant's kept one piece of Lubna's luggage if nothing was found in it.

"Negative. Not enough time. Got Owens ready to deliver." Grant is speaking swiftly.

"Send Levy. Female preferred." Riordan gives the order.

"Received." Grant is short.

Riordan isn't sure if it's because of their tiff earlier or because he's changed Grant's orders from Isaac Owens to their female agent, Constance Levy.

"Out." Riordan is fine with Grant being mad. He knows he's right, but now's not the time to admit it.

16
Relenting
Riordan & Demi

Riordan walks over to his office door but turns to swing by the desk for his papers. The phone is blinking with a red light. He sits in his high back swivel chair and takes the receiver to his ear. He pushes the button and puts in his voicemail code. One message is from Errol about meeting up in a few days if he can. Riordan closes his eyes and exhales. He really doesn't need surprise helicopter visits on the top deck helipad from his boss throughout this job. The second voicemail is from Captain Nero Ulfa, from the hidden deck, asking if all passengers and crew are aboard *Passionista*. He's prepared to depart at their four o'clock scheduled time.

Riordan calls down to Ulfa to confirm all crew are accounted for and decides he will not be calling Errol Adler back. He hopes the old kook gets busy and steers clear of the twelve-week cruise altogether. Being micro-managed is not something Riordan tolerates. He's too damn good at his work to let anyone interfere.

The door softly shuts, the lock clicks, and when he looks up he sees her, the deep blue of her eyes searching…lingering on his gaze. He feels as if he's been punched in the chest. The sight of her sends his heart aching to touch her.

"Good morning." Demi's smooth, sexy voice registers in his ears, and he feels his body respond. *Damn it.*

"Ms. Greer?" He's prepared to stand but sees her move first, causing him to pause.

She walks towards him, and he's unsure of what's happening. He hopes she'll take a seat but, that's not her idea as she eyes him and places her clipboard down on his desk, continuing towards him. He postures, his body responding tensely. He has no idea how to react to her coming at him so swiftly. She's locked on his eyes; he hangs up the phone just in time. She reaches out, pushing her hand against the corner of his chair. She moves so quickly he has no choice but to accept her in his hands. Letting his chair sway around towards her, she softly leaps into his lap before he can protest and brings her mouth down onto his with a consuming force he can't reject. Her hands gently run through his hair, and her tongue is suddenly in his mouth, exploring him. He feels a surge of her energy and, against his rules, finds his hands on her waist, then moving up her back, pulling her into him! She melts into him, her tongue gentle but arduous. He feels he may dissolve beneath the heat of her, their connection possessing, and perfect.

His hand finds her hair, then the nape of her neck where he grips her lovingly, wanting to devour her as his heart feels as if it might explode. He's already engorged, and she loves the feel of him snug and full beneath her. She sinks down more and presses onto his shaft with a pulsing, gripping energy, inhaling long and deep from his mouth so she can weave her energy in and exhale it back into him. He knows what she's doing and allows it as he presses into her, yielding… surrendering himself to her tantric dominance. He's cognizant that at this very moment he'll never be the same, she's penetrating his soul, and he's willingly relenting-

Riordan knows he should stop this…

Demi moves one hand from his soft, wavy hair to his neck, caressing, her other hand moves down his broad, muscular back and opens wide at his heart chakra, she presses her breasts against his chest, and he exhales into her, feeling her perfect bust warm against him. Her next breath brings with it a long, throaty moan. His shaft pulses in response, and she meets him with her own gentle squeeze. Riordan feels so much want for her. He's dreamt of her, dreamt of this moment for years. She slowly, steadily pushes forward on him, rocking her hips inward and gliding back. She inhales long and deep again, matching her exquisite thrusts with her breath, and then his. He allows her to lead, and he follows her movements to secure their new connection. She is exquisite…a goddess, and he knows he can relax within this knowledge. He has, unknowingly, prepared himself for years to be worthy of her at this moment.

Suddenly, she releases her kiss gently. Her eyes meet his, and he sees a deep desire within her. She brings her hand around to his chin, still slowly, longingly grinding into him. She moves his head to the side and brings her mouth down into his neck. She suckles and devours him, still keeping their breath synced with his and her secret squeeze. Riordan's eyes roll back and close, his hands sliding slowly down to find her perfect tush. He pulls her down deeper onto him. He knows he only needs to breathe her pleasure and pulse along with her. He wants to explode as she moans into his neck, but delaying gratification means more prolonged, savory pleasure, and every part of his body energetically fusing with her. He inhales her scent and exhales a throaty moan. She's still gradually and perfectly thrusting forward along his erection, squeezing him through her thin clothing fabric, allowing him to pulse in her warm, sacred region. There is so much give and take, so much balance and fairness, in their impassioned exchange. She moves slow across the front of his neck, circling his Adam's apple with her moist, warm tongue. He moans deeper. She continues sucking leisurely with her soft tongue to the other side of his neck, tasting his musk scent... inhaling him into her. She adores the taste of him and reveals so as she whispers, "Riordan....". He surrenders while releasing his shoulders, necks, arms, and back pressing his chest into her. The way she speaks his name for the first time almost unhinges him. His body responds to her soothing adoration. He can feel a pearl of precum glaze the head of his penis. He can't believe how much his body aches for her!

She moves up and takes his ear between her soft lips. Riordan's breathing tethers as he hears her softly exhale near his ear. He follows her breath and reestablishes their timing. Again she thrusts into his crotch, squeezing him as he grips her hips to hold on through the raw pleasure, *her* pleasure. He senses her goddess possession of him. He's now sure what madness feels like, but her rapture is worth every moment. He turns to her, searching for her mouth. She opens to him softly, and he inhales deeply, entering her mouth with his soft, velvety tongue...drinking her in. He runs his warm palms up under her shirt to caress her back in a slow, tantric massaging flow, pressing her into him as if devouring her. Chakras to chakras, universal bliss breaths rhythmically inhaled and exhaled in unison. She moans as she receives his flawless ecstasy, and she relents, molding into his large chest again. He's found the perfect touch, and she submits beneath it...

17

I Must Have You

Demi & Riordan

Demi releases from his glorious mouth to lay her head on his chest. She must take a moment to calm her eager orgasm. Men use "edging" to prolong their seed, and now suddenly, she must also try to ease her movements for fear that she may explode right here in his lap. Still breathing with him, she closes her eyes to ensure syncing with his long breaths in and out. His energy is powerful. He's a god beneath her, and she's so ready to devour him. She knows if she keeps thrusting along with him, her body will take over and lead her on a journey of pleasure waves, she'll have no choice but to surrender to, over and over again. She wants him more than anything she's ever wanted in her life, despite meeting him only twenty-four hours prior. She's now aware that she's dreamt of him…even though she didn't know who he was, she vibrationally attracted him to her. For two long years, she's meditated, manifested, and loved him *into* her life. When she locked eyes with him and shook his hand that first moment, the feelings of reassurance and familiarity were the first indications. He *feels* like home. Spending time with him for hours over dinner, feeling full in her heart, and laughing joyously were further attestations. Feeling free enough to kiss him no matter what the outcome, even a bit inebriated the night before, did not deter this perception. This, however, this complete feeling of soul interconnection, of intertwined sexual completeness, through every cell of her body…this is the certainty! She can never be apart from him. She knows she is meant to be his, and he hers. It's as if she's known him for lifetimes.

Demi picks her head up, moving into him slowly again and accepting him as he presses to her body, still following his breathing. She brings her hands to his face, looking into his light cocoa-colored brown eyes, watching as she grinds slow onto him. He looks tranquil with lust for her. She's never seen this from any man. She feels safe, desired, completely content. She continues to look into him, moving slowly against him, squeezing her sexual power up through her body and around him to claim him, possess him. He takes everything she offers and matches it, offering his own un-rivaled energy back to her! He's strong and impassioned, his body herculean and engulfing. He has her in his grasp, yet he's consider-ate and sensual, the way a gentleman should be. She wants him to possess her in every way, and she wants to own him, his heart, and his fiery soul. Freely.

"I-" She feels him pull her down by her waist yet plunge upwards into her erotically. His firm, bulge creating more pleasure making it difficult to concentrate. She's soaked beneath her cloth-ing. Her body aches deep within her insides for him. His seductive eyes make her want to let go. She knows he has the power to over-take her right here, even through clothing. He is a god to her god-dess. Nothing can stop this attraction.

He's still breathing, caressing, gliding… "Yes…*Ms. Greer.*" He's listening. Attentive to her every want.

She glares, a grin forming, it fades as the fervor again over-takes her. She's so willing, she can hardly focus. Her yoni aches and squeezes for him…the pleasure is indescribable!

He purrs in her ear, *"I'm listening…Demi…"*

He said her name! She can no longer take the restraint, she grabs his face again, "I-I want you…I have to have you!"

Riordan responds, stands without warning, holding her to him, his mouth crashing down on hers as he exhales and groans. He feels her words. He cannot deny her. *In the energy of tantric weav-ing, the universe overtakes and completes.* The familiar phrase, one that has stuck with him since Bali, resounds in his head. Kissing her hard, his tongue possessing, meeting her intensity, he protects her as he walks her across the large office towards the captain's dressing quarters, a secret hideaway. She presses into him to keep their fused rhythm as he steps with wide, long strides, his strong legs carrying them swiftly and gloriously through the bathroom to the uniform closet where various forms of captain's attire hang. It smells of him, fresh and manly. A small skylight brings in enough light for them to see their silhouettes in a sultry blue haze. He kicks the door shut behind them with his foot and reaches to lock it without re-leasing their kiss.

She presses and swings her legs down from his waist, reach-ing for the floor, pulling his face down with her, so she doesn't break their passionate kiss. She finds his uniform shirt buttons and fights the impulse to rip them open. She loves adhering to the erotic principles of tantra and can usually prolong discipline in every move, but the ache that this man has created within her core...she's not sure even orgasm can ease it. She's never felt her body throb so much in cadence with another. It's as if his every breath is a heartbeat to her soul garden.

Demi squeezes inhaling their bliss down into her sexual chakra while eagerly unbuttoning his shirt. His muscular torso that was pressed against the cotton fabric is now beneath her wanting touch. He lifts her shirt over her head, breaking contact only briefly, as the fabric of her shirt grazes their skin. Her plump, fevered lips return to his with magnetism. Her arms come back to pull his uniform top over his arms, getting the short sleeves caught around his well-defined biceps. She breaks their kiss to gently manage the plight. She sees his arms bare in the dim lighting. He's *very* masculine, without even trying. She looks up to see he's admiring her white lace bra, and she grins seductively, giving him permission to remove it. He is quite *the gentleman.* He reaches tenderly forward finding the front clasp. His hands feel massive in proportion to her chest. With one move, he frees her bosom and helps her bra slide off her arms and down to the floor. His crisp white undershirt is tucked perfectly into his uniform pants and belt. Demi unbuckles, unbuttons, untucks, and waits, allowing him a moment to kick off his shoes. She does the same with her flip flops. He takes his undershirt up and over his head as she swiftly removes both his pants and boxer briefs, tenderly freeing his manhood. She's never seen a more perfect engorgement. In the subdued lighting, she admires his flawless physique. The same color as the rest of his sun-kissed skin, his penis is remarkable! He's an adonis, and she is in awe of him. He wants her as much as she wants him. She gazes up at him, sultry and enchanted. He smiles and adores her through sleepy, bedroom eyes. He reaches gently to her waist, sliding his fingers along her hips, removing her sexy yoga pants and thong in one fell swoop while caressing her firm derriere in the process. He looks at her absolutely perfect curves, within his very touch, after so many years! He's wanted her for so long...

His body responds, coaxing him to possess her...to *belong* to her. He steps on his socks one-by-one, removing them, never losing his gaze or breath-connection with her. She reaches up, and as he lifts her, she hops up again into his arms, opening to him and feeling his glorious heat between her legs. He's fevered and firm, and the feel of her slick folds makes his knees want to go weak. There is so much he wants to do to her, with her, so much he's dreamed of...*with Demi*. He can hardly believe she's in his arms and how phenomenal this feels. He's almost overwhelmed with what's happening. Only yesterday, he repudiated this. He was ready to replace himself so he wouldn't have to yearn for her or make a mistake. Now, she's in his arms, and none of this feels untrue. Anything else, depriving this...would now be a falsehood.

She's kissing him forcefully, running her fingers through his hair, desperate for him. He again tries to match her breathing, which has now increased. This foreplay is definitely tantric, but he suddenly finds himself even more aroused! She's exceptional at leading him, even with just her breath. She releases, and he takes the opportunity to hold her in one arm, using the other to trace his palm down the front of her chest then sweetly cup her perfectly rotund breast. She gasps under his touch, and he thrusts gently up towards her, not quite entering her yet, just gliding, spreading her warm slick fluids between them. She arches back, and he lowers his mouth toward his hand to gently move her nipple towards his lips. He takes her into his fevered, wet mouth, and as he suckles tenderly, a desperate, throaty moan releases from her. His body pulses at the sound of her, and he glides again, further lubricating them both but not entering her until invited. *A woman's yoni garden is sacred, you must be invited...*

"Please!" Demi hisses in the quiet of the massive closet. Her command bouncing off the shelves and hung uniforms. She feels safe within his grasp and locked room.

He hears her plead and wants to please her. He musters his discipline and breathes for more patience. She's making it so damned hard to control his body and prolong their desire. He knows he must be strong for both of them. Tantra requires it. The longer their pleasure is drawn out, the deeper their alliance will be. He must protect their balance...their tantric bond, especially in this first encounter.

"Riordan...*please*...I-" Demi's words are cut off.

He bends and lowers her down to the carpet, she grasps his shoulders, trying to arch and pull him into her, but he's stronger and gently frees her arms from him, placing her wrists above her head. She exhales in weariness, he wanting to ravage her. He devours her neck, sending shudders up her body. She loves it and grabs his head to keep him close. If she could, she'd entwine him deep into her being, possessing *all* of him…but he is patient.

The scent of her makes him throb again within his core. He's leaning over her heated form. He again softly grabs her wrists and puts them over her head, this time clasping both wrists in his one hand to extend the energy of her body. He drags his left palm down slowly between her breasts, grasping one lovingly as his mouth suckles the other. She whimpers in arousal, aching as her body reflexively curves towards his mouth, and she moans louder. His erection responds to her voice, pulsing against his stomach, and then touching her outer thigh. Both are now trying desperately to withstand their desire for each other. He releases her breast from his mouth and trails kisses down her stomach and tiny waist. His hand drags and massages her skin, reaching her beautiful mound. He finds she's drenched with want for him, and he feels the scent of her will drive him mad!

Tenderly, he slides his two fingers into the genesis of her opening, pausing to make sure he's invited. Demi moans opening and arches pushing towards him, so his fingers slide inside just deep enough and rest curved at her g-spot. He presses his palm then towards her clitoral pith applying a little pressure. Demi moans louder, and Riordan exhales his heated breath on her inside thigh. He closes his eyes, rolling them back and around again, giving silent praise to the source for the goddess beneath his touch. He cannot believe this moment and how perfectly magical her response is to all he offers. She wants him.

Riordan kisses her thigh and holds just enough pressure gently inside her so her body can acclimate to his touch. She begins to rock back and forth towards his hand very slowly, using his offered pleasure how she needs. Riordan opens his eyes and sees the absolute beauty of her tummy thrusting back and forth, her pale pink labia sweetly grasping at his fingers. He wonders if she knows how exquisite her body is to him.

"Huhh...huhh...Rior..." She's lost control of her tantric breaths, and he knows that's quite befitting. Her body is taking over and beginning to breathe and respond on its own, faster and faster. He looks up, watching her face, and begins to move his thumb along the hood skin that buffers and protects the most sensitive part of her. Riordan loves that she's clitoral and vulva sensitive, which means she may be very responsive to the multiple types of female orgasms he's willing to give her. He's committed to exploring all of them over time. After all, she's a goddess and should be worshipped as such.

One of her wrists breaks free of his hold, and she reaches for his ear then clings to his hair to pull him onto her, a clear invitation. He's so very pleased to feel her desire. He releases her other hand and brings it to his lips, kissing her fingers while his circle inside her. She grabs the carpet as if trying to hang on. He recovers from her, swiftly moving his mouth up, careful to unfurl her legs wide and arrange his hands, palms up under either side of her hips, cradling her tush. Her arms are free, and before she can seize him, he kisses her abdomen, then around her mound of gorgeous silky dark hair, and then down the inside of one leg forced open by his austere body size. He's teasing her senses. Demi lets out a breathless whimper, and he knows she's ready for his oral pleasure. He's accepting of every tell she offers so he can entwine their passions and meld their universal energy. He knows who she is, and it's completely in sync with how she responds. She's authentically tantric, and he loves it!

He inhales her scent deeply, and his own body pulses achingly with desire. As he leans in, gently using his lips to part her opening, she arches to him instinctively, her hands somehow find his hair again. She hitches a breath inward, and as soon as his velvety tongue reaches her clitoris and he begins his first suckle, Demi's body reacts in an abrupt crescendo of intense full-body pleasure...breaking, emerging, convulsing gorgeously, her palms thrashing up to clutch the floor above her head. Her abrupt move is followed by a loud resounding cry of bliss erupting from her core. Riordan holds still, resisting his own lascivious desire, with the sight of how beautiful she is in her goddess indulgence. He lifts up and views her writhing beauty as fulfillment releases through her body from head to toe. He's honored to share such a moment of pleasure for her. He watches her in amazement and grins at her, gazing into loving blue eyes that hold such desire for him still. He knows he's going to enjoy providing her more and more pleasure. Tantric energy is all he's ever yearned for with her, and he couldn't be more pleased with their natural chemistry.

He feels…she is his *one*.

18

Queen Must Have Her King

Riordan & Demi

Riordan continues to observe her, pausing with patience, as a gentleman should. When she falls listless, he places his palm on her flat tummy radiating energy into her. He needn't do much, and that's why he loves tantra. The perfect timing and arousal produce such intense full-body orgasm. Sex becomes less about the act and more about making love completely. He's no longer interested in the energy being centralized in just the private areas…but rather radiated throughout her, *and his*, body. Once he learned tantra, he was hooked! It's why he'd gone so long without anyone…until Demi.

Her rhythmical breathing returns, she looks up at him in awe. He watches her blink slow, salaciousness in his eyes. His heart swells with endearment for her…he's only ever dreamt of this moment. It's actually real. Proof, his law of attraction, manifesting is real. He feels he will never be able to be apart from her. Ever. This moment proves the last two years were his own torment, and his patience now worth every breath.

She locks eyes with him, her arms limp over her head, her breathing returning to match his. He breaks eye-contact and gently kisses her shoulder, assessing her sensitivity after her full body orgasm. He's learned women need their ecstasy moments after releasing their greatest energetic body power. She purrs, exhaling. He continues slowly peppering kisses down her breast, her ribs, slightly over to her tight belly, and down her abdomen. He's cautious and steady, so her arousal can build. He can already tell she's multi-orgasmic. A woman like Demi needs more and more. She loves his lips, his soft, groomed beard, his delicious scent caressing her nostrils. She loves his *mouth* and how gently he uses it.

Riordan *knows* tantra. He's not only educated, but he's also mature and aware that he should "edge" tonight, or better yet, allow things to simmer down and not lose his energy right away. There's time for him later. He knows he'll have more clarity and power by remaining controlled. He's already incredibly pleased with how she responds to his foreplay, and after this moment, he's looking forward to many, *many* more encounters to see her so aroused. He knows it's rare to be so in sync so early on. First-time sex can be quite awful, but it's as if her body was made to complement his! She's exquisite.

He moves more towards her core, inhaling her essence, his erection still unyielding, *throbbing*. Her scent continues to evoke him even more than before, and he feels as if he may go a little dotty. He wonders if he should stop, maybe continue more of this after dinner.

Pushing his thoughts aside, he returns his focus to her needs. Perhaps another few moments of yoni attention would hold her over until evening. When he reaches her belly button, he feels her hands come down and sweetly cup his face. She pulls him up towards her face, and he follows her guidance. She parts her lips kissing his mouth fiercely, desperately, her tongue searching. She draws a long breath in and energetically refuels from him, releasing a begging moan from deep within her throat. He finds it difficult to concentrate as her lips move along his, her tongue taking him over. She's beginning to possess him again, moving her hands in his hair. She breaks the kiss, whispering, "I need you."

He adores her words as they echo in his mind, words every man *needs* to hear. He breathes with her and mutters along her mouth, "I'm here." He wants her to know he's fully present with her...

"I want you..." She abruptly pushes him up and away as she gets up, he tries to respond, resting back on his thighs. He's not sure of what she wants, so he allows her some space to move. She sits up and presses against his shoulders, guiding him sweetly to the floor on his back. She whispers in the echo of the closet, "You're breathtaking. I want you so much."

Riordan feels very treasured. He watches her precious face as she moves his hands above his head now for *his* submission. He relents, trusting her, "You are so beautiful, Demi."

She smiles straddling him, "No more Ms. Greer stuff?" She teases, hovering above him, her warm wetness hovering above his engorged penis.

"If you prefer...I certainly won't mind calling you-" His voice gruff, as the sight of her hair falling around her gorgeous face unhinges his defenses and halts his thought.

"I prefer you..." She kisses him hard, inhaling him, his musk scent, his energetic strength...his engulfing passion. She wants all of him and breaks the kiss to find his neck and tastes him at the nape. His chest rises with arousal, and she moves to his chest with her fevered lips. She instinctively finds his erect nipple with her mouth. She suckles lightly, investigating how he reacts to stimulation on his erogenous areas, making mental notes of how to drive him wild as he did her. She feels his shaft pulse against her stomach and enjoys the velvety feel of his shaft skin. Swiftly she runs her lips down his soft chest hair, over his rippled stomach muscles, and before he can catch his breath, she gently engulfs him in her mouth. Riordan's head arches up instinctively, his eyes rolling closed at the extreme pleasure of her wet, merciful mouth. He sinks down into his body, *trying* to breathe. Demi curls one hand tenderly around the base of his shaft, then the other to cradle his scrotum, moving her mouth slowly up...then down, up....and down his long length. She is in awe of his girth and size, the absolute heavenly feel of his silky skin, and mostly the sounds of pleasure she hears from his strained breathing. She slows, relaxing their rhythm, and to prolong his satisfaction. He's so firm, it's as if he's waited years to be touched. She creates a delayed tantric rhythm with slight twisting, her tongue exploring him at a pace he can hardly bear. He inhales long between his teeth, trying to stay controlled, his hips beginning to rock to the tantric rhythm she's created. He's so close, and she can feel he's attempting, in anguish, to extend their buildup. She's impressed with his resolve. He's truly a king beneath her hands... and *mouth*.

Demi releases from her lustful suckling, gliding off from him slowly. His hands come down to meet and softly caress her hips as she moves up, straddling his mammoth frame. She gives him a few moments to recover, kissing his neck, his jawline, and finally, her favorite warmth...his *mouth*. He spreads his fingers open and uses his palms to caress up her back, pressing her into his chest. His erection now so prominent between them both. He can't help but pulse as her tongue glides and explores his mouth, her stomach pressing along him. He hugs her into his soul, careful not to cause her any discomfort. He's felt this embrace in his dreams over and *over*. Even as close as they are, he can't get enough of her. He feels her above him, shielding him, her hair surrounding them, his embrace protecting her.   Again, she finds his hair. She loves the feel of his soft, wavy curls between her fingers. Releasing her lips from him, she looks and sees his sleepy eyes coming to focus on her. He looks up at her, wanting to hear anything she has to say. She whispers in a hushed seductive voice, "I want you inside me…".

Riordan sobers as he looks up at her. He wants that too. He's wanted her so long he almost can't believe he hears her melodious voice ask for him. He brings his hand up the front of her neck to hold her face to his. He gazes deep into her, touches his forehead to hers, third eye to third eye. He closes his eyes and begins to say something, but she kisses him eagerly, taking his wrist and moving his arm back up over his head…holding him down, willing him to submit to her goddess within…as she had done with him. She breaks their kiss, lifting up…locking eyes with him. Riordan searches her expression. She grins, staring deep into him. Before he can react, she arches swiftly and slides down over his erection, engulfing him into her wanting, aching warm yoni. He's doesn't stop her, her tantric energy fierce! He stares at her face as she pushes her hands gently down into his chest, lifting herself up then deeper down to the base of his shaft, sinking onto him. She moans at the same moment he does. He fills her completely, stretching her, and as she seizes him in a long tantric snug squeeze and rocks her hips forward s-l-o-w, she feels her eyes begin to roll back in ecstasy. She's never felt any man as good as Riordan! He's warm, and silky, firm, and completely…enormous! Riordan clutches her hips with his large palms no longer able to keep them over his head. She feels magnificent, a haven he can never describe with language. She's moving so slow, she overtakes him, and he submits to her lead. He looks up at her perfect silhouette, hears her drawn breaths, and knows he must follow. She's driving him to mania, and he's relenting. She looks magical, her body gyrating slowly forward…then back, her eyes tantalizing and possessive. He doesn't know how much more he can withstand. Her elongated strides claiming and wanting, her pleasure prolonged.

As if she can read his mind, she whispers through quiet moans, "I'm with you. I want you to cum for me…you have all the power now."

Riordan realizes she's giving him permission and holding her own release for him! He sits up abruptly, cradling her head with his hand. Sweetly, he turns them both, placing her down on the soft carpet and moving on top of her. He knows she wants him deep, and if he can manage it, he'll caress her clitoris with his slow thrusts while deepening their sexual energy.

Cradling her in his arms, he brings his mouth down onto hers and thrusts his hips forward, sinking fervent into her essence. Pure ecstasy! Demi breaks from their kiss and wails with a surprising moan, her hands grip his back, and she pulls him deeper into her with her legs up and locking them around his waist!

Riordan feels her squeezing his head and shaft inside her pool of velvety warm mounds. Her body is suckling his! He thrusts slow and long, pressing his energy into her…she accepts him and squeezes a long tantric pulse. He follows her tempo. He's trying to keep her pleasure their priority but, as she throat moans more and more into his ear, he feels as if he's losing all discipline. Tantra IS control, a beautiful control, a prolonging of gratification to allow for complete body, mind, and soul immersion. Riordan has no idea how he's hanging on. He feels as if he'll lose his mind…

"Demi…" He whispers breathlessly in her neck.

To quiet him and allow their release, she finds his mouth with hers, and with one last slide of her warm tongue, one last tight tantric squeeze around him, she pulls him in, igniting his eruption, and she let's go along with him…

pulsing…

throbbing…

thrusting…

pulsing…and pulsing…

crashing over the cliff together…

together…

a queen has claimed her king…

19

Favorite

Demi

Riordan brings his brawny arm lovingly around her body, holding her in front of him. He strokes his thumb along her taut tummy. The shower-head is pouring steaming water over them, wrapping them in a cocoon of heat. Demi leans back against his chest, feeling his length along her back and tush. He's such a massive human, with very large features, and she finds him extremely enticing and gentle. He brings his other arm around her to snuggle her close. He enjoys the nape of her neck below her ear and her long, wet hair against his body teasing his cock. She sinks deeper into him, beaming as the memory of all they had just shared. The immortal memory swarms around in her mind. She'll never forget this day.

She smiles at the thought of how convenient it is that he has a full bathroom and closet attached to his office. She's supposed to be up on the top deck with her clients as they meet for lunch and relax in the hot tubs. She'd gotten them both very distracted! And…she loves it. Riordan is worth every touch, moment, memory, sacrifice, and breath. He's the best lover she's ever, *EVER* shared her body and tantric skills with. She's proud of herself for going against her angst and approaching him in his office anyway. She'd considered avoiding him for the next twelve weeks, thinking it would be easier after his "kiss rejection" but, after really meditating on it, she realized that was not what would bring her happiness. Just thinking of him brings her elation, and after very little sleep, she dared herself to follow her desires. Leaping into his lap in his office chair could have resulted in being fired and an escort off the yacht but, the alternative of never knowing his energy and parting ways felt like an assault against her inner being. She giggles now at the happiness she's experiencing following her instincts. *Always follow your inner being. Your soul IS your compass.* This is the most compelling joy she's ever felt. Riordan is everything she's ever wanted…and *needed*. Whatever happens from here, she knows she'll never regret this day!

He releases from gently suckling at her neck. "That…*was*…" He whispers, unable to finish his sentence, exhaling long instead.

"Hmmm…*it was*…"

"I don't believe I have words to describe what transpired…" He trails off.

She smiles, "None expected. I'm comfortable with euphoric silence. Just being in your arms is communication enough." She snuggles to him, rewarding his honesty.

"I…I like silence, although, I must admit, I've never fraternized with crew on duty before." He exhales near her ear, then kisses her lobe. "You've pleasantly corrupted my rules…"

"Oh, you won't hear any complaints out of me." She turns, giggling, and reaches up to put her arms around his neck. "By the way, where did you learn the tantric ways?"

He stands up, locking onto her frisky stare, "I had a few months stay in India once and learned some things about self-love, intimacy, and tantric energy while there. I could never go back to the western ways of living fast, being unfulfilled, and sexually disconnecting after that trip. I'm ruined." He smiles, meaning in more ways than one.

"Well, I can't say I agree with you being ruined…more like an *expert*." She kisses him, parting his lips with her tongue and exploring his moist, sweet mouth. The yacht abruptly jolts, and their kiss is broken.

He looks down at her, regretfully, "That's the engines readying for our departure. I'm sorry, I've got to get this beast out of this dock and out to sea in the next thirty minutes." He feels torn and wants to prolong their intimate time. He wonders how well the crew would do with him, *not* answering a knock at his office door. After all, he is only stepping into the role of "captain" for now. He's waited so long to feel her in his arms this way.

She kisses his nose, "I have to get my butt up on that top deck and play referee anyway. I really want to continue this, Captain Tate, should you feel…" He kisses her before she can finish her sentence. She giggles into the kiss, sliding her hands along his sculpted hips and down around his divine tush, giving a loving squeeze, pulling him into her body closer. He willingly forms to her, hugging her snug to him, feeling her curves beneath his fingertips and against his body. His groin responds at the feel of her, and she grins with a small moan. Their desire is so natural. She drives him wild…as if he's known her his whole life. He breaks free from their closeness, reluctantly, surprised at how easily he could ravish her again. He's more than satisfied but, his body wants more. Demi is the kind of female deity you can't get enough of, and he's excited for what more could happen.

20

Her Tongue

Demi

Riordan appears fifteen minutes later down on the lower deck. His uniform fresh, his hair wet but combed back, curls hanging. He nods to various crew as he makes his way to Captain Nero Ulfa in the control room. As he approaches, the real captain stands and shakes his hand.

"Ah, Captain Tate, we're underway and right on schedule. I'll have us out to deep-sea by the time you sit to eat lunch, sir." Captain Ulfa has tremendous respect for Riordan Tate. In the marine world, Riordan's reputation is impeccable. His rescue of the twenty-three men aboard the vessel LEE, off the coast of New Jersey, six days into his own wife's kidnapping in 2007, is still talked about. He not only saved those men and one injured coast guard rescuer, but he did, in fact, also rescue his wife. Sadly, she died in his arms in the chopper on the way to the hospital. Her knife wounds too severe. An unforgettable tragedy no one should have to endure. He always thought of Riordan, as a true man's man. When Errol Adler explained this mission and the importance of the undercover agents being led under the leadership of Agent Riordan Tate, Captain Ulfa didn't hesitate to move aside. If he was needed to stay "under deck" for three months instead of two weeks, he'd do it in a heartbeat. Riordan is a hero, in his opinion.

"Great to be here, Sir. Is there anything you need from me, Nero?" Riordan looks exhausted but in a pleasant way.

"Oh no, sir, you continue with your work. We'll take care of the scheduled port docking and take care of all the necessary supplies, shipments, and customs issues. You're in good hands."

Riordan nods. He can't comprehend how such a nice man, with so much experience and education, could work for Errol Adler for so many years. Then again, he questions his own loyalty to the cowboy bastard. It's got to be the money.

"Ay-Ay, Sir. You know where to reach me." Riordan playfully points up at the ceiling, motioning towards Captain Ulfa's bridge and the office he has now taken over, and christened with the exotic Ms. Demi Greer, who he already misses. They shake hands again, and he leaves.

***

Riordan leans against the side of the bar, sipping mineral water and lime, admiring Demi in a white bikini under a gorgeous matching sarong that's almost see-through, clipboard in hand. She leans in close towards one of the couples in the larger hot tub on the yacht's bow. She comforts them with jokes and her glowing smile. He adores her compassion and care for their enjoyment, as the yacht begins to move away from New York and into the sea. He catches on to a few glances from the husbands, and some of the wives, at Demi's body, understanding the lingering looks all too well. Demi is a voluptuously striking beauty and obviously desired by both sexes. She doesn't see how breathtaking she is, but he can. He wants to take her in his arms and carry her back to his room to reenact all the pleasurable things they'd done earlier. His body reacts, and he cooly sips his drink, trying to calm his inner yearnings for her already.

"She's quite a host, that instructa dere." Maurice points a shot glass towards Demi, then dries it with his towel, smiling at Riordan.

Riordan nods. He crunches ice between his back teeth, taking in her beauty and also watching the various behaviors of the new guests. He sees Demi certainly has an interesting group to transform. "Hmmm…" is his response.

Maurice continues, "I'm going to follow her lead wit dees drinks, sir. I don want da poor lady to hab a hard time, mon. Dis a special group." He giggles in his deep Jamaican voice.

"That's a good deal, Maurice. Thank you." Riordan puts a toothpick in his mouth and rests his foot on the wrung of the barstool he's standing near, his forearms leaning on the bar. Demi hears his deep voice and turns to lock eyes with him. She smiles at him in the middle of speaking with Alan. Riordan winks. He wants her to know he's thinking of her, that what they have is between the two of them. *She's amazing.* He remembers her scent, her mouth, her moans.

Demi excuses herself and walks alluringly in his direction. He feels his body relax as he exhales. Her being near calms him. She's responsive to him even in her work-mode. He's pleased to see her approaching.

"Good afternoon, Captain Tate. Would you be willing to take a moment to meet everyone?" She winks and waves her hand in the direction of her large group.

"I'd be happy to, Ms. Greer. Maurice and I were just having a drink. Can I offer you anything?" He looks down at her through tired bedroom eyes, his energy depleted but recharging by the minute. He wouldn't reject a late afternoon nap though, with her in his arms.

Demi smiles, tilting her head attentively, "I'll wait until later when I'm not working, thank you though, that's nice of you to offer."

"Aw, Ms. Dey-mi, it is fi o'clock somewhere." Maurice chuckles deep in his throat. Riordan grins, keeping his eyes locked on the woman that has brought him so much pleasure. He can't get her sounds, her movements, or her energetic lure out of his mind. His groin reminds him yet again.

"That's true, Maurice. *So* true. I need to get through this meet-n-greet stuff, and then I'll come to see you for that drink." She flashes her bright smile in the bartender's direction and looks up at Riordan, "Shall we, Captain?" She nods her head towards the large, rowdy group of hot tub talkers.

"After you."

Demi turns away from Maurice and gives her new lover a flirty smile as she makes her way toward her guests. Riordan follows her, stealing a quick glance of her waist and tight tush swaying in front of him. He looks up at the four couples and runs his hand down his beard before letting his arms rest at his sides. He's delighted that the faint scent of her still lingers on him despite their tantalizing shower. She looks back and whispers just loud enough for him to hear, "I'm missing those lips already." He tries to maintain his composure, despite the vivid memories flashing through his mind. He feels a surge of her energy flash through his chest. She's enchanting.

"Just say the word, Ms. Greer." And he means it. He'll please her anytime she desires it of him.

She stops and turns, smiling up at him. He slows, wondering how he'd explain her kissing him in front of an audience, let alone the cameras. She leans to him, presenting her clipboard as if she's showing him information. "I want those lips…on me, Captain." He looks down at her paperwork and then back at her exquisite blue eyes, seeing the want she has for him in her dilating pupils.

"Noted, Ms. Greer. It's now my highest priority. Your comfort is extremely important ma'am."

She blinks slow and exhales as if he's just freed her. "Hmmm…" She's pleased by his admission.

He hears her soft moan and finds their flirting extremely arousing. This mission is fast becoming his favorite, quite a switch from him refusing the very thought of her the day previous. She turns, leading him the rest of the way to the group. As he approaches the first hot tub, he pretends to adjust the watch on his wrist, signaling Grant to plant cameras in Lubna's room while Owens and Levy search the rest of the cabin for the jump drive or serum vials. He'll be sure to monitor the couple here on the top deck with the beautiful Ms. Demi Greer.

Demi watches Riordan conversing and listening intently to the couples as he goes from one to the next. He's very personable, and he looks so tantalizing to her. More so now that they've been intimate. It's a risk, especially after meeting only a day prior, yet she can't ignore her fierce intuition…or *desire for him*. She feels such a vibrational pull to him it's almost painful to be out of his presence. She's learned, in her tantric education, when the universal feeling comes to you, you act on it! Energy is real and not to be disregarded. He feels like home to her. That moment he shook her hand and looked into her eyes. She felt as if she could finally exhale. Now… she feels as if he is her air, although the sight of him can take her breath away.

"Isn't that right, Demi?" Sagrid touches Riordan's forearm and calls out to Demi. "Captain Tate is very uh…how you say? Taut? Tight…no taut, yes? He should join us for tomorrow's ten o'clock morning Yoga, yes?"

Demi moves closer to them so Sagrid will cease her obnoxious shouting. She softly obliges, "Captain Tate, you're more than welcome to join us for chakra balancing yoga each day if you'd like." Her voice is melodious, her eyes intense with a sassy challenge.

He's staring at her half-smiling, "Thank you, Ms. Greer. I have other ways I stay in shape, and by ten o'clock in the morning, I'll be steering this tiny boat in the direction of the islands you all want to land on." He gives her a quick wink. Demi clears her throat, her insides pulsing unexpectedly.

"Of course." She likes him. He even flirts properly.

Sagrid makes a loud raspberry sound with her over-injected botox lips, "Ah, I guess our captain prefers his alone time with da veights?" She squeezes a bicep, getting Riordan's uniform shirt wet. He spots how quiet Lubna is and catches her look of annoyance towards her outrageous wife. "You like alone-ness Captain Tate?" Sagrid slurs the words and drops her drink off the side of the hot tub onto the deck.

"I do what works for me." Riordan keeps a pleasant smile but nods to Maurice. He looks at Demi and assures her with a smile, he's going to take care of Sagrid's behavior. Maurice picks up a phone behind the bar and readies a rag for cleanup. "Well, ladies, it's been a pleasure meeting you, but I must get back to the bridge and make sure we're still up for clear skies this evening. You all enjoy your afternoon, and let my staff know if there's anything you need." Riordan steps away from Sagrid and turns to wave to all the couples. In unison, they all wave and murmur goodbye to their uniformed captain. Demi smiles and lowers her eyes as he leaves. She tries not to seem too obvious and steals a glance also of his luscious, exiting backside.

Sagrid downs the rest of Lubna's blood-orange martini, "Oh, I don't want the captain to goes, but I like the view when he do!" She laughs, lowering her sunglasses to follow Riordan's perfectly sculpted back and rear as he disappears into the stairwell. Lubna leans into her wife's ear and scolds her. Sagrid pushes her off with an elbow and begins to stand, dripping hot tub water on her spouse. A very large crewman appears from the stairwell and walks right to Sagrid to help her out of the hot tub with a towel.

"Oh my darling, thank you, aren't you a big boyz." She thanks the crewman, squinting at his name-tag, reading the name "Hemmel" in her Swedish accent. He continues to guide her across the deck and over to Maurice, who has a large glass of water prepared. Hemmel takes the water and Sagrid's elbow and disappears with her through a door behind Maurice's bar. Lubna frowns and looks to Demi. The exit was so swift, there was little time for Lubna to react, let alone follow her wife.

Maurice bends to Lubna, "Ms. Nayhan, Hemmel is going ta help yur wife to de elevator and den to yur cabeen. Dey Captain do not allow intoxicashon on de tope deck. She be bery safe...and mooch more comforbul in yur suite." Maurice explains, and Demi catches the conversation silently praising Riordan's discreet orders.

"Well, shouldn't I go with her?" Lubna is visibly uncomfortable.

Maurice's deep voice is very soothing, "If you feel you most, but I'd hate fer ya ta miss out on Ms. Greer's activoties." He motions toward Demi with one hand, the other behind his back.

Lubna frowns at Demi with agitation. Demi offers Maurice a sweet smile, "We're going to meet over at the floating hammock area to enjoy dessert and more ice-breaker exercises. After that, we'll turn in and will reconvene in the morning for our first Toga session. Tonight is a night at sea and time for us to get comfortable with our couples."

Maurice helps once more, "Oh, yu don wanna to miss dessert, ma'am." He shakes his head, grinning wide-eyed at Lubna.

"I-I guess. My wife booked this trip, and now she's not even here for the first afternoon! I'm getting so tired of this." Lubna's irritation resounding.

"It only anudder hour miss. You complete de activoties, and den tell yur wife about it at brefas no?" Maurice shrugs his shoulders. Demi thinks he is very professional and appreciates his assistance.

"Yes, yes, I can do that. Okay, where do we go?" Lubna stands up, and Maurice runs a few steps to get her a towel. He helps her out of the hot tub and shows her the way to the floating hammocks aft.

Demi watches them depart, then turns towards the tinted bridge windows where she's sure Riordan is watching. She mouths the words "thank you" and rolls her eyes while smiling.

Riordan enjoys every part of her interaction and makes a mental note to praise Maurice in front of his peers at the staff meeting. Lubna choosing to stay and not being frenzied, or running after her wife, is a better outcome. He notices she's not overly concerned about her wife or a crew member going to her cabin, so she either has the billion dollars of stolen information on her person or hidden elsewhere on the yacht. He's betting Grant and Owens will find very little in Lubna's cabin now.

Riordan touches his watch, and Grant keys up, "Phone Errol and patch the call through to Sagrid. Make him think *she* called him, and her think *he* called her. Let's see if they reveal anything while Lubna is busy. I'm getting a strange vibe."

"Received. Out." Grant disconnects.

Riordan remembers Grant is still pissed at him from this morning, which he can allow. He has him to thank, really. His pep talk warmed him up and helped him relent to Demi's advances. Grant will still do his job despite his emotions, as he's always done. And Riordan knows he'll come to see him if anything comes out of the recorded call between Errol and Sagrid. He takes a seat in his captain's chair again and watches the woman who's now changed his life in just a short twenty-four hours…well, technically two years back.

He gazes down at her, enjoying the way she's eating an ice cream cone with her students while laying in a floating hammock. He smiles at the memory of her crawling on his lap, kissing him… their union in his dressing closet when she surprised him by making him *her* lick-able cone. *Oh, the feel of her slow, loving tongue.* He can't get her out of his mind.

21

Satisfy Her

Riordan

Riordan studies Captain Ulfa's charts and understands the routes chosen, the islands they'll dock at, and the potentially dangerous areas for pirating, rogue waves, and marine life. He leans back in his desk chair and looks around the spacious bridge office. The hours have passed, the sun has set, and darkness has taken over most of the lighted areas on the deck below. Demi has left, as have all the couples, and he wants nothing more than to go find her. He checks his watch and realizes why he's so hungry. He picks up the phone and calls down to the kitchen.

"Hello Gerdie, it's Capn' Tate. Have all our guests eaten?" He's trying to see if Demi has already retired to her cabin.

Gerdie clears her throat, "Yes, sir. Well, Ms. Greer has requested her dinner in her room this evening. She did not eat with her guests in the main salon."

"Oh, she didn't? Is she ill?"

"I don't believe so, sir, quite the opposite."

"Oh?" He hopes she doesn't make him fish for information. He pauses.

"Well, I don't want to be a snoop, but she may have a guest." Gerdie lowers her voice as if telling him a secret.

He smiles on his end of the call, "Oh, okay."

"I only say so sir, because she is so slim but asked for two dinners and a bottle of wine….oh, and two desserts!"

He's thrilled at the information but realizes Gerdie is one to watch out for as she repeats details, "I see, well she does have many students on board. She's probably dining with one while she conducts a private therapy session. As long as she or any of the guests are not sick, we're good. Right Gerdie?"

"Oh, yes, sir. You're right."

"Okay then, you have a good evening. Great job today, by the way. Excellent attention and service to our guests." He knows how to incentivize his staff with praise.

She sounds proud, "Thank you, sir!"

"Good night, Gerdie." He hangs up. He has one more phone call before heading to his cabin. He pushes a tiny button on his watch and waits. The phone on his desk rings, and he picks it up. "Hey."

"Hey."

He's aware Grant may not want to talk, "I'm going to head to my cabin and turn in. You good?"

Grant knows Riordan is checking in. It's been this way since they were in fifth grade. Even when they're mad at each other, there's still a check-in. Grant will always answer about work, but he can't be budged to discuss personal feelings unless he's the one bringing it up. He'd said enough earlier and, by all rights, should be thanked. Grant's outburst helped Riordan understand the magnitude of his feelings for Demi and how his decisions not only affect him, they affect Grant as well. Demi advancing on him, of course, sealed the deal. He's not sure he could've resisted her, and now knowing Grant supported him beforehand, he's even more grateful for their friendship.

"Yep. Nothing new. Sagrid and Errol sounded like a bunch of idiot blamers. Spent more time trying to figure out who butt-dialed who, then saying anything important or anything we can use as evidence. She hung up on him after he called her a drunk. They've got some interesting relationship dysfunction."

Riordan is pleased to hear Grant elaborate, "Okay, I can't say I'm surprised. It was worth a shot. Great job."

"Yeah."

"Okay."

Grant hangs up. Riordan looks at the phone, wondering how long it'll take Grant to ease up this time…and when he should tell him about the most incredible encounter he's ever had. He may just keep it all to himself. Evelyn was Grant's sister, so he was a part of their life and marriage in a family sense. Her death just about killed him, but Grant was destroyed too. Neither of them could save her. Riordan thinks for a few moments. Perhaps keeping Grant farther away from this would be best. Grant loved his little sister deeply, and Demi wouldn't be the first woman he'd try to "friend" in an effort to replace what he's been missing in a sister. Then again, it might be what Grant needs.

Riordan straightens up his desk, pushes in his chair, and makes sure nothing is left out. For the first time in years, he feels excited to leave his office and looks forward to activities outside of work. He turns off the lights and heads towards his goddess.

Moments later, he knocks on her cabin door, a small box tucked nonchalantly in front of his stomach. No need for the cameras to identify more details of his extracurricular activities. His other hand is tucked behind his back in a habitual military stance. Riordan hasn't lost his integrity, despite his heart suddenly distracting him.

Demi opens the door, and when he sees she's barely clothed, he steps to the right to block her, so she's not exposed on the cameras, although *he* certainly doesn't mind her appearance. He smiles and is patient, the view is incredible. Demi smiles bright and gives a small wave inviting him in. She closes the door behind him, and then jumps into his arms to show him how much she's missed him in the last seven hours. He happily catches her.

Demi kisses him intensely yet somehow remains gentle, her lips soft and relaxed, her tongue searching. He carries her in his arms to the living room and sits down in a huge high-back chair. She's straddling him yet again, and he smirks, thinking how erotically immersive she is and how this is the way things heated up earlier. She exhales and breaks the kiss that's already taken effect on her, beginning to moisten her treasured female parts. She gazes up at him with bedroom eyes, and he realizes it's fast becoming his favorite look from her. Her outfit is as sexy as her sultry gaze. He holds her away from him to see that underneath a gorgeous cream-colored bohemian lace half-robe, she's wearing matching g-string panties and a see-through lace bra. It's as flattering as her earlier white bikini, and he loves the way her dim cabin lighting illuminates the outfit against her skin. She has curves that should be illegal, and he is incredibly grateful they are beneath *his* hands.

"Wow, this looks exquisite on you. Is this how you sleep every night?" He grins, moving his palm to cup her cheek. He doesn't remember her dressing this way when he had her ex-husband under surveillance. Admittedly, he would often excuse himself from the surveillance room and keep another employee on shift through difficult nights. It tore at his heart to see such a beautiful soul entangled with pure evil. He looks at her, knowing he will never allow evil to enter her life again if he can help it.

She's happy to see his appreciation and hear it in his deep, rhythmic voice. "I try to feel good about myself now and buy clothing my body reaches for. When I saw this tonight in my closet, I thought of you. I've had it for a while, but you're the only one I've wanted to take the tags off for.

"Well, I'm in awe of you. Thank you for including me."

"I can't stop thinking of you. This afternoon was more than I could've ever hoped for. Do you know what it feels like to connect with you and find out you're tantric too?" Her eyes are wide, like she's revealing found treasure.

"I do now." He smiles wide.

"Who taught you so much about the female body?" She cups his face, caressing his well-groomed beard. He's so damn good-looking.

He didn't want to get into too much detail, "A guru in India, and her female students of course, but that was years and years ago. I'm a bit rusty."

"I don't think you're rusty at all. Were you okay with me wanting you to be satiated?" She knows true tantric men try to remain powerful with ejaculatory release control and only when they choose. She knows she begged, and she's so happy she did. He's beautiful when vulnerable. He's powerful because of it!

He's enjoying their exchange, "I *more* than enjoyed how things went. Your energy is magnificent."

"I feel the same. Have I ever met you before yesterday, Captain Tate?" She smiles teasingly.

"You're going to at least call me by my first name when we're alone, right?"

"If you prefer. I kind of like the sound of Capn' Tate!" She giggles, and it makes him happy.

"I would prefer, at least in these private moments." He really loves the way she purrs his name…even if she calls him Rior, just hearing her address him with her sexy, throaty voice makes him excited.

She looks down, "Is that for me?"

He jokes, "The pretty box or the bulge in my uniform pants?"

Demi laughs out loud and throws her head back a little, she jokes back, "Well both, and I think the bulge is pretty too!"

"Oh?" He feels great about her enjoying his body; he's certainly enjoying hers.

"Oh yes!" She nods, and he slides his palm along her beautiful neck. She grows serious with his touch and allows him to pull her lips to his. He meets her halfway, closing his eyes to caress her mouth with his own. A small moan escapes her, and he's reminded of how she sounds, his body pulsing in response. She's breathing slow, but her tongue begins to explore at a faster pace. She takes his hand and slides it in her lace lingerie opening, clearly inviting him to touch her erect, wanting nipple. Gently, he caresses around her areola with the warmth of his large thumb pad. She arches in. He obliges and draws her closer. Exploring her moist, hot mouth as he begins to match her breathing. Letting her set the pace.

Slow…

Sensual.…

She loves to inhale and exhale completely through each exploration. As if she's committing every touch to memory.

Suddenly, she melds closer to him, pressing deeper into the kiss and pressing him against the chair. Once pinned, she slides her hands around his neck, running her fingers up and through his soft hair and then down his defined neck muscles…caressing, massaging tension from him. He feels his shoulders relax beneath her heated touch. Now fully erect and breathing to her rhythm, he feels her pressing and squeezing his lingam through their clothing. Demi moans in his mouth, kissing him deeper, and he takes her cue by grasping her curvaceous rump to press her down onto him as he then stands up. He huffs mildly and smiles; he finds himself walking her to a more private area to rapture her for the second time today. She smiles through her kiss, pleased he's taking the initiative to move forward with their night. She is loving everything about this day!

Demi allows her hands to work at his buttons and uniform while he kicks off his shoes and socks along the path to her bedroom quarters. He finds her massive bed and is impressed by the warm glow in the room, with soft light bouncing off their skin from the floor lights. He moves his hands to protect and cradle both her head and tush, gently laying her down in front of him. She reaches out to him, not wanting to lose their attachment. He follows her gaze and stretches along the splendid length of her body with his own, careful not to crush her. She's so beautifully delicate yet fierce in her femininity.

She's got his shirt almost off, and his undershirt untucked from his pants. His stomach ripples with taut muscle. She enjoys the feel of him beneath her fingers. She could explore every inch of him with just her palms and never get enough. The energy running off of his body makes her pulse within. Her yoni is throbbing with fevered heat. Unbuckling his belt with one hand, she gets into his pants with the other, hearing him gasp as she slides her palm in along his firm, warm shaft. Gently, she frees him and glides her soft thumb over his drop of precum. He's so ready, even after their afternoon tryst. Tantric men rarely lose stamina, and she smiles at how she has attracted and found her match.

Demi enjoys undressing him. He's slow, gentlemanly, and incredibly serene for such a giant. She finds this *very* alluring. He's not impatient. His movements sultry and timed within their slow breaths. Prolonging gratification can be torturous, but it's a glorious torment with him. Every throb is as if she's feeling mini-pulses of orgasm before the actual surrender.

She breaks their intense kissing so she can glance at him, now naked, his chest and neck exposed, near her fevered lips. The glow of him in the dim lights make him a sight before her! A god draped in golden hues of color, protective and warm against her wanting body. She revels in the pleasure of how her body pulses rhythmically to him while she studies him, an aching need contracting within her soul. She wonders if he knows how attractive he is to her. How much she's built intense desire for him in such a short time of knowing him. She takes a pause to really admire him, drink him in, running her fingers along his face, neck, down his shoulder…bicep, stomach, and along his wanting lingam. She likes that he's on his side so she can view him in front of her and prop her head on her hand. He's breathing long and relaxed, watching her eyes, letting her massage him with her tantric expertise. His engorged penis, resting between them, delights her with silky, warm fluid she hopes to enmesh with her own momentarily. She knows he'll try to control himself and put her pleasure first, but she'd much rather feel him surrender with her. He seems to have controlled himself enough prior to meeting her.

His face is tranquil, and his eyes are admiring her hair, her face, her neck, and her spherically, rotund breasts. She's captivating, her physique arousing him as much as her loving caress. They drink each other in. The visuals of their body parts that brought so much pleasure earlier in the day are now glowing in the shadows of the low lighting and flowing bed fabrics. The cool air from the window breezes along their skin and feels like velvet. She licks her own bottom lip, slowly from left to right, as she's exploring his magnificent face with her eyes, his rock-hard erection with her soft palm. She feels him squeeze in a tantric breath and keeps in sync with him. She is aware of how they're bonding and possibly creating a secure attachment that may never be severed. She wants that. How tantra can commit two souls together for a lifetime is absolute bliss.

She's *thinking*…keeping eye contact, while letting her hand now explore his hair, ear, neck, and chest… Her palm opens wide, sliding down his pectoral, the erect nipple, encircling it slowly with her finger pad. He's very well sculpted and so *very* appealing, yet doesn't seem to notice himself too much. Riordan seems completely content with his fixation upon her.

He's caressing her cheek, trailing down along her shoulder. Her long hair drapes forward and falls, leaving strands against her waiting, swollen breast. He turns his fingers and runs his nails sweetly along the side of her neck and down her chest. Her eyes roll closed, the pleasure causing her yoni to ache. He sees how she responds to his feather-light touch. This Tantra technique prolongs arousal, and he's excited to know her orgasms are building. He loves relaxing her while waking all her senses at the same time. She lets out a long, exhaled moan, and she instinctively reaches again for his shaft, using the same feather-light touch on him. He pumps beneath her grasp and watches her respond to touching him. She smiles so lovingly, she's gorgeous to see, and he thinks of how honored he is to finally be with her. Oh, how he's dreamed of this for so, so many nights. He's filled with gratitude, as he was sure he'd never see her again. He wasn't aware he could feel so strongly for her just being in her presence. He knows now, dreaming, yearning, visualizing her in his mind drew her closer and closer. He knows now the power of intention, the importance of attraction. No matter the circumstances, energy begets energy, and their vibration matched and found each other despite the world. He knows now she was meant to walk into his office yesterday, that they both dreamt each other into being.

As she grasps him just a bit more snugly, he responds again. Her touch is so soft and loving. She *knows* how to touch him. She's the kind of woman a man can trust.

"Riordan…"

"Hmmm…"

She focuses her eyes on his, "What do you want?"

"You…"

"You are so…*hard*…" A tiny smile appears under sultry bedroom lashes. Her deep blue eyes are looking exquisite in the glow of the room. She gives another tender squeeze.

"I am…because you…" He's trying to answer, his eyes slightly rolling back with the pleasure she's gifting. He finds it almost impossible to even whisper.

"Yes…" She waits.

"I-I'm so happy you joined me…in my office today. I'm really happy you came onboard yesterday. I'm so…" His deep whispers trail off.

She smiles and glides her fingertips like silk, then her hand, taunting and arousing him, "I was unsure but **very** happy I ignored my fears. I knew touching you would be worth the rejection if you had-"

He leans to kiss her forehead. She was worried about being refused even more than he, "There's no way I could reject you…I had decided to try and distance myself from you…but-" He knows how incredibly strong of a woman she is. It's one of the reasons he's so attracted to her. She's got a quiet fire.

She chuckles softly, "You're very intimidating, Captain Tate."

He moves down to softly kiss her nose, "Ahhh, just titles. I don't bite."

She then moves her head back to look in his eyes, giving him another long pump, massaging his foreskin ever so gently. He blinks slowly with the tingling sensations and surges she sends through him. "No, your fierce eyes, serious look, your...absolutely massive...*size*." She glides and squeezes more intensely on his girth.

"I haven't hurt you, have I?" He asks. He looks at her, concerned, tracing his thumb along her bottom lip. She delights in the way his eyebrows hitch up slightly, feeling a surge in her heart as she sees how much he cares for her comfort.

"Oh my, no."

He feels better, letting out a small sigh and letting his shoulders relax. "Oh, good. I do not want to hurt you."

"A bit snug...and exceptionally sexy. I had to *have* you. I felt as if I've known you, as if my body yearned for you...for years somehow."

Riordan leans forward and onto her, pleased he can be vulnerable and admit things to her so freely and early on. Demi makes it easy for him to be himself.

She brings both her hands up under his arms to spread her palms on his back and press his back into her to be closer. She loves the weight of him on her. The immense heat radiating off his chest and into hers warms her to the core. Oh, he feels so good, his muscles bulging between her long fingers, his wanting lingam strong and fevered against her stomach.

"We have a deep connection Demi...I don't know why. I only know it feels really good. I felt it from the moment I met you." He chortles, meaning years ago when he met her himself, through surveillance feed. "This feels comfortable and just..."

"Yes. It feels really, **really** right. I had learned of this...I mean, it's taught in every tantra class about how aligning your own intense energy will draw your perfect match to you, how you need to do nothing but focus your own energy and healing. Now, I really get it!" She arches her pelvis into him. He knows what she wants. She guides the way, and he follows her invitation. She communicates predominantly in touch, and he absolutely adores her types of conversing.

"You are so lovely…very, very, *very* special Demi." He leans in and kisses her with so much feeling, it's completely instinctual. She arches down and slides around him in one motion, slick and velvety with want and desire for him. He glides and molds into her body snug and begins to gently thrust, making love to her slowly and poetically, with long rhythmic strokes as she squeezes gently around his girth. It's all so perfect, the right pace, the right timing… the aching pleasure with each firm squeeze and release. Their bonding is taking hold and so early on. He sinks deeper…and *deeper*… into her snug yoni, passion grasping at them both. Their ebb and flow of lovemaking seeming to follow the tide of the ocean just outside their yacht window. Slow and natural movement…incredible pleasure, so enjoyable the rest of the world simply disappears.

An hour later, Demi latches around him, drawing her orgasmic energy yet again, up and serpent-like through her chakras… her kundalini flow offered slowly through him and he through her. He's building his power again, in no hurry, as this pleasure is divine. His aim is to satisfy her, and only her…

22

A Man

Demi

Demi breathes in deep, stretching her arms above her head, her toes pointed out towards the bottom of the bed. She opens her eyes and senses him near. His heat is magnetic. A smile tugs at the corners of her mouth, and her sleepy eyes fixate on him. As she begins to focus, she takes in the sight of him next to her, his arm tucked under his pillow, his bicep ample with sculpted muscle. His other palm down on his stomach, the beautiful silk of the sheet just covering his manhood resting beautifully plump yet flaccid on his inner thigh. She rolls quietly closer, careful not to wake him. Her head sinks into the plush pillow, and she stares, taking in the absolute glorious sight of him, a god in her bed. Her body throbs inside for him *again* causing her to smile at how much she desires their connection. Never before has she felt such balance with a man. He so quickly completes her body, mind, and soul weaving. She wants to do so many things with him and *to* him…

His breathing moves his muscles rhythmically up and down along his ribs. Demi resists the urge to reach over and caress the ripples of perfect muscle, knowing full well he needs rest from her keeping him up so late. She continues to enjoy the sight of his smooth sun-kissed skin and follows his physique with her eyes. As she syncs her breathing with his, she notices their connected energy stirs him, and he stretches and turns over away from her, exposing his perfectly V-shaped back. There are a few markings she wasn't aware of, most likely because each time they've explored each other's bodies, she's been completely preoccupied or in low lighting. They're still exploring each other, and she realizes she's committing each inch of him to memory.

There's a scar near his left lower rib area that looks very much like a knife injury, a second similar yet longer scar peeks out from under his armpit. She squints, trying to guess how this evidence of trauma came about on such a decent human. She thinks how it appears as if he's been in close hand-to-hand combat. Eyeballing from his head, down his spine, to his perfect tush, which admittedly made her raise her eyebrows and linger a moment, she wonders how a military man has not one tattoo. He's damn near perfect, except for his two slight scars, there may be more, but she's pretty clear that she'd see him as flawless regardless. She makes a mental note to ask him sometime, and as she reaches forward, almost touching him, she retracts her hand begrudgingly, knowing if she wakes him, she may very well *not* make it on time to teach her morning yoga class!

Demi quietly leaves the warmth of the bed and tiptoes to the shower, her body already aching for him despite the multiple orgasms he'd provided just hours before. Riordan Tate is definitely the most amazing lover she's ever encountered. As she reaches into the shower to feel the temperature of the water, a smile overtakes her. She's finally able to admit to herself, she's ecstatic to be divorced!

Already forty-five minutes into the yoga root chakra stretches on Deck A, Demi quietly guides the class, "...and with a long, drawn-out master breath...come out of your chin-to-chest neck stretch, raise your chin up...third-eye up to the sky. At the same time, you want to curl your tailbone and root chakra up, as well... great job...".

Demi sees Sagrid briskly walking towards the group. She lays her yoga mat out, bends down on her hands and knees to lift her head and tush, mimicking the group. She appears awkward and a bit abashed.

"...let's take another long drawn breath, please don't forget your tantric squeeze...use your body's greatest energetic power, class...you'll thank yourself later as you experience the dopamine, oxytocin, and serotonin boost...just from a properly drawn breath!". Demi peeks again, and Sagrid is looking around, trying to correct herself, comparing her moves to both Alan and Roderick. Seems odd that she's not alongside her wife, as Lubna did get to class on time and is at the front of the class with a space next to her that she obviously saved for her wife.

"...and with another beautiful breath...I'll ask you all... when you're ready, to lower yourselves down to your mat, and onto your backs..."

Sagrid scoffs so the whole class hears her, obviously dissatisfied with having to move out of the position she had just worked so hard to copy.

Demi smirks, knowing a student who isn't fully invested in the energy and breath of a move is still on their logical brain side and not even near being relaxed enough to transition into a new pose. Sagrid has missed the entire class, so she's not going to like the next part either.

"...as you sink down into your mat, feeling the floor beneath you, please allow your legs to relax, your feet to fall open... take a deep master breath and move your arms out in an a-frame with palms up towards the sun. Deep breaths going through that root chakra, spiraling all the way up and through all your chakras surrounding your spine and out...". Demi sits back on her ankles and scans the group. She stands and begins to walk around, monitoring the couples and watching them ease down into their meditations. "Okay, everyone, you have the next ten minutes for you. Please take your time, make the best of your self-care, and really allow those deep masterful breaths to heal you. I'll be back in a little while to close out the class...you all did such an amazing job..."

Demi walks through the class as everyone is laid out on the mats. She's pleased to see all her students are finally relaxing. Even Sagrid has found a slower breathing with her eyes closed and her overly large sunglasses on. Her hangover must feel as rough as she looks.

Demi continues her silent steps around the area and through the group. Electricity reaches her, and as if being hit by lightning, she senses *him*. Looking up, she locks eyes with her beloved. Riordan gives her a look that she recognizes is only for her, and she smiles curtly, knowing he's headed to his office and just wanted to share a moment with her. He's getting a late start, and she represses a giggle, aware that she's the reason why. He turns and heads up the stairwell in his freshly pressed captain's uniform. Demi catches a glimpse of his rear and sighs. She loves how their tantric connection continues to increase her attraction to him. *If that's even possible.*

Riordan takes another sip of coffee as he leafs through the report Grant left for him. He looks up towards the soft knocks at his door, and he knows it isn't Grant. Even her knock has become familiar. Demi peeks in before he can answer. Riordan smiles and waves her in. She enters, closing the door behind her. Fighting the urge to jump into his lap, she instead ops for the deep navy blue chair in front of his desk and takes a seat.

"Well, there you are!" She whispers.

"Good morning." His voice is deep and smooth, his sweet smile just for her.

"Good morning. How are we feeling?" Demi leans, resting her chin in her hand, elbow tucked on the armrest.

His eyes are dancing, "Really great. I have no complaints."

"I can see that, although there's a bit of a sleepy look happening here…" She swirls her long fingers towards him and chortles. He looks somewhat sleepy but in pleasant spirits.

"Yes, I slept in. I don't get to do that very often. Thank you, by the way."

"I enjoyed seeing you rest. You should get more sleep. And you are most welcome."

He smiles wider, enjoying her playfulness, "I agree, but there's just something about losing sleep for the right person…and then regaining *strength* later."

"I'm not really thinking that there's *anything* wrong with your strength…or your control for that matter." She likes his compliment and returns one back at him.

"Well, thank you, I do try to exercise control at all times, but there are some special situations that truly challenge me." He gives her a small wink, returning her flirtatiousness. "Yet, I'm always up for a challenge."

Her eyebrows raise, and she looks at the floor, "Yes…that you are." She laughs, and he joins her. Her eyes meet his, and she leans in, lowering her voice, "Seriously, you have incredible edging control! You know you don't have to-"

"Uh…yes, yes I do. Especially with how things are going, which are amazing, by the way, but I will be building my resolve as I can. Don't worry, I'll be sure to meet your energy and be vulnerable when it's appropriate…just not every…day…"

Demi loves that he understands the importance of a man "edging" to keep his stamina and control. It's not an easy tantric practice, and many men, especially her students, get very frustrated trying to have an orgasm but not ejaculating…or just allowing an intense build up, and no orgasm, over a few days. Society has taught men to always go for it, get to the goal, overindulge…and then they wonder why they feel weak in their body, their minds, and lower energy in life. It's amazing to her how so many have been conditioned and taught incorrectly about male and female energy and given the opposite knowledge of what is actually needed. Riordan knows so much. *Soooo* much, and she realizes what a turn-on it is that he not only understands and practices tantric principles, but it shows up first in his demeanor and then in the bedroom. She feels slightly greedy that she gets to enjoy so many orgasms, and he edges to enjoy one for her three. She knows that this is the way true energy was meant to be. *Female before male.* He understands the worshipping of his goddess and how her slow, long, tantric orgasms increase her power…the way a woman was intended to be. In her eyes, he's a real man, not a coward like her ex-husband, where everything was about him, his life, his work, *his*…orgasms. She knows now what she's been missing in life. To her, there is nothing like the energy of an authentic man. She hopes to bring this feeling along to the couples and teach them the **truth**. There's always a risk of them splitting up, truth can do that, but it's better in the end. Truth creates an undying bond between two lovers…or brings one to the right lover and away from the wrong one. She looks at him with gratitude. Not only is she able to teach her students from her authentic experience, but she's sure the love that's growing for him in her…will come through her energy.

"I look forward to you matching me." She sits back, "So what's your schedule look like today?"

"I've got a few meetings. I'm preparing for our docking at the Isle of Verde, but after four, I'll be free. How about you?"

"Well, I finished yoga. I'll be sending my couples off for an afternoon of swimming and lunch as I see each of them privately in their own couples session. We'll all reconvene for dinner and dancing on the top deck. Could I interest you in a slow dance? I'd much prefer you as my dance partner."

Riordan knows that he shouldn't be seen in uniform dancing with another employee of the crew, but a larger part of him doesn't want to let her down. "I'll try to conveniently be lingering on the top deck around then…looking like a preferred dance partner." He smiles. A loud one-knuckle knock sounds as the door opens. He looks up and nods.

23

My Goddess
Riordan

He knows the code knock and tells Grant to enter. Demi turns and smiles. She stands, "Well, I'll let you get back to work. I've got to go wake up the sleeping beauties out there on their yoga mats."

Riordan stands, "Have a great day. Let me know if there's anything you need."

"I will, thank you." She turns, "Crewman Apton, good morning."

"Morning, ma'am." He steps aside, giving her room to leave. As she does, he closes the door behind her and turns to look at his best friend. A smirk is forming at his mouth.

Riordan smiles, "Grant." He waves his hand at the chair she just left, offering it for him to sit in.

"Sir." Grant slumps down the way he always does when they're alone.

"Sir? You still mad?"

"Nope. Pointless, I guess."

Riordan smiles. He loves it when Grant finally stops being mad. He's terrible at any negative emotion. "How so?"

Grant brings his fist up, resting his cheek on it, "You know how so, dick. You finally listened to me…but you had to get me all angry and pissed."

"I can't take responsibility for your feelings…but I will admit I am grateful you can express them to me, even if it is a bit aggressive."

"That wasn't nearly as aggressive as I should've been. And I regret not doing it sooner. You've fucking been in love with her for years, Tate." Grant leans back against the chair.

Riordan clicks his pen a few times. They both pause.

Grant sighs and crosses an ankle at his knee. He's chooses not to speak.

Riordan eyes him, "Thank you."

Grant's eyebrows raise, his face softening. It was unexpected but definitely nice to hear. "I got you, brother."

Riordan nods. He knows Grant can be the worst drunk, sometimes the biggest fuck-up too, but he's never let him down when it mattered. Missions, deaths, business, secrets, loyalty, and now love. He's a best friend for a reason. He's got what it takes, for over thirty-three years. "Same...but really, man, thank you. I- I can't even describe-"

"No need. It's the real deal. I know you."

Riordan smirks, "Uh, about that-"

"I took care of the footage. No worries. There really wasn't much."

"Right on."

"I mean, it was cute, but there wasn't much." Grant's eyes squint as a big smile shows on his face.

"Cute?"

"Okay, not cute. More like inhibited...*visually*. Hopeful."

"Hopeful?"

"Yeah, well, first she was hopeful with deep throat kissing you. Then the locking of eyes here and there, the hallway footage, hiding the box in front of your stomach, entering her room shielding her from view and never leaving...at.........*all*...." Grant teases.

"You made your point, Apton."

"See? Cute."

Riordan sighs and smiles, "Cute, huh."

"Hmmm...yerp." Grant watches Riordan, pauses, and bursts out laughing. Riordan tries not to laugh but ends up joining him. "Right?

Riordan shakes his head slowly, "It's so...not cute."

"What do you mean?" He leans in, watching his eyes. There's a look he hasn't seen in Riordan in years.

Riordan leans back in his chair, running both his hands through his hair. He looks elated yet dumbfounded at the same time and sighs, "I-"

"Yes?"

"I'd dreamed of-"

"Riiiiiight."

"Grant, I fantasized about her, I mean I dreamt of her…you know in my arms but-"

Grant's voice gets higher, "Right." He smiles, extremely happy for his friend who spent so many years alone. "But what?"

He leans his head back against the chair now, looking at the ceiling, blinking, and trying to find the words, "It's unbelievable… she's- she's just remarkable Grant. I don't even know how to describe it."

"Yeah, I can see that, dude. I feel like I'm falling off a fucking cliff over here."

Riordan smiles, coming forward to lean his elbows on the desk. He folds his hands together under his chin and looks into Grant's eyes, "I'm done, man. Stick a fork in me and serve me up on a platter *done*. I've never felt this way."

"Well, you're referencing food, so I know it's serious." Grant smiles, making a joke, but he can see a change in his best friend.

Riordan chuckles at how ridiculous his own words are. He's not usually at a loss for them. "I mean, I fucking loved your sister, you know I did, since like seventh grade."

"Oh, I know. In fact, the last time I saw this look in your eyes was probably that many years back."

"No, really, I loved Evelyn, for most of my life-" He tries to explain.

"It was that first love, childhood, and high-school-sweethearts stuff. You lucked out, man. You had the relationship everyone yearned for. It was great stuff…"

Riordan nodded, "It was a great marriage, absolutely…"

"Listen, it's a step forward to hear you say that. It means you're making peace with that whole part of your life. That's what someone like Demi brings along brother, you needed to appreciate it. She's helping that door. It's all good, man. Doors have to close, and new ones have to open. It's just how it is."

"I thought so, like putting that motherfucker who killed her in the ground…legit too…I thought the closure would come… faster." Riordan frowns at the memory of the bastard that kidnapped his wife, frightened her, threatened to rape her, stuck a knife in her slowly, letting her suffer and bleed out, the bile killing her, slowly…in his arms as he rescued her. To finally reach her, let her know she was his everything, his priority, that he'd found her… only to have her perish in his grasp. That's pain beyond pains. He's never been able to explain it, and he never will…he couldn't put Grant through that. He's had to make peace with the injustice, the unfairness of life.

Grant keeps Riordan from going back down a very dark road, "But you need Demi."

Riordan's face immediately softens. He sighs, "Yeah."

"Closure, man. It comes differently than we think, in ways we'll never know."

"How'd you get so smart?"

Grant smiles, "I've had a lot of time to watch you…and to think. I don't have a Demi yet."

"Are you saying you need closure, Grant?" Riordan was doing what he normally does, turning it on Grant to give him the presence he needs.

"I'm fine, dude. Loved my sister, always will, but we're fuckin' talking about you now. Don't leave me hanging here. Why can't you *describe* it?"

Riordan shakes his head slowly. He thinks of Demi and seems to lose his words like there aren't intense enough words to describe what he feels now that he's been with her. How she feels like home. He remains reserved.

"Really, man?"

Riordan shrugs, a small smile forming.

"Holy fuck, dude, Riordan Tate is at a loss for words?"

He closes his eyes, pinching the bridge of his nose, his eyebrows raising as he feels the sleep deprivation thick in his head. "It's uh-"

Grant stares. He's really surprised. He leans farther back in his chair, the legs coming off the ground, stretches with his chest wide, and lets out a strained laugh.

Riordan looks at him, "Well, remember the tantra stuff we were discussing?"

"You mean the amazing fucking awesome tantra energy shit *YOU* learned while we were on that mission in Bali?" Grant lowers his chair and focuses on Riordan's face. "Yeah, we started talking about it at the bar the other night, but you sent me home."

"Grant, it's hard to know if you're paying attention when you're sauced. Why do you think you have no memory of all this tantra stuff from Bali? You were in the class with me!" He laughs.

"That was more like a sleeping class Tate, you had me up way too much with the damn wire on whats-her-face's husband."

Riordan huffs, "It was a bit more than needing sleep. You had help from other…uh substances."

"Oh right…aw man, that hookah shit was-"

"My point exactly, and that was no normal tobacco, sparkles. I should've fired your ass. You're lucky you work for me…oh, and that I don't pee test your ass. Anyway, do you remember any of that class?"

"Like?"

Riordan rolls his eyes, "Related to tantra?"

"Could you just review for me again? It was super interesting to hear some of it again."

"You're killing me. We need to go over this security detail, so when we get off this raft and onto that island, we can recover the stolen items and complete this mission before it's even gotten started."

Grant points to the report he placed on the desk earlier while Riordan slept in, "We are so good on that, it will literally take five minutes to get through. Come on, you got me all curious again with your speechlessness about Demi. Don't leave me hangin' now!"

Riordan smiles, "Okay, first off, you can go google all the history and countries of origin stuff if you need to know all that. Basically, Tantra means "interweaving", and it's about interweaving energy."

Grant smirks, "But look at you, man, it's like you've been sexually reborn or something."

"True, but you can't just have sex and call it tantra. It doesn't work with just anyone."

"Seriously?"

Riordan sighs, "Seriously. Remember Jeanine?"

"Jeaniiiiiiiiiiiiiiiiiiiiiiine…" Grant gets that hazy, sultry look in his eyes again.

"Right. So there's a connection…an unmistakable energy sometimes. You're energy, I'm energy, everything is energy. Energy begets energy…"

Grant gets sarcastic, "Oh, like my best friend thinking he wasn't good enough to be with a certain hottie…so he didn't get the hottie until I convinced him?"

"Hey, focus, Einstein."

"No disrespect, man, but she's fucking gorgeous, Tate. How-"

"Would you pay attention?"

Grant sits up, "What I mean, *sir*, is it took your *best friend's* energy to change *your* energy so that you'd go submit to *her* energy! You actually think you could survive this mission being near her and not…"

"I don't want to think about that now. Thank you…again, by the way. I do appreciate the love. I know I can be difficult."

"You're welcome." Grant smiles genuinely.

"Can we fucking move on here? I'm on a tight schedule."

Grant snorts, "Yeah, okay. Proceed, Captain Tate. But, don't rush through the juicy parts."

Riordan wants to reach across and smack the shit out of Grant, but he's fun to be around, and deep down, he really wants Grant to have the gift of a tantric woman. Nothing would make him happier than seeing him in love and bonded with the right woman. "Okay, can we get back to your lesson, A.D.D. boy?"

"You're hurting my feelings." Grant pretends to wipe away a tear and laughs.

"So…back to energy. It's a huge deal. Especially with the right woman."

"Go on, Professor."

"Well, if you remember, in those classes in Bali, it was expressed *on the daily* about feminine energy and how it's the more dominant…err…, the more *powerful* energy. Basically, the soft, accepting, receiving feminine energy…which is *vulnerable, giving energy*…well, that's actually the more dominant. The goddess energy. In our country, we're taught that men are superior because we're physically stronger, firm, and should be in charge."

"True." Grant's frowning, very curious as to where this is going.

"Well, in actuality, women in their *feminine energy*, are the more dominant species. They can create life, they can birth life, they can empathize easier, show compassion and emotion, cry…and because they have the power to *be vulnerable*, to be soft too…they actually live longer, and they are the origin of creation and power."

"Wait, men are actually the weaker sex?!!"

"Not exactly. Both men and women have male and female energies…it's more of who chooses to…use the feminine energy and how." Riordan leans back, stretching, and lets Grant absorb the information.

"Okay, so are you telling me when you're with Demi, you're being more like a woman?" He lifts an eyebrow.

"Nooooo, no, no." Riordan smiles, "Not in the way you're thinking. I'm able to be ***fully*** me, both energies as we were meant to be…and she likes it! Because I allow my vulnerability in, *I'm* receiving the best of her. More of her. *Her* completely."

Grant nods, "Okaaaaay."

"All right, let me explain it this way. There's sex, and then there's *tantric sex*. The difference is sex as regular sex is mostly physical…but tantric sex is more a body, mind, soul immersion experience. It's…it like "soul sex". That's the difference between the girls you're with and then Jeanine. You'll never forget her, right?"

"Oh my gawd, no…neverrrrrrr."

"There ya go. She's in your soul, man."

Grant raises both eyebrows, "Dude, she sooo is. Even the way she *cums*." He bites his knuckle and then sucks air through his fingers.

"There's that too. Women are taught early on the wrong ways of approaching pleasure. Shame is used so there's no self-pleasuring or understanding of how they can have seven, or more, different orgasms."

"Are you serious?"

"Oh hell yeah. Women should be worshipped, cherished, *pleasured*…it's how they can truly be their true essence."

"Someone's in love."

"If you were present in that class years back, you would've remembered all this." He jabs a finger at Grant, lowering his voice and ignoring his comment. "Anyway, none of this is explained to us early on. Religion, family pressures, societal views, even fucking sexual abuse are huge hurdles for young girls. It's no wonder over half have some sort of orgasmic dysfunction when they become sexually active. We are taught to go for it with women, and it's expected that we freely do it whenever, with whomever, and however many times we need to, but there's still a double standard when it comes to a women's pleasure. We're encouraged to actually be hyper-sexual, which takes our energy, and thus our own power, away and messes us up, so we have difficulties bonding. Women are taught to go against their truth and desires and live a conservative, hypo-sexual life or be labeled a nymph, loose, a slut, or worse. None of it works for either sex. We're conditioned to go against our own energy…and we wonder why there is so much miscommunication and damn DISCONNECTION!"

"Unbelievable."

Riordan folds his hands together on the desk, "Now, you know how we learn a lot about opposites on our missions?"

"Yeah."

"That applies here."

"What? With pleasure, I mean orgasms?"

"You're getting this finally. Good."

Grant smirks, "I absorb everything you teach me, Tate…just not when sleep is involved, or uh, you know, a cocktail or thrice."

Riordan's eyes squint, a slight smile lingering.

"So opposites, yin yang, black-white stuff?

Riordan just stares, waiting.

Grant lowers his tone, "Oh…you mean women are supposed to have *many* orgasms and men *fewer*?"

"When a woman has an orgasm, they become more energetic, more *powerful*, and more balanced. Their bodies are designed to have multiple…and as *many* as they can, in many diverse ways. Orgasm is no joke. It works directly with who they are, **mind, body, and soul**. It elevates their oxytocin, their dopamine, even their serotonin levels! Now, isn't that interesting that they are encouraged to protect their bodies, hold off, even be celibate to ward off pregnancy, when they can only have one baby a year…yet men can father over a hundred and forty-nine pregnancies in a year." Riordan chuckles and shakes his head.

"Holy fuck, I never thought of it that way. It's sad, but if we really consider the facts, we should be the ones concerned about contraception and trying less to bang as many females as we can."

"It's comical how we function here compared to other countries. How we're taught opposites of what it is we really need."

"You learned all this in that Bali class?"

Riordan smiles, "They were much nicer about it, then I confirmed it in the states with a guru in Los Angeles I befriended. The tough part is…finding, or rather attracting, a partner who gets it!"

Grant puts his finger to his upper lip, "Oh right, the one you said they bumped off when she started to get rich and speak out about Tantra. Accidental suicide is what they let us think, right?"

"Well, that's what they want us to think…but I know differently."

"Sad, man. Really sad."

"Well, it is what it is. She was a beautiful soul."

Grant looks overwhelmed, "This is incredible. I had no idea you thought or knew about all this shit, and I figured you just didn't know how to stop working so much."

"I think I'll take that as a compliment." Riordan smiles.

The phone on Riordan's desk buzzes. Grant stands up to stretch his legs while Riordan takes the call. He walks over to the windows and looks down on Deck A. There he sees Demi taking the younger newlywed couple into an office to the left. She's got a confidence about her, a gorgeous balanced walk with her little clipboard and files in her arms. He's happy for Riordan. To find another, he can be so bonded with and on a completely different realm seems extraordinary. He knows what he needs now too and decides after this job he's going straight to Jeanine to sort some things out.

Riordan hangs up, stands, and meets Grant over by the control panels. He leans against one of the stools and stretches, looking down for her, the one who's ignited his soul. He sees her come out of a side office door, rushing slightly. His chest flutters in a way that almost makes his knees go weak. She's everything he's ever dreamed of. They watch her reach the other side of the deck and lean into the bar where Maurice greets her. Her yoga outfit is flattering on her in a pale purple that brings out the rich darkness of her hair. Riordan watches as her long strands down her back wave in the wind and caresses the curve of her tush. He blinks slow, remembering how she gently flipped her locks out of the way, and he felt them rest, tickling across his chest and stomach. He could smell her shampoo as she received him in her moist, loving mouth. She has the slowest, most exquisite rhythm with her breath and tongue and brings him pleasure with her eager desire to tantalize yet protect his most sensitive body part.

He stares as Maurice hands her bottles of water and an extra pen. She smiles sweetly and steps long and confidently back across the deck. Just before reaching her office door, she turns and looks up towards the windows. She smiles, with one small wink, just in case he's sitting there. It's as if she senses where he's at and that he can feel her energy.

Grant huffs a tiny breath of happy envy, having witnessed her loving maneuver. "Okay, brotha, tell me more."

Riordan smiles, "Okay, where'd we leave off? Admittedly, I'm a bit distracted."

"I totally understand. I hope to be distracted, *incredibly* so, now that I know it's worth it."

"Well, just not on the job. I'm not as interested in this mission as I was a few days ago. I need you."

Grant nods, "Love can put everything else second, can't it?"

"There truly isn't anything better. It makes success, money, material possessions, people...all seem so small in comparison. I thought fulfillment was doing all this, being the best, running the show..."

"Well, you've done pretty damn well in life, bud, despite the setbacks."

"It's all small potatoes, Grant. There is nothing comparable to the beautiful, vulnerable soul of a woman. Nothing."

Grant stares long at his best friend. He's never respected anyone more than Riordan, and now he's even more envious. "I believe you, brotha."

Riordan sighs, "Okay, so...orgasms.

"Oh, yes, my favorite.

So guys are different, obviously. But basically, the more we have them, the weaker they...and *we* become. We lose our seed, we lose our power."

"Oh fuck, yeah, I can totally see that. It's like my brain shuts down." Grant taps his temple.

"It's natural...orgasm is healthy, of course, but our bodies aren't like a woman's. We have to be smart about our release. All that crap we're sold early on is bullshit. We probably wouldn't have done half the stupid shit we did in our teens if we had any education about jackin' off. If we had any sense to relax and let things build, we probably wouldn't have made so many dumb decisions. Recouping, gaining strength and our power, so to speak, would've given us the clarity to satisfy...better."

"I probably would have had way fewer partners and a better reputation." Grant laughs at himself.

Riordan agrees, "I was not always this controlled. I feel bad now for Evelyn. In our early years, it was always the first one was for me, the second for her and me. I never knew it should have been double for her, and I could wait it out until the next time...let things build. Delay gratification. I bet with less, my orgasms would have been longer and stronger. There were only a few times I was multi-orgasmic, and come to think of it...it was the times after we were interrupted by your parents or we had to stop and wait until later. When later came, it was so much more intense. *Damn*."

Grant looks curious, "So, holding out gives you more intense, satisfying orgasms?"

Riordan nods, "Holy fuck, yes."

"Women are incredible creatures, with multi-orgasmic needs."

"They truly are...we think they can't. I mean, we've been conditioned that way, but in truth, we're even fucking better when we lead with our feminine, more dominant energy." Riordan shakes his head slowly. "All right, so we've been fed the opposite of what we actually need, it's been proven. We've also been taught to ignore our feelings, stuff them away to be a *man;* we're weak if we show emotion...or we aren't a real man if we're vulnerable in any way. We're fed values and ideals that not only sabotage real connection but ultimately affect our health…and it's no wonder we fucking die younger."

"True! Women statistically outlive us by twenty or more years."

"Right! And *most* illnesses can be directly linked back to emotion."

Grant lifts his eyebrows, "We could learn a thing or two about feeling."

Riordan nods, "I certainly am. I feel so free. Like she's healing me."

Grant smirks, "Oh, I don't doubt it. You know if the guys from Delta heard this conversation, we would never live it down."

"True, and I understand that. But, if it were our sons, our family…"

"I would want this for mine…this understanding and thought process. Fuck." Grant stares at the floor for a moment.

"I learned this all so long ago, and it was mind-blowing then. But something was diminished in me after losing Evelyn. Just death and life and going on, I'd forgotten about the practices and how to mindfully execute them and how to breathe and edge. All the ancient teachings of how incredibly powerful our souls can be when we allow them to guide us. The vulnerable, interweaving process of tantra, and breath, and *living* a soul love."

Grant looks up, "Wait, what's *edging*?" Riordan smiles, happy his friend is still listening.

"This is where our power comes in. Edging isn't easy. Infact, porn was invented to distract us from it and from controlling ourselves. In a nutshell, no pun intended, edging is when you connect with yourself or tantra partner, and you bring the pleasure to the point of climax…"

"Right."

"Here's where it can get tough. Ladies go first, yes?" Riordan asks, checking Grant, hoping he's not a selfish prick in bed.

"Well, of course." Grant raises an eyebrow, assuredly.

"So you let her crash over her cliff, so to speak, the second or third time, and you orgasm too…right?"

Grant is hesitant to agree now, "Okaaaaayyyy…."

"*But*, with no ejaculation."

"What!?"

Riordan can't help but chuckle at Grant's reaction, "Yeah, edging is keeping your *power*, your seed dude…no ejaculation."

"Fuck dude, wait…are you telling me you can do this?"

Riordan raises his eyebrows, "Yes."

"Easily?"

"*Nooooo*. Not easily. I didn't say it was easy. It gets easier, but…we learn all wrong, so unwinding that clock after its ticking… takes perseverance and control…edging is *essentially*, delaying gratification. It increases orgasm when you do decide to have one. It helps one focus on the bonding and the time spent instead of the end goal." Riordan gives him a few moments to soak in all he's presented.

Grant looks at him, "Bro, I don't get nearly enough sex now, with this work, the stress. Now you're telling me I'm supposed to "suck it up" so to speak…when I do get close?"

"Listen, it's not a stress thing. It's about power, keeping your mind straight, but more importantly, pleasing your *goddess*."

Grant laughs abruptly. "Seriously, Tate? *You* edge?"

Riordan confesses, "Listen, Demi drives me wild, but she *understands* tantra. She's…well, never mind."

"Holy shit. It seems like torture." Grant puts his hands up in a surrendering motion.

"It's really not, Grant. We lose our power when we lose our seed. Ejaculating is losing it all, and the bonding is put last. If we can prolong the pleasure, both can truly experience soul immersion."

"Oh."

"There's a healing…a *power* in two becoming one. This is a true power that's scary to other undesirable energies."

"You mean the evil bastards of the world." Grant squints, remembering some unsavory types.

"Right."

Grant takes in a deep breath and exhales, "So, she orgasms as much as she can to increase her power, we follow her lead, prolong our *pleasure*…but keep our strength. And, weaving this together is…

"It's nature. It's how we were intended to be, as a species. It's true love-making, man. Indescribable pleasure. You won't even look at another woman. Your soul will be fulfilled." Riordan opens his hands peacefully.

Grant studies Riordan's face. He's overwhelmed, feeling juvenile, excited, anxious, and incredibly curious. He trusts Riordan with his life. He has many times, and he would die for the guy. If anyone else was saying this, he'd probably walk away, shaking his head at them. But, Riordan is a true man's, man, a walking specimen of energetic power. Always has been since they were young. He commands respect and grace with just a glance.

Riordan sees what's going on in Grant, "I bet I know what you're thinking."

"How the fuck am I going to…"

A smile grazes Riordan's mouth, "Edge?"

"Dude! I-"

"Relax, this is all a gift, man. Open it only when you want… with the right partner, *preferably* one who doesn't enjoy running with scissors!" Riordan chortles.

Grant laughs out loud, "Aw, come on, not even you knew Mindy was a little cuckoo until the scissors incident. She kinda put off that chill vibe at first. I won't ask her to cut the ribbon for my gift wrap everrrrrr."

"Mindy was a little too "windy" between the ears, Grant, even for you. We all saw it. You just needed a shiny pair of shears coming at your face to get it." Riordan laughs harder.

"Yeah, yeah, yeah…thanks again for holding her back. That girl had a titty out and was still swingin' at me."

"You're welcome. She's kind of the type that should wear a lil' sign that says "do not feed tequila". Riordan holds his chest, still laughing. "It always seemed to turn into TE-KILL-YA, from where I was standing."

Grant brought his fist to his mouth, laughing the hardest he has in a long time. "Dude, if I farted wrong, she'd go off."

"Definitely won the shortest fuse award, man." Riordan calmed his laughing, wiping a tear from his eye. A wave of gratitude for Demi washed over him. With all she's been through, she's certainly more emotionally balanced than most. He looks at Grant and sees his smile fade. He's again concentrating on all he's taken in. Riordan waits a few moments.

Grant points at him, "So you're telling me you're an expert in all this?"

"No, there's no expert stuff here. Just like all your skills here in this job, in life, it starts out as practice."

"How the fuck do you know that?"

"Well, while you were crashed out in that Bali class, *sleeping beauty*, the rest of us were learning meditation, self-love, self....*pleasure...*"

Grant huffs, "You mean...*rubbing one out?*"

"Ah, now that's what we're taught when we're young, but when we're learning to be disciplined, mature...a, man, we're encouraged, given homework even, to self-pleasure as a way to love ourselves, our bodies, know what we like...from our *own* mind, not what society tells us to like...*in porn.* It's how we build up the control to the edge. Porn completely distracts us from prolonging the pleasure. It teaches us to always reach a goal...have an ending." Riordan shrugs slightly.

"I kinda like porn."

"You're allowed to like it, but it's not the way real connection is. It's certainly not how real women are...or what they want, right? It's all acting...*fake.*"

Grant nods, "I can understand that. I don't need that shit. When I think of how I felt with Jeanine, it was a whole different level of..."

Riordan sees Grant can't finish the sentence, "I bet you didn't want those moments to end, right?"

"Oh, no way, dude! No fuckin' way."

"I bet you didn't think of her in a nasty, ass-slapping, name-calling, howling, nut-busting manner, right?" Riordan's voice is low and monotone.

"No. And when you say it like that, I feel a bit defensive."

"Right, because you'd wife her up, yes?"

Grant stares into Riordan's eyes. He understands now. He gets the "soul love" part and has the realization that he's been the one sabotaging it all these years...like Riordan almost sabotaged his connection with Demi. He feels as if his brain is going to explode. "*Shit…*"

"It's all good brotha, Jeanine's been waiting."

"She's married, Rior."

"Believe me, she's waiting." Riordan smiles. He knows for a fact Jeanine's asshole stockbroker husband does not please her and that he's headed to jail soon. He's got plans for Grant.

"So, you're an expert at this edging now?"

"Noooooo. She tells me I'm pretty damn impressive, though. I mean, she drives me wild. But goddamn, it's so great prolonging the gratification because it makes things ten times better. She's commented on my control. I get so caught up in the bonding with her it's not difficult to WANT things to go on and on…it's becoming natural. I don't need to work so hard. It's so pleasurable. What's really nice is we can decide, together, when to…well, anyway-"

Grant releases his shoulders and smiles, "I'm really happy for you, man. You've got me convinced!"

"Sometimes, I just don't even try."

"What do you mean?"

"She's super fair you know. She wants me to have as much pleasure as her. I do have the same, if not *more* pleasure. I just don't always edge. I enjoy just bringing her to her pleasure. I can't explain what it's like to satisfy her."

"You're killing me here."

Riordan smiles, "It's not just a puppy-love or honeymoon phase feeling. It's something more. Like I finally found the secret to wanting to *live…*"

"Purpose?"

Riordan smiles, "Yeah."

Grant smiles, "Yeah. Wow, and this is what your girl is teaching down there with those couples?" Grant jabs a thumb towards the lower deck.

"Hmm, yup. More discreetly, I'm sure. You know, in a professional capacity. And she's certified." Riordan wavers his eyebrows with a tiny smile. "Expert level."

"Impressive." Grant smirks.

"Well, it's intimacy coaching. So, body conditioning, hence the tantric yoga this morning, then couples coaching, which is for their minds, and then the best part…"

"Whoa, does she…you know, demonstrate tantra for them?" Grant lowers his voice, unsure if he is offending his best friend.

Riordan huffs, "She gives them coaching homework based on where they're at in their relationship…for when they go back to their cabins."

"Oh, so no forcing you to lay there and take it while they watch?" He snorts, happy with his comical question.

"Hysterical. No, she likes a *reserved* relationship like I do, just us. I think we need to get back to this report. Lesson over."

"No, but seriously, how does she help the couples if they're having a struggle or can't get something right?"

Riordan shakes his head, "I'll ask her for you. They *are* adults Grant, they can get along just like the rest of the world…I feel these couples are brave, though. They're certainly vulnerable enough, deciding to come on this lil' pleasure cruise. She mentioned that these retreats usually help their energy sync up, or they help them find that they really need another partner. A *different energy…* when they get back home. Energy begets energy, right? I guess the helpful part is knowing for sure if you're with the right person or not. I can see divorce is not as bad as we're taught. Living a lifetime with the wrong person could be really bad for one's health."

"Wow, that's kind of incredible! I can see how getting…err attracting the wrong people can begin the downward spiral. I can't even imagine that in marriage. Really, man, thank you for sharing what you know. I'm kind of fascinated…and interested." Grant stands up slowly, looking at his watch.

"Interested?"

"Yes, sir. The first challenge is the uh, edging. I'm sure I'll feel like I'm in a special class with this fuckin' body."

"You'll be fine. Just know that it takes time. You have more control than you think. And besides, if you need help, you've got an expert here on the ship. Remember, men have been doing tantra for centuries. Porn has only been around since the 1500s. I don't know about you, but I want what's worked for over 10,000 years, not what creates a psychological block." Riordan shrugs.

Grant stretches his arms up to the ceiling, placing his palms on the wood of the yacht decor. "Dude, I'm not gonna talk to your woman about my junk."

"Suit yourself. There's always google." Riordan stands, grabbing the folder with their plans for the island excursion, and steps around the desk to follow Grant to the briefing room.

Grant lightly slaps Riordan's back, "Really though, thanks for all that. I didn't realize you had more hidden *Steven Hawking* stuff in that brain."

"Hey, what's the worst that could happen? Jeanine somehow ends up in your arms because you balance your energy, and it finally matches hers?" Riordan steps through the door, Grant following behind.

"I didn't think about that! Hey, Tate, can you *imagine...*" Grant muses, his eyes glazing over.

"Anything's possible grasshopper, *anything.*"

24

Natalia & Chance

Demi

Demi notices Natalia is quieter today, while Chance is still his same bubbly self. As she hands them both bottled water, she makes a mental note that Natalia chose to sit in her own chair instead of next to Chance on the couch. Demi sits in the high back chair across from them. Their energy is much edgier then she'd hoped, especially after a tantric yoga class, but she's used to it on these retreats. Sometimes things get worse with the couples before they get better.

"Make yourselves at home. I'm just going to read over your answers on your intake paperwork real quick." Demi opens their file folder. She's already read through most of their information, but she wants to observe how they've settled in. Chance nods, then turns his attention, and his body, towards his wife. He reaches for her bottled water and smiles. She shakes her head and says she's got it. Demi observes she's in full "push-pull" mode, and knows she can help them. She familiarizes herself with a few more facts about the couple and dives right in.

"Mr. Rubins, how does it feel to be on your father's superyacht?"

He tilts his head, surprised at the question. "Call me Chance, please. Well, it feels all right. I mean, my father has always had money, and I wasn't raised with him, so it feels the same as anyone else's experience, I guess."

"And how's that?"

Chance shrugs, "Easy, for him. I paid to be here like the others."

Demi searches his face. He has such a warm smile, but she senses resentment. She presses. "So, Chance, did he pay for your medical education then?"

"That's an interesting question, Ms. Greer."

"I'm just trying to establish what we're working on here in your relationship with Natalia."

His eyebrows furrow, "What would my father's money have to do with Natalia?"

"A lot, actually." Demi softens her voice.

"*Okayyyy*, my father didn't know about my education until my sixth year. He cleared all my student loans in one phone call. Paid everything for my eight-year run, before I was even done."

Demi makes notes in their file. "So, you would have preferred a relationship with him instead of him paying to get out of his guilt…from not being there to raise you?"

Natalia huffs a laugh, "Oh, you're good. She's good, babe." She smiles at her husband and drinks water with a clear I-told-you-so glance.

Demi smiles at Chance, "Is that why you try so hard to make Natalia happy, Chance? Because you felt *not good enough* for Errol Adler to show up? You don't want Natalia to feel the same way?"

"What the fuck? Why do I suddenly feel like I'm in trouble…and you're some weird psychic!" Chance slides back in his chair, looking pretty defensive, yet a small smile hints at the corners of his mouth.

Demi mimics his movement and slides back against her chair, crossing her leg and lowering her voice to soften him. "You are not in any trouble, Chance, and I'm not a psychic. I understand energy is all. I'm reading right from the answers you wrote. I'm just digging through the details…getting down to business. After all, we only have twelve weeks on this retreat. Is that alright, Chance?" He nods, unsure, and she moves on to Natalia. "Natalia, how do you feel about Chance being a successful pediatric surgeon?"

"I'm proud of him, of course. He's amazing!"

"And how do you like your position as a manager? At, what is it, Club Risqué'?"

Natalia laughs out loud, "That's an exotic dancers club. I run Club Noir, Ms. Greer."

"Oh, my bad." Demi opens the file and pretends to check her notes. "Club Noir, yep, there it is. So tell me, Natalia, was your father…or mother the absent parent?"

Natalia turns her head slightly, bringing her ear towards Demi. "What was that?"

"Which one of your parents was the absent parent, either in or outside of the family unit?"

"My mother."

Demi could already sense it. Natalia is in a strong female role at work but, needing significance enough to work in a sexy night club while asking for BDSM at home from her new husband. Deep down, they both trauma bond in their relationship over not feeling good enough, but her trauma is slightly worse since she thinks her mother left because of her, and she needs to punish herself to try to reason and make sense of the abandonment. Demi hopes they haven't gone too far into pain and sex. To where it's something Natalia enjoys. "You do know her leaving wasn't because of you, right?"

Natalia presses her lips together. Chance answers, "I tell her all the time. See sweetie, she left for her own reasons, not because of anything you did."

Demi softens, she knows the mother left for some sort of addiction or selfish life, and Natalia thinks if she were more special, better behaved, or...was a boy, her mother would have thought her valuable enough not to leave. "Have you enjoyed pain in the bedroom, Natalia?"

"We haven't tried yet."

"Okay, good." Demi is relieved.

"I can't really get into that, Ms. Greer. I want to make my wife happy, but I just-" He shifts in his seat. "I just don't want to hurt her. It breaks my heart when she cries. I can't be the cause of more tears."

Demi smiles sweetly at Chance. She leans forward and places her hand on his knee, "I know Chance, that's very loving. You're a sweet guy." She soothes him away from the anger she'd sparked in him earlier. "You've got a great guy, Natalia. He wants to heal you, not hurt you."

"I know." Natalia looks down at her fingers.

"That's why you're here. To heal each other. Many relationships can be about hurting the other for some sort of life lesson. The best relationships are when two souls come together to heal wounds. Looks like you've got a great start! I'm here to help you, okay?" Demi looks between them both. "I'm going to give you some homework before you begin any BDSM stuff. If you don't like it my way, we'll try it your way. Can we agree?"

They look between each other, unsure if they want to trust Demi, unsure they want any of this...*work*. Couples generally start out thinking the retreat is going to be one big, long vacation, but the work soon changes that, for the better. They won't know that until the end.

Natalia answers first, "Yes, okay."

Chance searches his wife's face for validation, then follows her lead. "Okay, I'd rather try it your way, Ms. Greer...if it means not tying up my wife and whipping her. Don't get me wrong, Fifty Shades of Grey was hot but..."

Demi smiles, "That story was actually more about growing in *love* than most people think. How forgiving and loving unconditionally, allows healing for each other, no matter the circumstances and childhood wounding. I actually know the author. I'll never forget her calm smile as she explained how oblivious unevolved-evolved lovers can be judging her story, spending so much time being loyal to their *opinion* instead of digging deeper within themselves AND within her book. She laughs all the way to the bank, still making millions off of negative publicity, and yet still positively changing lives. Her example of one couple growing together to meet each others' needs and so then changing the course of their journey...well, it's just damn brilliant. To me, I felt the story showed exactly what I do in my work too. Most come into tantra in pain, or inflicting pain, and find that they no longer need to be loyal to suffering once they find the freedom of meeting their OWN needs."

Both Chance and Natalia raise their eyebrows, completely inspired.

"It's like that saying, IF YOU DON'T HEAL THE WOUNDS THAT HURT YOU, YOU'LL BLEED ON THOSE WHO DIDN'T CUT YOU." Demi gently moves her hair passed her shoulder shrugging and smiling. "We truly must love ourselves enough to love others. What's nice is, sometimes you see the love another has for you, and it can give you the drive to make yourself a priority. You both have a lovely start. I'm excited for you!." Demi smiles looking between them

Natalia turns to Chance and smiles, submitting, convinced enough her shoulders and body begin to relax. Chance takes her hand in his and kisses his wife on her forehead. They look to Demi, pleased.

"Great! Look, I know it's hard to trust me. We've just met after all. But I want to see you both happy and fulfilled. I have to go to your core foundational issues to understand how and why you both function the way you do. If we can admit where we come from, we can heal and deal. Make sense?"

They both nod, looking like a couple ready to embark on learning a new skill. Demi watches them closely but finds herself sensing something out of her peripheral vision. Outside on Deck A, she can see both Sagrid and Lubna in some sort of altercation. She focuses, turning her head fully in the direction of the windows, and sees Sagrid with her hand behind Lubna's neck, her forehead touching Lubna's in such a way that Lubna can't really get free. She presses her hand against Sagrid's chest to break free. Sagrid's other hand holds a mimosa; they stumble a few steps.

"Just a moment. Excuse me, I'll be right back." Demi stands and briskly walks out of her office.

25

Attention to Detail

Riordan

Riordan hangs up the phone with Maurice. He watches as Maurice does as he's instructed and moves towards Sagrid and her wife on the top deck. Demi appears suddenly, and Riordan stands up, slightly alarmed. He was hoping she'd not been interrupted from her session. Maurice removes Sagrid, and Lubna follows as Demi directs her to do so. Riordan rubs his brow, convinced Sagrid is only getting worse.

Demi turns, looks up towards his windows, her face searching. His chest aches. Even though he sees her, being distant from her affects him. He remembers all too well this feeling. Being able to see her and only *yearn* for her. She is his now, and admittedly he still yearns, but only until he can hold her again. He reaches for the phone and punches in the four-digit code for the phone closest to where she's standing on the deck. It rings, and he sees her walk towards the wall to answer.

"Hey."

"Hey yourself, everything okay?" His voice is deep yet soft, trying to decipher her feelings.

She huffs a small laugh, "I guess you saw all that?"

"I tried to send Maurice before you were interrupted but, you're too quick for me." Riordan chortles.

"Well, I try to go slow, Captain Tate."

His mind remembers, and something deep in him stirs. He smiles, "Uh, yes…ma'am." He pans his eyes along the whole deck to see if anyone was in ear-shot of her.

"Thank you for your efforts with our guest…err, my student?" She clears her throat. "I'm beginning to think the lovely cocktails on this ship don't bode well with Ms. Sagrid Hamsum."

"I agree. Even a mild morning mimosa seems to be a bad idea."

"Yeah, well day-drinkin' being what it is an all." She laughs.

Riordan chortles, "I hear ya."

"Well, thank you for enlisting Maurice's help. I appreciate your *attention to detail*…even during the daylight hours." She's flirting again.

Riordan clears his throat, a smile grazing his lips. "Well, you're very welcome. I hope the rest of your day is less…eventful."

"Thank you. In this way, yes."

"Hmmm…okay. Talk with you soon."

"Hope so, Captain Tate."

26

Jade
Demi

The water is beautifully searing, almost unbearable yet...*not*. Demi exhales a long and languid breath, sinking down all the way to her earlobes in the soothing bathwater. She smiles, looking up at the little gift box, classy and metallic. It's a beautiful shade of hunter green that glistens in the light of the moon that peeks through the round yacht window. She almost didn't see the cute little gift Riordan had left for her. Somehow it had landed on the floor under her bed. She'd never have found it if she weren't searching for an earring. He really gets *her*. She smiles, gazing towards the window again as her jade egg charges in the moonlight. He chose a perfect size and a perfect crystal for her yoni. What a man! She smiles in the water, elated to have someone so attentive to her needs.

Demi fans herself with Diana and Claude Turner's file before opening it to finish her notes. She's still slightly over-heated from the bath. Despite her skimpy negligee and a tall glass of ice water, she's damp from the much-needed detoxing perspiration. An hour and a half later and still a bit overheated, she chuckles. It's possibly the effects of the now-inserted jade egg. She does love the healing of a crystal in her sacred yoni space but has recently decided, only when Riordan is not already occupying that space. She squeezes again at the thought of him and feels as if her eyes will roll back.

Pulling her feet onto the couch and closer to her body, she decides to get serious and finish some work. The first day of coaching went well, in spite of the Lubna and Sagrid fiasco. Not only were they encouraged to leave the top deck early, they never made it to their session and had to reschedule. Demi feels they are the "trouble-couple" in the group already...there's always one couple that is.

Claude and Diana are the typical baby boomer couple, struggling to shake off too much parental influence. Demi knows she must only suggest things and validate that patience will bring change with their *least* resistance. Diana is more impatient and has great difficulty with Claude's independence. She doesn't understand that he needs his alone time in his shop to fill up his creativity and interdependent areas before he has a need to share with her. Diana takes it offensively that Claude doesn't think more of *her* needs. Demi knows she has to consistently give Diana homework, after each session, of offering phrases of positive affirmation to Claude. Demi smiles as she writes, knowing that by the time Diana gets to the fourth compliment, Claude will be all over her. The man just needs to hear that she appreciates him, and he'll jump her bones. Demi makes a note that they may actually be her easiest couple.

Next, she opens Allen and Rod Hamilton's file. She finally feels as if she's cooling down...but only on the outside. She secretly wishes for Riordan to join her and hopes to hear his knock soon. She hadn't been able to find him, so dinner together isn't certain. The two plates of food on the cart by the door smell amazing, but she decides if he can't make it and doesn't show in the next thirty minutes, she'll at least open the bottle of wine for herself and sleep with her jade egg instead.

Skimming over her notes, she remembers how appalled Rod was at Allen's request for them to try introducing a young lover AGAIN into their relationship. Demi feels Allen is making such a request to somehow return pain to Rod for his affair, which was over nineteen years ago, so there may be another underlying reason. She wonders if Allen has already been with the young college student friend of their daughter's. She wishes she could talk with young *Paco* and see where he's at in the scheme of things. He may not even know of them, really, and Allen may be using him as a pawn. She wonders how they will do with their homework. Rod, who is starving for touch, is to give Allen a pedicure while listening to him explain A-Z his reasons for why he feels so strongly about a polyamorous relationship with a nineteen-year-old college student. Rod is not to interrupt or leave at any point in his "act of service" pedicure for Allen. Demi hopes they connect in the ways she knows they can from *touch*. She scribbles in her notes about their not having had sex in months and wonders if they're even sleeping in the same bed. This couple could be truly challenging since there's been so much respect lost from Rod's affair with his secretary which resulted in their daughter.

Demi's stomach growls. She picks up Chance and Natalia's file and decides they will be the last of her work for the evening. She writes how she had instructed them to use a blindfold only this evening and extremely slow touch. No bondage, no fast movements. She wants Chance to learn he can meet Natalia's needs without having to hurt her, and she can enjoy not knowing what he's going to do and, best of all, not anticipate pain. Both can create the trust they need without all the distraction of an engagement and wedding *and* buying a house. Stress puts a huge strain on a relationship. Now the real work starts. They both have abandonment issues that they can help heal in each other…*without* more pain and trauma. They need to learn that loss and rejection are a part of life, but it doesn't have to be a long term pain or carried over into the bedroom because it's *familiar*. She writes that she hopes they can mature together in this step. Tackling it so early on in their marriage will ensure they'll stay together through all the other tough stuff that may come. She smiles at how couples think marriage is an end goal when really it's the beginnings of a whole bunch of growing together.

27

Days End

Riordan

Riordan buttons his shirt up only halfway, hoping it won't be on too long. He smiles to himself clutching the rose he confiscated while walking through the dining kitchen on the main deck, and steps into his Italian slippers. He heads for the door, freshly showered, eager to see Demi now that the day is over and all arrangements for tomorrow's port docking are underway. He makes a mental note to try to find the jade yoni egg he had brought to Demi's suite for her; somehow, it had disappeared during their tryst. Walking down the hall towards her door, he chuckles at the memory of how he'd gotten separated from her gift as he was going to hand it to her.

He taps on the door lightly so she'll know it's him. The door swings open, her beauty staring him in the face, her energy welcoming. Feeling safe and invited, he steps in and to the side, his gaze quickly scanning the environment before locking eyes with her. Demi slams the door and jumps into his arms, her mouth on his neck, nibbling deep yet gentle. He catches her and lets his body lean secure against the wall, cradling her and feeling her warmth cling to him. Her jumping into his arms seems to be a theme for her...and he doesn't mind at all. She feels divine, her mouth searching his, silk fabric covering her curves beneath his palms. He allows a breathy moan to escape his throat. He's missed her.

She inhales and soaks in the glorious smell of him. He hears her and cradles her head in his palm. Her warm, wet tongue plunges deeper into his mouth. He accepts and tastes all that she offers...slowly...like velvet beneath his lips. Holding the small of her back with his other arm, he makes his way to the couch this time and sits down with her still clinging to his large frame. She's delightfully trim and small but feels every bit his equal, and he adores the feel of her body molded to his frame. Damn, she really gets him going.

Pressing him against the couch, she lifts away to break the kiss and see his beautiful light brown eyes beneath her. His finger tracing between her cleavage. He smiles lazily up at her, "Good evening…"

"Thank you…" She cups his face and kisses him again, slowly…powerfully.

Riordan frowns and tries to make sense of her gratitude. The rose he brought lay on the arm of the couch. She looks at him again, and he's not sure how to respond. "Uh, no…*thank you*. That was a very nice welcome."

"I love your choice. The color is exquisite."

He's searching her eyes as the color of the rose is red…a very rosy red. He waits.

Demi kisses him again, licking his lips, teasingly, "I needed a jade egg for my collection, and the size is perfect."

Riordan smiles wide as she continues to pepper his lips with tinier kisses. He's relieved she found the gift and even more relieved he chose the right size egg for her magnificent yoni. Admittedly, he wasn't absolutely sure as she feels incredibly tight each time they're together. He remembers his teacher in Bali explaining how sacred a woman's womb is and that you can never go wrong gifting the right tantric woman an egg that calls to you when you think of her. He loves her validation and that his instincts were right. "I'm happy you're pleased."

"I am, very much so…and I have a feeling you will be as well!" Demi reaches towards his few fastened buttons and begins to undo them. Locking eyes with him, she instinctively continues to his jeans and zipper. He had dressed down thinking he'd be her dance partner but found out from Maurice that she gave the couples the night off to work on their personalized homework.

Riordan reaches up gently, cupping her face in his hands, guiding her lips to his once more. He buries his tongue deep within her moist, heated mouth and easily syncs with her breath. She moans and frees his erection, causing him to throb beneath her hand. He kisses her deeper, her tender hands perfection around his most sensitive body part. As she inhales, she releases from his kiss and slides down his body swiftly, her mouth sinking down over his fevered, engorged lingam. Riordan's arms raise up as he grabs at the back of his hair, a swift inhale in response to the incredible pleasure that surges through his body. Demi tastes him, beginning a slow suckling down his long shaft. Riordan's eyes close at the ecstasy she bestows, every inch of his body stimulated.

Demi continues her soft, slow rhythm caressing, rewarding him for how he's made her feel. She releases, pulling his jeans and boxer briefs to his ankles, removing his slip-ons, freeing him of his clothing. Her hands travel up his legs, caressing the muscles of his quads while reaching between his thighs and opening his legs wide. She likes how his shirt is open, his gorgeous body peering through the fabric…wanting her. Massively sculpted chest muscles and rippled abs peek out, his skin an alluring tan contrast to the white cotton. Demi smiles, his surrender pleasing her. Moving her hand to him yet again, sweetly grasping his shaft. She guides him, careful to keep his pleasure a priority. Lowering, she glides her tongue along the length of his swollen shaft then down in search of a testicle to suckle. Caressing him with her hand while gently nursing on his scrotum is almost more than he can bear. Riordan pulls air between his teeth, his stomach clenching in response to her slow, torturous bliss. The pleasure she gives is exquisite. Demi releases continuing back up along his shaft with her tongue again, circling around his head and suckling it to create even more arousal. She encircles her fingers around him and rests them, squeezing slowly, causing him to grasp the couch cushions. Demi loves hearing him pleasured. She takes both her hands, creating C's with each thumb and index finger, bringing them together at the head of his beautiful penis and dragging both opposite each other lightly down, down, down towards the base, then spreading her palms through his groin muscles and down his inner thighs, knees, calves, and to his feet. Riordan exhales what seems to be years of stress as she begins the warm-up to her expert lingam massage. Caressing up his long legs with the back of her nails, she creates tender sensations, knowing she's forcing his brain to explore more of his right-side dopamine and oxytocin hormones. Demi is coaxing his body into delayed gratification, her focus being *his* pleasure.

As she reaches the base of his shaft again, she moves up then in, lightly caressing his penis in between her plump cleavage. She slowly finds his stomach with her mouth and kisses each inch of skin, moving upwards, letting his erection glide along the silky feeling of her stomach. Ever so slightly, she places kisses into the soft dark hair that leads a trail up towards his chest. Her mouth instinctively finds his fevered nipple and encircles it with her indulgent tongue. Riordan reaches forward and places a gentle hand on the back of her head, cradling her scalp and long hair in his palm. Inhaling again between pursed lips, he gazes at her, his eyes wanting and sleepy. She sees the bliss she's gifting and locks eyes with him. The bond being forged between them is becoming dangerously addictive.

Riordan brings his other hand to her face and guides her up his body to his lips. His mouth engulfs hers, and even more emotion spills from his heart. He'd hidden so much inside for years as he'd watched her. He grabs her to him and stands up carrying her, mouths exploring, tongues gliding in unison. He hugs her close to him, walking naked from the waist down towards her bedroom. He finds the door with his foot and kicks it open to find her bed. He places her down, his body molding to hers. She opens to him, pulling him onto her, wrapping her feet and arms around him, exhaling at the pleasure his body feels on top of hers. Riordan swipes her hair away from her cheek, his mouth still exploring hers. A breathy moan escapes her, and his body throbs in response. Demi reaches down his stomach to find his engorged member with her soft hand, she gives a gentle squeeze, and Riordan moans.

"You're driving me mad, *love*..." He whispers into her ear.

"That's not madness, Rior...that's perfection. Our souls finally finding each other..." Demi whispers back to him, her breath caressing his lips and mouth. "I feel like I've wanted you my entire life. This...this right here...is *everything*. Everything in the past, every moment, every little trauma or mistake...it's all okay now. This connection, our pleasure, it means everything to me..."

Riordan understands exactly what she means. It's as if all of life's *meaning* is complete for them now. She pushes his chest up, and he lifts to see her in the low light. Demi grabs her nightie and lifts it up and over her head in one fell swoop, letting it land on the floor. She smiles and grabs him under his ears, pulling him to her, arching her pelvis to guide his penis towards her aching and begging yoni opening. He leans on one arm and frees his other arm from his shirt. Trying to wriggle free of the other, he feels Demi's fevered mound press into his stomach, her silky wetness causing him to throb again. Clenching for control, he throws his shirt to the floor. He lifts himself up on his forearms and cradles her head in his huge hands. She looks up at him sliding her hands around his hips and to the clef of his glorious tush. Demi pulls him inside of her, they both gasp at the feel of finally uniting again, her warm, moistness engulfing him, his engorgement strong, possessing her.

Riordan's eyes widen as he feels the heat of her velvet inner mounds around him and the silky roundness of the yoni egg caressing against his head! She smiles up at him as her eyes roll back and blink slow. His lovely girth fills her, his length pushes the jade egg up and snug to her creating blissful pressure. Demi's breath hitches in her throat, and Riordan looks down at her, concerned, still cradling her. He's trying to match her breath and unsure of how far to move forward. She guides him deeper…than deeper. This is the first time he's felt the incredible pleasure of a yoni egg.

"Oh…uh…wow…you feel incredible, baby." Demi grasps his hips again pulling him into her deeper. He goes tantra-slow, allowing her to guide their pace. Demi begins to tremble, "This…*this is…*" Demi inhales abruptly and stops breathing. Riordan watches her face as she unexpectedly crashes over the cliff of orgasmic insanity. She can't breathe, she can't make a noise, she shakes and locks eyes with him as if begging him to not let go. She was not expecting such a sudden, fierce full-body orgasm…or the intensity of such pleasure so quickly!

Riordan smiles at her, praise in his eyes, "Yes…how *beautiful you are.*" He slows his movement, careful to follow hers, appreciation for her orgasm after-glow. He halts all motion to be considerate of her sensitivity. His gratification voluntarily delayed.

Demi takes in a breath. Her orgasm racked her entire system with unimaginable pleasure. She falls limp with welcomed exhaustion. Riordan rests within her, pushing her hair aside, finding her gorgeous neck to softly suckle. She caresses his back slowly with her fingertips, trying to regain her normal breathing.

"*YOU* are beautiful…" She murmurs breathlessly. "That was intense. It came on so strong and abruptly…you get me so…". She manages a sweet smile, unable to find the words. She turns to kiss him.

Riordan feels a twinge as she swipes his mouth with her tongue, her body still tremoring every so often beneath him, "Well, the egg."

She nods, "Hmmm, it's a perfect fit for us. I've always worn them, but this is the first time…you know, I've wanted to share the energy."

He looks at her with soft eyes, "Really?"

"Yes, I'd always used them to keep healthy…*inside*, but my Ex ignored most of my interests. Anyway, I wasn't willing to share this…" She huffs quietly.

Riordan knows what she's talking about and is flattered he could be her first with this. He remembers how her asshole husband used to talk about her to his crew. A real tough guy when he wasn't around her, putty in her hands when he was. Riordan realizes he's been inside her holding on and decides he should give her body a break. He begins to slide away, still fully engorged.

Demi grasps his shoulders, "Where are you going?"

"I-I thought I'd give you some time."

"Ohhhhh, no you don't." She pulls him back to her and kisses him deep intensely. Her body is thankful, welcoming…she pushes her pelvis towards him, squeezing him and the egg, pleasure coursing into them both. Riordan thrusts slowly forward, following her command. She's even more warm and silky, and the egg against the side of his head now is heavenly.

Riordan manages a whisper, "Are you sure?"

"Oh my baby, yes, you feel so…damn…gooooooooood…." Slowly, intricately, she's drawing him in and squeezing him tight. Electrical pulses seeming to be surge through her body, and she wants him to feel it too. "Oh….hmmm…" She's building again, the sounds of air escaping through her tense lips.

Riordan feels her. He has no idea how he's holding on. Every movement, every thrust feels as if it will be the last before losing control. He feels so connected to her. Whatever her movement, he falls into it, kissing and caressing her neck, burying himself deeper and deeper. Following her every guiding breath. Her fingers begin to dig into his back, creating more vigor.

Demi feels as if she's going to come again, "Wait."

Riordan stops immediately, hoping he didn't hurt her. "I'm sorry, are you-" Demi presses her hands to his chest, and he moves away, pulling out of her. She's smiling and pushes him gently to the side, rolling him on his back! He relents.

"I want you to relax and feel me now." She climbs on top of him and slides down over his shaft again. His eyes close slowly as the feel of her cradling womb surrounds him again. Instinctively, he reaches for her hips, and she rests her hands atop of his. Demi looks down at him with intense passion blazing in her eyes and begins a slow, steady circular thrusting...controlling his pleasure yet giving him so much of it. She locks eyes on his and syncs her breathing, every part of her being possessing him.

Riordan can hardly whisper, "God, you're gorgeous...I've always needed you...*I've wanted you for so long.*"

Demi smiles. She knows down to her soul they will never be able to part. This is tantra! This is *true* love-making...the kind only a few understand and allow. The bond is forged. "You've got me, Riordan, I'm *yours*..." Demi grinds deeper, suckling on his most sensitive erogenous member. She takes his hand and brings it to her mouth to kiss him. Dragging his fingers along her mouth, she suckles his ring finger pad, nibbling it between her front teeth to activate the meridian. Riordan's head tilts back. Her taunting is almost more than he can handle. She takes his hand then and drags it down her face and neck, slowly letting him feel her skin. She places his hand on her breast, letting him sweetly squeeze her beneath his hand. Caressing and holding her perfectly plump breast, she secures his hand to her and the other to the hand on her hip. She begins to grind him in deeper circular motions, ever so slowly, swirling the egg around his head. She's going around and around, swirling her hips to the rhythm of their matched breathing. She feels him hard and masculine inside her, her familiar buildup getting her closer to the edge.

"Dem..." Riordan is losing control with what she's doing.

"I am...*all yours*..." She feels he's getting closer, as is she. She picks up the pace ever so slightly. "I-"

"Demi..." Riordan's trying to keep up with her. She's grinding him in a clockwise motion, completely aligning his chakras with hers. She feels exquisite...he's losing control.

Demi picks up the pace, grinding more and more...she's watching his face. He's so good looking to her, especially in the throws of their love-making. She's losing control. Her breathing begins to catch in her throat. Suddenly Riordan sits up, grasping her face and plunging his tongue into her mouth, his breathing fast and his hips moving in sync with hers. She kisses him back.

Riordan can't take it any longer. He begins to crash over the cliff, she let's go just as he does, both halting, locking onto each other, lips releasing, foreheads together…moans of ecstasy ringing through and into the room…

Pure

     tantric

        bliss…

28

The In-Between
Demi & Riordan

Days pass, turning into weeks. The tantra couples enjoy their excursions on and off the yacht while Riordan and Demi's connection intensifies. Demi decided easily to rework her schedule so that she was coaching less and spending time with Riordan more. He didn't mind at all. The case had gotten stagnate. What was supposed to be a week's worth of casework turned into many, Riordan didn't mind. His team was unable to find the jump drives or the missing vials. Riordan was barely keeping Errol Adler away from flying out to the yacht and appeased him with mini check-ins and reports of small activity. He felt as if there was too much communication from Errol. Almost as if he wanted a play-by-play from Riordan daily.

The energy of the crew had calmed, and Demi's four couples seemed to settle more into being family, with the exception of the drunkard, Sagrid. She spent most of her days sleeping off her hangovers, while her wife Lubna, struck up an unlikely friendship with Rod of all guests. They'd spend afternoons speaking Spanish at a back table off the bow, working through their journals Demi had required as homework. Occasionally, they would each get a visit from their spouse, take a bathroom break, or end up napping in a chaise lounge, but, for the most part, they seemed content with each others' company and humor. Riordan noticed it was more of a dry humor as he often turned on the audio near them to listen in, just in case Lubna confided in Rod. With limited knowledge of Spanish, Riordan was at the mercy of his agent Constance Levy to interpret what was being discussed. Grant updated him from what Constance would report each day, and for the most part, there was nothing Lubna shared of a disgruntled nature. It was almost as if she didn't even work for Adler Industries. After all, she was on a three-month vacation, and Riordan didn't know what kind of company allowed its employees twelve weeks vacation! He'd asked Errol Adler to verify Lubna's employment on four occasions and still hadn't received an answer beyond her taking a lengthy trip. He thought this very perplexing.

Demi was becoming more and more brazen with her romantic needs. Riordan obliged her. She'd frequently pull him into a private laundry room, lock the door, and have her way with him. He rather likes her spunky nature as they were *more* than comfortable with each other, their connection magical. On occasion, he'd have to unlock the door, signal Grant on the cameras, and head back to his uniform closet to find a newly pressed uniform. He didn't mind appeasing her. Demi's sexual appetite and prowess were as insatiable as his. She met all of his desires, and he hers. Their bond melding deeper and *deeper*. Truth be told, he'd never been happier. For the first time, he'd put work last.

Nights were reserved for their slow, quiet tantric time. In the tub, out of the tub, in bed, on the furniture, countertops, shower, and even in *her* closet a time or two. At times they'd take intermissions to order room service and wine, or meet up with the couples out on the deck for dancing and a nightcap, only to end up back again in her cabin. Time seemed to slow down, and neither minded much. He let up on being so prompt and rigid, Demi relaxed in her scheduling. Life had become very enjoyable.

Demi loved to slip into his office unseen, whispering to him from the closet when she could hear he was alone and rustling papers. He'd appear with a deep chortle and a passionate rewarding kiss, ravishing her body with love and adoration. Riordan believed Demi to be his ultimate mate. She pleasured every inch of him. Their unexpected romance grew into a love neither had seen coming but always dreamed of. They shared childhoods, teen years, relatives, jobs, sadness, gains, losses, wins, and learned lessons.

Demi shared, with tears in her eyes, how she had met Teo while she was in her third year at the University of New York, studying Kinesiology. Teo Luczano happened to be picking up his nephew one afternoon from NYU for winter break. He took one look at Demi exiting her dorm building and had to have her. She told Riordan how Teo pretended to ask her if she'd dropped a scarf in the doorway and later admitted taking it off his bodyguard, so he could meet her pretending it might have been hers. She remembered seeing his nephew, standing with another "uncle", who she thought was the kid's father at the time. She admitted she was drawn to his cool demeanor and sharp Dior clothing. She thought Teo a doting uncle and agreed to having coffee. Coffee turned into dinner, and dinner turned into ice skating in New York City. She told Riordan how Teo had courted her, pursued her slowly, waiting for her sexually until she decided it was time. He was ever the gentleman, oddly meeting all of her needs as she had them; pretending to give her the freedom she desired as an independent woman. They were young, and she had no idea his "working for his father" meant he was being groomed to run the Loczano Cartel. When his father became too ill, Teo eased right in. He seemed confident, happy to run his father's orchard's and business pursuits by day, romancing her by night. Their early life together was filled with weekend trips on his family jet, to long college-weekend vacation time off on his sailboat. She grew to love being spoiled with sleepovers at his mini-mansion, to his sacrificing nights in her tiny dorm room bed with homemade Rob Roy's and Pho from the Vietnamese place down the street. Teo seemed every bit a respectful, young Mexican stallion for her, listening intently to all her needs and desires. Pretending she was his everything…*pretending*. He showered her with gifts of jewelry, clothing, lingerie, and travel. She never knew it was too good to be true and just thought this was how a rich, firstborn son of wealthy Mexican coffee bean farmers lived. He proposed to Demi exactly two years after their campus encounter, and she agreed to marry on the family plantation in Mexico. Her sister, Deidre, and her crew of college pals, all made it out to stand with her as she unknowingly stepped into a life with one of the most dangerous cartel leaders in Mexico. She admitted to Riordan how easily she was manipulated because she thought most of the Loczano family to be "good people" and just thought they needed a high level of security because of the area of the country they had their business in. She recalled how it was easy to dismiss anything out of the ordinary because she and Teo continued their whirlwind beginnings in their neat little penthouse apartment in New York. They didn't move out to their Hampton's home until their fifth year of marriage, and that's where things started to get tough. Her freedoms were fewer, and her friends were too far away. Running her businesses got more and more stressful with Teo's watchful eye and pressure for her to keep short hours. He wanted her to be at his beck and call but rarely seemed able to be there when she needed him. His anger and outbursts seemed unreasonable, and although he never hit her, he often took out his stress on her with hurtful words and lengthy interrogations! She mentioned to Riordan, how over time, she no longer wanted to have his children and often faked not being on birth control when she, in fact, was. Riordan allowed Demi to vent, his heart aching that he couldn't tell her how much he already knew most of her pain. He feared he would lose her if she found out too soon he'd put Teo away. He promised himself he'd explain it all to her when the time was right.

Riordan felt enough love and trust for Demi that he did open up to her about Evelyn. He explained how she and Grant were his childhood friends and how they all grew up together, running around the Hamptons tiny bikes and big dreams. He'd admitted how he and Evelyn were each others' firsts and how he was too late to save her. Demi cried for him and wrapped her arms around him, her heart breaking for his loss of his childhood sweetheart and first wife. She spent time with him and Grant on the top deck after hours, smoking cigars and drinking whiskey, listening to their hysterical stories of lives well lived, both of them admitting Evelyn would have loved her. Although odd, she knew she'd love her in return. Riordan vibrated truth and love, even if he lived mostly in a world of secrets. He seemed to command respect from others without even trying. Demi watched him, often feeling admiration for this beautiful man who somehow walked into her life weeks back. She gave gratitude out that he was hers. She'd experienced the most fraudulent of men in Teo…and here stood Riordan. A man's man. Her reward for surviving the deepest of betrayal. She loved Riordan with every ounce of her being.

Riordan fell deeper and deeper in love with Demi daily. They'd fast become a favored pair amongst the crew and couples, no longer hiding their feelings from everyone. Life was good, and the weeks passed at a lovely, leisurely pace. Riordan realized he no longer wanted the case to be over. He had full confidence in Grant and had silently decided to turn the business over to him as soon as they all returned to New York, whether the case was solved or not. This was out of character for Riordan as he'd solved every case he'd accepted since opening Tate, Inc. He knew for certain, Demi was his future, and he'd finally found a reason for all the millions he'd invested and doubled over the years. He dreamt of a life with her that would take him to his dying breath. He now intended to give her a future that'd take her breath away.

As for their tantric interweaving, he really could want for nothing more. Demi's slow, sensual ways mesmerize every cell in his body. He's able to withhold and build his seed during their daily trysts, by night, she insists he experiences as much pleasure as she. Demi likes "fair" and although she is wise to the ways of tantric men, she sees no need to overly prolong his gratification. She enjoys his happiness. He's already calm and cool in his natural demeanor. Little does she know, it's her energy that keeps him tranquil by day, submitting to her by night completes him. They're perfect for each other.

Riordan was especially enamored one evening. Demi had guided his hand from her yoni egg in its beautiful display, to her body. She wanted him to experience filling her with the healing crystal he'd gifted her. She guided his large fingers to help push, ever so slowly and sensually, the jade egg in and slightly up until it nestled in her g-spot. From there, she guided him and his lovingly aroused lingam to her anal area, pressing close to him. Cautiously he whispered, asking if she were sure. She loved him, and although she hadn't yet told him so, she was intent on showing him how much she trusted and wanted him in *every* way. Demi submitted to him knowing he could be trusted. Riordan did as she bid, stroking his ready manhood along her silky wet opening, lubricating them both to ensure there was no pain to diminish the pleasure. *She* set the pace and slowly slid onto him as both their body's allowed. The pleasure was incredible, almost indescribable! They both experienced that when done tantrically, and with the intent of a true healing connection, love will take over. Trust became their primary language…with little words needed.

Riordan held onto her hips, the rapture mind-blowing. She was sensual and tight, griping, and breathless. She wanted him that way, and he felt enamored…captivated even. She moved sensually and with love, he with mindfulness and passion. She guided his hand in front, over her tummy and moved so *he* was pulling *her* onto him. He breathed smoothly and into her hair, she moaning and loving the new type of orgasmic sensations they were building. He'd pleasured her daily, for weeks, in so many different ways. Anal seduction was now another to add to his godly expertise. Riordan doesn't seem to notice how magnificent a lover he is. Demi finds his low ego incredibly arousing.

Riordan would often rest during their intimate hours and hold her incredibly close. He'd remember to give gratitude, immersing them both in the energy of their interwoven bliss. Multiple, full-body orgasms often ravaged them in the ways tantra allows. Demi showed her need for him daily. Riordan looked forward to all she desired. What he'd learned in Bali was nothing short of spiritual, but with Demi, it was *perfection*.

29

Admission

Demi

Just about their ninth week in, Riordan decided to accompany Demi on the Island of Myrel for lunch and a little sight-seeing in the town. Grant, and the security team, were with the couples and on task looking for any clues as to Lubna's quest to sell the stolen information. Riordan and Demi free to explore.

They purposely made their way to the opposite side of the island and found a quaint little cafe along the water where the stone roads allow only mopeds and pedestrians. Riordan scans the area and was on alert since he'd never been to the area before. Demi watches him with admiration.

"Is everything up to your standards, Captain? Can I order us some wine and perhaps a little lunch of lamb, cheese, fruit, and bread?" She reaches to stroke his long curls. His hair had grown longer in the two months aboard the Passionista.

"Yes, that'd be wonderful Dems. You've got me famished from last night. And this is my treat, by the way." He swirls his hand in a circle around their menus, indicating he's buying their lunch.

She strokes his beard and then his full, plump lips with her fingers. "As you wish. Last night was magical…yet again. I don't think I've ever experienced this much affection or such a skilled lover." She smiles.

Riordan blinks then smiles back taking his eyes off his surroundings to find her beautiful blue eyes, "Really?"

"Hmmm…really."

"It's been the best time of my life."

She gazes at him. He's serious. She leans forward from her chair to reach and reward him with a kiss. Sitting back, she feels an overwhelming feeling. "I'd have to agree, Rior, I-"

He notices she stops, and he slides his hand into hers. She grasps it tight.

"I… I'm in love with you, Riordan Tate. I have been since the moment you shook my hand in your office. I just want you to know that today…and for all your days after. You are greatly loved."

Riordan feels as if time slows. He feels his body stand. He comes around to her side of the tiny bistro table and guides her hand and body to stand. Looking deep into her eyes, he pulls her into his arms and kisses her with the deepest gratitude he has in him.

Islanders looks over and smile, whispering to each other what a stunningly beautiful couple they make. The waitress pivots and walks away, deciding their order can wait. The bartender across the patio wipes his hands on a rag and smiles enviously at them. Demi, small but mighty, is wrapped up in Riordan's embrace, their kiss stopping time.

He breaks the sultry seal of their lips to whisper to her, "I love you, Demi, here…now. No matter what happens or where we end up on this tiny planet, I've fallen for you, and I'll never be the same. I don't want to be without you."

She looks up at him, enthralled with his admission, both of them there at a caribbean island street cafe…tears welling up in her eyes. Knowing she'd waited all her life for Riordan Tate. He made all the pain, lessons, and hurt disappear. She wants for nothing more.

30

Danger

Riordan

Their near perfect afternoon stroll after lunch is diminished by the feeling that they're not alone. Riordan can sense, looking through the town's people, that they are being watched. He isn't sure why and thought it to be because they're American. He decides to quickly to squash anything that may try to erupt.

Riordan leans in and whispers to Demi that they need to find a safe place. He guides her through a side alley and up narrow stone steps towards a sign that says, "Guzelle Art Museum" under a title written in another language. Demi submits and clasps his hand as he pulls her in front of him and looks behind them to make a visual profile. A figure ducks into a doorway, and Riordan is now certain they're being targeted. He lifts Demi by her waist and hurries her up the stairs, moving them quicker than originally planned. She quiets wishing he were being his playful self, but she can feel by his hurried strength that he's turned intensely serious. Demi has no idea of the danger they could encounter. These parts of the world are known for appearing relaxed and slow, but Riordan is painfully aware of the many abductions and muggings that ensue on beautiful little islands. Foreigners exploring new areas don't always understand the culture or dangers within them.

Riordan reaches the top of the stairs and puts Demi down, pulling her through another alley-way and then into a small doorway that leads to a bar. They enter. There's turtle-shell drums playing in a unfamiliar song on the radio behind the bar. A small, dark-haired woman flips her hair over her shoulder and continues to clean the bar with a damp rag. She smiles and looks down. There's an old couple sitting near the wall and a few other men playing pool towards the back. Everyone eyes Demi, and *then he*...his frame towering above her. He waves politely and pulls her through the bar and out the side door, looking for an escape. Demi tries to keep up.

The door opens, and he looks left then right, choosing to go right and a little farther up the alley. He's unfamiliar with the area, but the infrastructure is common to many cities he's been to before. He has to keep her safe from whatever this situation is. He knows they're being followed but cannot understand why. He's not usually one anyone tries to rob or mess with. His size tends to keep him out of such trouble, so he considers that it may be more *personal*. He begins guiding her back towards the Passionista, this island doesn't feel safe.

31

Black

Demi

Demi's eyes open, she peeks through her hair to his empty pillow next to her. He's not there. Sadness runs through her. She exhales the way she does on all his early days when he's had to leave her for staff meetings and dealings with Errol Adler. A large carnelian crystal lays aside a note. She smiles, stretching her arms out to reach it, yawning wide. His frisky pleasure from the night before is still indescribable to her this morning…she smiles remembering his silhouette in the dark. How the impending danger on the island ignited something within him, causing him to be more protective, yet fierce. His thrusts intense, his embrace tighter. His tenderness still a priority. Her body feels incredible! As if completely satisfied yet hungry for more.

His passion seemed to really kick off after her cabin door shut. Reaching to caress her leg beneath her skirt he was ever the gentleman…until she moved his hand and he discovered she'd been without panties under her dress the entire time they were traipsing through the alleyways and up stairs. Something stirred him and he swiftly had her up in his arms then on top of her desk! The thought of him entering her, nesting within, burying himself and his full size deep within her sacred space now reserved for only him…made her clench within. She wants him *again*. Grasping at her sheets, bringing them up to her mouth…she can smell his scent. She takes another deep inhale, her eyes closing revealing again his memory…his massive chest, his breath on her skin, his mouth on her neck… When he turned her around and took her from behind. Demi bites the sheets, replaying his forceful yet tantric rhythm again in her mind. Her body pulsing, remembering every moment of his slow, exquisite love-making.

She reaches for the note and opens it:
ALREADY MISSING YOU
R-

Demi rolls onto her back smiling, admiring his stunning handwriting. She wonders if there is anything this man isn't good at. He printed, yet his words look almost calligraphic on the pretty paper.

Suddenly something moves in her peripheral, her head instinctively snaps towards the figure, fear washing over her! She feels the negative energy. The carnelian stone falls to the floor as she brings her arms up to protect herself!

A large hand covers her mouth! She kicks high at the dark figure, and a sharp pinch comes from inside her thigh! She feels the stab...a needle? Something stings. Suddenly, Demi feels her racing heart begin to slow, and all that is in the beautiful room around her begins to close in. Tunneling...

to *blackness-*

32

Discrepancies

Riordan

Riordan peers down onto the main deck as he sips his coffee. A sharp pain sears through his chest at the top of his stomach. His brows furrow a moment, and he takes a deep breath, wondering if he'd overdone it last night. His mind moves to her, and the pain sharpens then stops. He scans each guest, watching them laugh and stuff their faces with breakfast foods. All are accounted for, and the staff is readying the stairwell for disembarkation to the Port of Evy on Island Mar. He's been asked to join the group for a luncheon. He'd normally decline but Demi asked.

Riordan is uneasy at ports because of the added security dangers. So far, it's been a great two months, the mission being successful safety-wise…as for the stolen formulas, that's the only snag in his plan yet he's confident things will work out.

A twinge ignites again in his gut and brushes it off. He doesn't see her down below with her clients. She's never been late but, last night was a most intense time together. He smiles at the thought that she may have taken a little longer in the shower this morning. He certainly had to as waking up was not as easy as he'd hoped. He already misses her.

Grant knocks twice and enters, "Yo, you see that on camera?" He points to one of the camera views for the back of the ship.

Riordan frowns, sipping coffee. He moves his head in towards the screen and squints, looking at what appears to be a small vessel up against the back of the ship where the delivery doors are. "Hmmm, I'll call down to Captain Nero and see what's going on. I didn't have any deliveries on the manifesto. Maybe he does."

"Yeah, I just happened to notice it a few minutes ago. Thought I'd come and ask you." Grant looks Riordan up and down. "So, okay if I turn on the cameras near your cabin door now studley?"

"What? Oh, well, yes. Hey, have you seen Demi on deck yet?"

Grant smiles, "Rior, your lookin tired, man. You getting any sleep?" He's teasing.

"I sleep just fine."

"Oh, I can see that."

"Have you?" Riordan isn't amused. Something doesn't feel right.

"Have I wh-…oh, your main squeeze? No, no, she hasn't greeted the couples yet if that's what you mean."

"Okay."

Grant turns on the camera in the hallway to Riordan's room from his phone and sees it come up on the monitors. He points to her door, "She's probably running late, is all. Listen, I'm gonna go get the couples off this canoe. I'll see you down there?"

"I'll make an appearance at the luncheon after I speak to Nero. Are we set with Lubna and Sagrid?"

"We're set. We won't let her, or her lush of a wife, out of sight. Levy will stick close to Demi for you until you can join us. This island could be tricky. It has a reputation of being controlled by groups other than it's government. Who knows what they're willing to do to Americans." Grant is gearing up as he does before the adrenaline takes over.

"Ten-four, I'm gonna give a call to Nero and see what's up with that vessel down there. It's not like him to forget to notify me." Riordan can still see the rear of some sort boat bobbing in the water up against the yacht. He wonders if he's been too distracted or if something is off.

"Alright. See ya down there."

"Yup. Be careful, man."

Grant opens the door, "You bet." Closing it softly.

Riordan dials Captain Nero and takes a seat at his desk. The line rings. While waiting, he pans in closer on the camera facing his hallway and narrows in to see Demi's cabin door not latched. The phone continues to ring. Riordan wonders if she forgot something and stepped back into her room. The line rings, and Nero picks up.

"Cap'n Nero."

Riordan clears his throat, "Sir, Tate here. Hey, I see a vessel stern sticking out a ways from the Passionista near the delivery doors. It's not on my report. You have an unscheduled load?"

"No, no. Not that I'm aware of."

Riordan slams the phone down and takes off towards Demi's cabin. Two odd occurrences in the last five minutes are more than he'll allow. He's been at this job too long to get comfortable with little discrepancies. He takes the staff stairwell down and runs towards her room.

33

Alone

Demi

Demi stirs a moment. Pain sears down her neck and back. She lifts her head up and squints at the light overhead. Her wrists hurt...her whole body hurts. She blinks, trying to focus on what's around her. She jolts suddenly, frantically looking around. She looks up and sees her wrists are tied, and she's hanging! Her breathing becomes erratic, her body in pain. She looks down to see why she feels cold. Her toes just graze the floor; her heels don't reach. The silk nightie hangs on her, and she can see a blood trail from beneath the edge of it and running down her inside thigh to her calf. Her mouth is covered with what feels and smells like duct tape, her rapid nostril breathing making noise against it. She squeezes her inners, hoping to hell she's not been raped. There's no pain except for the inside of her thigh, where the blood seems to be originating from. She remembers being stabbed with something right before everything tunneled out.

She tries to free her wrists, but they are terribly tight. Her hands hurt so bad, and her body aches from hanging. As if all her bones have separated. She wonders how long she's been out and if she should try to scream. Her heart pounds against her chest and seems to be escaping through her ears. She tries to calm as she recognizes she's terrified and in full-blown anxiety. When she wriggles, her breath catches, her rib! It hurts as if a knife is impaled in her side. She relents and tries to hang still.

"There you go. Being still is best little darlin'. You keep wiggling like a fish. I'll have to throw you over the side of this here yacht!" Errol Adler's voice is unmistakable and as nonchalant as always. He sounds comfortable, as if he's done this a thousand times.

Demi turns her head left, then right. She can't see him in the dim light. It sounds as if he has her in some dungeon or machinery type room. She's breathing erratically again, and her rib is stabbing her with each exhale.

"Now, now. You just calm yourself down ya hear. There's no reason to go gettin' all worked up." Adler's voice comes from behind her. She can hear him lighting up a cigar. The stench already in the air. "I'm sorry it has to be like this…well, not really, you're looking mighty fine in that little nightgown there. I can't say I'm not enjoying the view from this angle." He sucks long on his fat, putrid cigar and continues. "I guess you don't much care for sleeping in underwear…you know, that's just not common enough amongst you split-tails if ya ask me, very nice to see a woman so free."

Demi hears him chuckle, then open and close the lid to his lighter. She's in tremendous pain, and he's speaking low and calm as if his torture is appropriate. She thinks of Riordan and begins to feel tears coming on. He has no idea where she is! *She* has no idea where she is! She tries to calm her breathing, not knowing how long she was out or even if it's day or night.

"Anywho, like I was sayin', I am super sorry about all this. Truth be told, lil' fish, you're just bait…kinda for a bigger, much more muscular fish, really. Oh, and Teo told me to tell you hello."

Demi's face cringes as she fights back tears. Hearing her ex-husband's name, knowing he's behind what's happening sends fear shooting through her every cell. She realizes he has reach beyond the walls of prison. Her chest heaves.

Adler stands up, and his voice begins to come closer, "Aw, now, now…it's all right. I had a hunch you'd be the perfect choice for the great Tate! You see, that ole' stud cost me a shit-ton of money when he took your hubby down."

Demi's breathing hitches. Her body stiff.

"Oh, you didn't know, darlin', not even your hubby knew about the great Riordan Tate until I told him. It took some digging…than some burying…some more digging…and, well, you can see how these things get all discombobulated. Hell, I was even scared. Everyone is scared of ole' Tate. That boy is one bad mother-fucker. He's so good, not even I knew he was undercover with your main squeeze. Your old man…ball-n-chain mexicano there. Thank goodness everyone can be bought. I mean, it was a pretty hefty price to get one of Tate's FBI buds to crack. Then again, it wasn't until after I got the $750,000 back because…well, death is cheaper than life sometimes." Errol cackles, giving Demi a break from his babbling.

Her mind races. There's so much she doesn't understand! The pain is torturous, and all she knows is she wouldn't be hanging and freezing if she hadn't met Riordan! Or...Teo for that matter... she can't *think*. She just wants to smash the fuck out of this mother-fucking Yosemite-Sam-looking douchebag. He steps around her, grazing the cleft of her ass with his pudgy fingertips. She shivers with disgust, wriggling away from his putrid touch.

Errol Adler steps into the low light facing her. His over-sized cowboy hat is not quite hiding his wrinkled fat face. He exhales, blowing cigar smoke into her already-suffocating nostril area. She's never wanted to kill someone until this moment. Rage doesn't come close to what she's feeling. "You sure are a pretty one, aren't ya, Ms. Greer. I bet you bring that ole Tate to his knees. I know ya must have somethin goin on cause your ex sure was interested when I mentioned we needed to recover some of our millions. Don't get me wrong, I don't much like the cartel...and your Teo will probably be better off to me six feet under, but for right now, everyone is fine right where they're at while I get some of my millions back."

Demi picks her head up and leans it back to try and alleviate some of the pain. She wishes he would just shut the fuck up. He prattles on and on, almost making her wish she's just pass out. Glaring up at the ceiling, she sees pipes. She feels the rock of the ocean, which relieves her since that might mean she's still on the yacht and not in some warehouse. She can hear waves against the room mimicking the sound and timing of the ocean she'd come to love. She's hoping she's still on the Passionista, still docked at the Island Mar. *Is it the same day?* She has no idea how long she's been out or suspended from the pipe above her. By the feel of the dislocation in her wrists, it could be days.? She's disgusted by him. She picks her head up and forwards, locking eyes with him, the duct tape half blocking her airflow. She feels completely alone...*helpless-*

34

Cost Me Money

Riordan

Riordan reaches her cabin door; it's not latched. He unholsters his .380 ankle gun and cautiously enters, scanning the entire area. Her shoes are still on the floor, and a small framed piece of art is facedown on the carpet. Riordan's heart is racing as he's hoping she's just overslept.

He silently clears each area, doorway, and finally, the bedroom and bathroom. She's not in the cabin! He sees the crystal he left for her on the floor, his note still in the middle of the bed, the sheets bunched up near the pillows. His chest hurts, another piece of paper is in place of where his body had been just hours earlier. He reaches for it:

TICK TOCK TATE
DON'T MAKE HER WAIT

Riordan crumbles the note and throws it against the wall. He pivots and runs towards the door. He raises his wrist radio to his mouth, "Code PGreen, I repeat Code PGreen!" Riordan makes it into the hallway and finally hears Grant key up with "Received." He gets all the way to the stairwell and heads down three flights before the alarms ring out. He knows Grant will evacuate everyone. Hopefully, most of the passengers are already on shore. He feels a rage inside he's never felt in his life before! More fierce than when Evelyn was taken. He begins missing steps, taking longer strides. He has no idea where to go or what's waiting for him but, he does know that the vessel at the back of the ship didn't belong there! The first deck is the best place to begin searching for her.

Riordan jumps from the last steps cautiously to the floor. He sees the crew ahead, running towards their evacuation areas. He turns in the opposite direction back towards the engine rooms. His training reminds him it's the only area of a yacht she could've been taken with not much camera coverage. A surge of pain passes through him. He can't bear someone hurting her or even scaring her. He hears whispers ahead and hides his body alongside some crew lockers.

"How the hell are we supposed to get her to the boat now!" A voice, in a slight Spanish accent, whispers hurriedly.

"This guy's a fuckin' idiot. I'm not going down for some dumb redneck. He better not move her until all this alarm shit is over…and the price just went up!" A second voice whispers back, and Riordan is fuming. He is furious that they may have man-handled her are even thinking of taking her away from the yacht…or *him*. He decides he's already gonna take them out.

He holsters his gun. Looking back at the exits, he sees a few more crew members evacuating. He tucks himself back into the corner again so as not to be seen. He hears the two henchmen again.

"What the fuck is he doing in there with her anyway. That goofy mudda-fucker better not be touching bossman's wife. He'll kill each of us slowly." The second voice whispers, and Riordan seethes realizing Teo is the connection to these two idiots. *Fuck, she's in this because of me.*

He swings around the lockers, crouched down, and picks up speed as he approaches the two men. Assessing and sizing up that they aren't as big as they should be, he decides to use one against the other. Torquing to the opposite wall, Riordan runs up the wall, turns, and side-kicks the taller one in the back, sending him violently into the smaller one knocking the little one out on impact. The crash their bodies make isn't helpful, but Riordan hopes the alarms drown out most of it. The taller, skinny Mexican pushes himself off his now useless partner and reaches for a gun very visible in the belt of his jeans. Riordan steps over him, trapping his wrist to the floor and placing his knee in his back, rendering the man immovable. Through clenched teeth, he calmly commands, "Don't fucking move. I'm going to ask you questions you're going to answer me quietly nodding yes or no…you got it?"

Riordan snatches the gun out of the man's belt and sees it's a 9MM PeraBellem. The Mexican tries to move beneath Riordan. He cries out as Riordan forces his thumb into his jaw joint paralyzing movement, "You got it?" The man relents, putting his fingers up in a surrendering motion. Riordan checks on his little side-kick and sees he's not waking up anytime soon. He may have hit him hard enough for brain damage, Riordan doesn't give a shit. He looks down again at his victim.

"Who the fuck do you work for?"

"No...no habla...eng-"

Riordan presses into his joint and up, causing another excruciating level of pain, "Who!?"

"Loczano! LOCZANOOO!!"

Riordan knew the answer, hearing Teo's name out loud makes him clench his teeth, fighting adrenaline and the want to kill the man beneath him. He knew then Demi should have been put in witness protection. Guilt sears through him. "Where is she! Who's with her!!" Riordan's rage is coming through his grasp and his knee into the man's spine.

"I don't know him, puto-" The man starts to cry. Riordan reaches over and snatches a second gun from the little one's waistband, another parabellum luger but in black. He cocks it and puts it to the man's jaw this time.

"I'm not asking you again!" Riordan has an idea who could be in the room with her but needs to know how many.

The man shakes, "Some Adler cowboy fucker! I don't know him!"

Riordan loses his temper at the confirmation that his very own boss took Demi. He grabs the man's hair and smashes his head against the floor. His body goes limp, and Riordan grabs his shirt, lifting him up and throwing him on top of his partner against the lockers. The gun is ready, and Riordan is more than happy to use it on Errol Adler, confusing Teo with why his very own employee's gun killed the cowboy. He steps around the pile of cartel henchmen and finds a door fifteen feet away down the hall. The light bulb outside the door is shattered, and Riordan hopes it's from Demi fighting and kicking. He squeezes his eyes quickly, trying to push away the guilt he feels for how he's responsible for all this. He prays she's alive, even if she hates him forever. He just needs her to be alive. *Please...please!* He can't have another woman die because of him. He slams his body against the door and barges in. His head snaps towards the light, and a gun cocks.

Adler looks over, a revolver tucked under Demi's jaw, her jade egg in his other palm, "Ah, there you are, Tate. You believe this old girl just literally laid a green egg! You put that gun on the floor, or I'll blow her pretty face all over these pipes."

Riordan has the gun pointed between Errol Adler's eyes, rage pulsing through his veins at the sight of him near her body. He knows he can make the shot, but he can't chance the old fucker's finger won't squeeze the trigger of the revolver pointed at her terrified face. His jaw clenches.

"Go on now, let it hit the deck."

Riordan wants to kill him more than he's ever wanted to kill a man. Demi's head and hair begin hanging forward, and her hands are purple! He feels indescribable pain in his heart. He relents, releases the hammer, and throws the gun to the side. At least he has the second gun still in his waistband. He opens his hands in surrender, trying to distract Errol with his obedient submission.

"And the one in your ankle holster, I've known you too long."

Riordan uses one hand to get to his .380, never taking his eyes off of Demi. He wants to run to her, take her out of pain…

"You know it took ya damn long enough to get here. Guess those two out there gave ya a run for my money, huh?" Errol laughs. Riordan watches her, moving his eyes back to Errol then back to her.

"I'm gonna end you, Errol." Riordan squeezes his fists.

"Now come on, friend, none of that. We've known each other for a long time. There's no need for hurt feelings. I just have to do this shitty revenge crap. You see, you cost me a lot of money when you messed with Laczano and put him away. That 51 million you seized was not all his you stupid fuck."

Riordan exhales disgustedly, "I didn't seize your goddamn money."

"Yeah, I thought that too. And, it took me a while to shake down the right FBI guy on the case. So, here we are. You fuckin' Teo's wife, which by the way, infuriates him even more Tate the Great. When he found out about you, there was no talking you up. That man has a damn contract out on you lil' buddy."

"So you set me up."

"Well, I didn't want to. You know, you and I go way back. But…I owed him a favor, and well some pesos. So, here's what I'm gonna need you to do. You get on your little ear thingy phone there, and transfer the money back. In fact, transfer *all* the money you've made from me…back. We'll call it even and we can all go home, call it a bad day."

Riordan squints at him, "I told you, I didn't seize your money."

"See, now you're making this difficult." Errol takes the gun and points it at Demi's knee.

"How's Teo going to feel if you shoot his ex-wife." Riordan hates this part of dealing with psychopaths. He has to keep Errol engaged until he can somehow find a window of opportunity.

"Well, I don't think he's gonna want her much now that you've spoiled her. Sagrid tells me it's pretty damn serious the way you two look at each other. He's still a pretty pissed off at her. He's a "mexi-can't" sittin' there rotting in prison because of you. *Real mad*, she went on and divorced him while he was in jail and all. I don't think he'll mind that it was your fault she ends up dead."

Riordan keeps it going, "So you set this all up yourself? There are no stolen vials, no missing jump drives right? That's why my crew can't find anything, right? All this was about trapping me so you could get money back…and keep yourself in Loczano's good graces?"

"Oh, that, yeah no, all that was just to get Lubna here so Sagrid could get rid of her and try to take me to the cleaners. Twat-waffle that she is. Kill two birds, one stone type shit. I'm sure you understand."

"And your son? You bring your son on a voyage where he could potentially get hurt? What's wrong with you?"

Errol chuckles, "Boy, his momma is costing me too much… besides Sagrid won't shut up about her, so the boy is here, I'm here, Sagrid's here…who knows what will happen to his Momma while we're all away. You don't need to worry your pretty-boi face about it. Let's get down to brass tax here and have you make those trans-actions *now*." His voice turning serious.

"I don't have any seized money, and I don't have a phone."

"Aw, come on, old friend, you really gonna make me blow a hole in her? She'll never do yoga again, let alone bend over for you or be able to put one of these up her keister. What the hell kind of kinky shit you two into anyway?"

Riordan doesn't answer. His mind racing, rage searing, his eyes darting, scanning the room. He has to get her out of here!

"Here, I'll tell you what, we're gonna have you use my phone. I bet..." Errol looks at the gun pointed at Demi's knee and the jade egg in his other hand. "I bet, just in that one off-shore account I send your payments too, you've got way more than enough to cover all you've taken from Laczano and I'll take the rest...just for shits and giggles." Errol turns a bit to figure out where to put the egg so he can throw his phone to Riordan, suddenly Demi's legs shoot up, still bound at the ankles, and she kicks Errol hard in his face with both feet knocking his cowboy hat and frame backward! He comes forward and points his gun-

BAM!!

Riordan stands, the gun from his waistband pointed at Errol's forehead. The shot reached its mark. Demi looks at Errol. He stares blankly at Riordan. Riordan watches as he falls face-first on the floor, his gun...still in his hand.

35

Got You

Demi

Riordan runs to her, lifting her up so her hands can be freed. She winces loudly. The pain is unbearable even with the feeling in her hands gone. Her body feels as if everything has dislocated.

"Okay, baby, I've got you. I'm gonna free you okay…just give me-" Riordan lifts her more, but her hands are bound too tightly and with duct tape and rope. He sees the tape on her mouth and gently rips it off.

She squints in pain, "*He-* He has a knife…there on his belt." She looks down at Errol Adler, a pool of blood growing around his head, face down in it.

Riordan lowers her gently, her body stretching again, and she yelps. "I'm sorry. I'm so sorry baby." He bends down and unbuttons the pocket knife casing revealing a solid gold Swiss knife. Riordan is disgusted and kicks the gun out of his hand as he stands back up and opens the blade. He lifts Demi up again and cuts the duct tape. Her arms fall around his neck. He cradles her to his chest and steps over and away from Errol. He walks her to a large generator and places her half-naked body on it. He cuts her feet loose and the rest of the tape from her hands. Demi lies limp against the wall along the generator. Riordan looks at her face. She won't look at him. He knows not to say anything else. He turns and walks over to pick up the other two guns. He puts his .380 back in his ankle holster, grabs the yoni egg, and puts it in his pocket. Rushing to the door, he peeks out to see if they have a clear hallway. Riordan quickly wipes his prints from the little guy's gun and puts it in his hand. He does the same with the second guy. It's not his best scene, but it'll confuse any investigation enough to keep'em busy. He doesn't know how many others are on board, who works for Teo, and who's working for Errol. He knows he has to get Demi off and to safety.

Demi tries to open her eyes but, whatever Errol stabbed her in the leg with keeps making her go in and out. *Exhaustion.* Riordan comes back and picks her up as gently as he can. She cries out as her body hurts all over, "I know, Dom, I'm sorry. I'm going to get you out of here. I'm going to keep you safe baby." Demi knows she needs to be mad at him, this man she loves more than anything... but, everything goes black-

Demi feels sprinkles of water falling on her eyelids and face. She opens her lids a little, but the sun hurts her eyes. She looks and sees Riordan staring at her as he's steering the handle of a boat, hitting waves. The spray of the water falls on her skin, and it feels tingly. She sees him, and he's standingg tall and mammoth above her, protective. He's so gorgeous, one hand on her leg holding her nightie down, the other hand steering the boat. He looks up and out at the water. Behind him, she sees the Passionista getting farther and farther away. She wants to move, but her body feels so heavy. Everything aches. She feels her limbs moving with the waves, but she can't find the strength to stop them. She looks at him again. He's not smiling. The look on his face is stern and serious. She's never seen his eyes so dark. He's still so beautiful...but she wonders, does she really know him at all?

Everything closes in again...the tunnel comes, and the sun disappears-

36

Heal

Riordan

The breeze flows in again, causing the sheer fabric curtains to slowly flap and waver on the bed surrounding her. He stares and watches her. Riordan sips his drink and takes a deep inhale admiring the strands of hair that get to wave and touch her face each time the wind blows. Her hand twitches, and he is reminded of the purple and yellow bruises thick around her wrists. She moves a leg, and her eyebrows furrow as the pain comes. She stops moving then opens her eyes, fluttering them, trying to focus on the ceiling fan moving overhead. It's too much. She closes them. Riordan stands and quietly walks to the side of the bed. He keeps his distance. He watches her breathing, sees the movement of her eyes beneath closed lids realizing she's finally waking. She's been out for two days. He wants to take her in his arms…kiss all her pain away.

She opens her eyes again, lowering them, resting them on his familiar face. She stares at him, trying to make sense of his gaze. He watches her, guilt deeply engrained in his empathic eyes. He knows he has to explain many things…and that she's *traumatized*. She may never be the same. For now, he has her safe…and only he knows where they are.

"I'll be back in a moment. I'm going to draw you a bath." Riordan speaks softly and watches her eyes to see if she understands him. He wants to lay down beside her, pull her into his arms, and beg for her forgiveness. Because of him, she is hurt. Wounded deeper than all the physical injuries. He did not keep her safe, and he doesn't know if he can forgive himself for that. He steps away, familiar regret hanging on his defeated frame. She follows him with her eyes until he disappears.

Riordan fills the tub with hot water, puts in eucalyptus oil, Epsom salt, and spearmint sprigs he found from a lady in town. The island is secluded, but it has almost everything one needs and only 13,450 people inhabiting it. It's the safest he could find on such short notice. He walks back to her bed to make sure she's okay. He has a difficult time when she's not in sight...even for just a few moments. The bliss from the last months flash through his mind...now this. His heart is heavy.

Demi tries to roll to her side but winces from an over-stretched spine. Her muscles feel strained in a way she's never felt before. She looks down and sees the same damn nightie, the lower part on the right side stained with blood. She looks up to see Riordan staring, water welling up in his eyes.

"He didn't rape me-" she tries to talk, her voice cracks.

It's not the first words he thought he'd hear from her, relief washing over him. Her voice sends electric through him. He's aware she may continue with warranted hateful words...and she won't be herself for quite some time. But, the relief at hearing her speak makes it hard to hold back tears. He opens a bottle of water for her half-whispering, "The needle to your inner thigh tore the skin as you were kicking. I bandaged it. "

"What did he shoot me up with?"

"A knock-out drug-like gamma-hydroxybutyric acid."

"What!"

"GHB or a liquid ecstasy. You've been out for two days so it's got to be one of those. One more day and I would have brought a doctor in. I'm so happy you're awake, Demi." Riordan doesn't smile, but the sound in his voice is sincere. "I need to move you to the bath. It'll help repair your muscles. I want to reduce your pain."

Demi looks at him. He's lovely. She knows she wants to be mad at him, but she loves him so damn much. He walks around to her side of the bed and moves the curtains aside. Bending down, he gently puts her arm around his neck, careful not to touch her wrists. Demi holds her breath and tries to be strong, she looks at him, but he can't make full eye-contact. He cradles her and lifts her gently into his arms. His hands spread wide and gentle on her skin. He smells fresh and has some sort of glorious musky oils on his face and neck. Demi inhales deep, closing her eyes as he moves her across the room; she opens her eyes and catches him looking down at her. He looks away and stares straight to where he's walking. He's stoic and could easily be someone she doesn't know, but that just doesn't feel right. What they've shared, the unmistakable bond they've forged can't be ignored. She takes a chance and places a hand on his cheek. His breath hitches and his eyes close to her touch. She moves his face and reaches up to kiss him. Riordan stops in his tracks and kisses her back. She deepens the kiss, suddenly his face contorts, his lips pull away, and he lays his forehead to hers. Beneath her hand, she feels his cheek tighten and his teeth clench. She pulls back to look up at him in the dimly lit bathroom, and Riordan looks at her, his eyes filling with tears. She moves her hand up his cheek despite the wrist pain, her other hand running through his hair. She looks into both his eyes and sees he's in gut-wrenching anguish. Riordan feels so broken, guilt riddling throughout his body. He continues to the claw-foot tub and sweetly places her in the water to distract them both from how *he* feels. Easing her down into the water, he tries to slowly lift her nightie up and over her head. Although she once looked breathtakingly beautiful in it, he felt it best to get rid of it. Demi lowers her arms into the water and sinks down to her chin. The water feels incredible, painful, but in a good way. Riordan turns the water off, then walks over and throws the nightgown in the trash can. He's not making eye contact, wiping away tears. Demi wants him close.

"Riordan?"

He freezes, his back to her. Hearing his name flow out of her lips is *everything*. He can't find his voice to answer, fearing as she comes out of her drug induced sleep she'll begin feeling disdain and hatred towards him. He thinks how he might not be able to live with himself if he has to go on knowing she once loved him and grew to hate him.

"Riordan? Do you love me?"

Riordan hangs his head, his shoulders slump, they begin to shake, and he brings his finger and thumb up to his eyes and pinches his tear ducts, trying to keep more tears from forming. He's breaking down, and she's half-across the room.

"Oh baby, come here…come here, please." She splashes the water lifting her sore, battered arms up, begging him to come to her.

Riordan goes to her and falls to his knees. He reaches in, cupping her face. His gaze showing unendurable pain, he places his forehead to hers again. Demi grabs his hands to secure them to her and let him know she's not letting him go. He silently cries, holding his breath, having trouble finding words. His body tense with shame. Guilt coursing through him at an unbearable level. He begins to speak, "I'm so, so sorry, Demi. I'm so sorry. I-" His voice cracks, "I'm so, so, so, so-" He begins to cry, shoulders convulsing, his heart feeling as if it's breaking in his chest. Years of pent up hurt and guilt rushing out. Remorse spills through deep hyperventilating sobs. He's tormented by the thoughts of her filled with fear and terror at being *taken* from their bed. He can't unsee her helplessly bound and hanging in that cold, dark room. Rage fills him when he thinks of Adler's fingers near her sacredness, the secrets, the things he's not told her. His spirit begins to break for what she's been through...*because of him.*

"Riordan..."

He looks to her, sobbing, almost unable to breathe. He's never broken down like this with another.

"Do you love me?"

His head begins to nod, his mouth falls open, he tries to find the words to which he knows he doesn't deserve to say. He doesn't deserve her, but he *does* so love her, "Of course I do. I love you so much, Demi...I-" He can't seem to continue. She deserves better.

"Because...I love you, Riordan! I love you from my soul." She tries to look into his eyes. He sees her through swollen, red eyes. "My soul Riordan! I love you! I fucking love you. Do you hear me?" She whispers, "I love you."

He stares at her, unable to believe what she's saying.

"I don't know or understand all of what happened in the last three days, and I'm sure there are upsetting things that'll come out...but, I do know I have never loved anyone the way I love you. Now, you say you love me, you've made love to me in indescribable ways my body can never be without, you found me and brought me here and kept me safe. I don't know much, but I do know anything we need to get through would take us both loving each other. I'm going to trust that there isn't anything we can't get through if we feel the same for each other."

Riordan looks into her eyes, her words melodious. He leans in and kisses her deeply, his tears warm and wet on her skin. She kisses him back...long and needing. He finally exhales, gentle so as not to hurt her. She pulls away and looks at him with wanting eyes.

"I need you."

He sees in her eyes she's desperate for him now, as he her.

"Will you hold me please?" He can't refuse her. He nods and stands up, removing his shirt, one she's never seen, and jeans that are also new. His body is toned and just glorious to see naked. His long shaft rests against his leg as he throws his clothing aside. He walks around behind where she sits in the big tub and climbs in very slowly, sitting down behind her so he can hold her as she's requested. He wipes his tears away, guilt still fresh within. Her words beginning to heal him. Her need of him helping release the self-loathing he so strongly feels not only in this situation but in the other areas where he felt he could have done better for her. He instinctively brings his palm around under her breasts, and places it gently on her stomach. Pulling her to his chest, he cradles her and then guides them both back, leaning against the rear incline of the tub. The water covers them, the steam rising up caressing them. The heat cocooning them in. Riordan brings his other palm forward and places it over her heart. She very cautiously brings her arms around to cover his and lays her head back on his chest. She sighs and feels that they can finally breathe. Again...together.

37

Again and Again
Demi

Demi opens her eyes and feels his palm protecting her head and face. She's facing him and nestled right into his chest. Her fingers are splayed, his chest hair intertwined and curling around her fingers. Her cheek is pressed against his pec, her mouth an inch from his lovely plump nipple. She can't remember how they got naked and in the bed together but, she feels it's just perfect after all they've been through. She has her leg up and draped over his. His large quad muscles warm against her yoni lips. His bicep supports her neck, and he's cradling her as if he'll never let her go. She thinks how she's never been held by anyone the way this man holds her.

A breeze flows in and covers them giving her an idea. She can feel his penis lying against her thigh, and even though her body still aches, she aches for him inside her. She, despite all they've been through, still feels the familiar stirring within her soul for him! . She exhales a slow, hot breath across his nipple and waits. With the hand on his chest, she gently moves it down his chest and stomach, caressing his mound of pubic hair and finally lowers arriving at his shaft. Moving her sore fingers up and down his shaft, she feels his velvety soft skin. His magnetic pull stronger than the pains she feels. She ignores her bruised and battered frame, taking pleasure in his sleepy, sexy physique. Another exhale, but this time with pursed lips directing the air to the core of his nipple. His penis pulses beneath her fingers, and he begins to stir. She lifts her head to gaze upon his sweet face. He stirs again, inhaling a long awakening breath. Demi again drags her fingertips down and up his shaft, then encircles the head of his seductively engorging cock a few times, slowly and softly. She again exhales warmth on his nipple, and he responds by gently hugging her closer. She winces as she's still sore but doesn't let him hear her. Demi continues her pleasureous assault, resulting in her own wet arousal. His member hardens inch by inch beneath her caresses, and she likes how he responds to her touch. Slowly she starts moving against his leg, pressing her lips along his thigh, ignoring the soreness of her spine. His breathing begins to increase, his heart beating a bit faster. Her arousal begins making the soreness in her body disappear. He always makes her feel such desire. She languidly strokes slowly up, up, up, circling her fingers in his soft curly hair, then to his stomach sweetly reversing back down, down, down, running feather-like fingertips along his hardened shaft. Her body pulses and aches for him.

Riordan inhales sharply, waking and runs his hand down along hers to softly capture her fingers and hold them still. His voice melodious in the large room, "We should talk."

"This is all the communication I want right now, Riordan." She moves her hand from his and continues her caress. His jaw clenches, and he exhales.

"Do you remember how we got into bed, Demi? Do you remember me washing you, taking you to the bathroom, trying to feed you?" He reaches up overhead to the opposite pillow and grabs three empty water bottles to show her, "Do you remember me giving you these? How you guzzled them down?" You need rest…and we need to talk when you're ready. He's speaking low, but she can sense his unease. She wonders if she was out again.

"I only remember moments here and there. Thank you for taking such good care of me. Now, I want you to heal me in *our* way." She reaches up to his face and pulls him into her kiss. His mouth is hot, and she can feel his want for her despite his chivalrous rejection.

Riordan again gently grabs her hand to return it to her, "I don't want to hurt you. You're injured, and you need to recover." She senses he isn't talking more about her physical injuries.

"You've never hurt me this way. I need you now…I need us. This…our bond. This is what heals me, Rior. I can feel you want me…don't make me beg for you." She's looking into his eyes, tears welling up in hers. He can't bear to see her cry. He doesn't want to selflessly take from her while she's in such a vulnerable way.

Riordan turns to her and brings her into his chest, "Of course I want you, I just don't want-" Her mouth turns up, and she covers his words with her lips. He presses back and parts her mouth with his warm, fevered tongue. She's so hard to resist. Her arms wrap around him, pulling him towards her request, she guides him on top of her. Arching into him, she finds what she's wanting and slides her palms down to his plump tush pulling him into her. Riordan lets her surround his cock with her wet, tight velvet beauty, a moan escaping his mouth into her. He holds his weight up on his forearms careful not to press onto her with his weight. She squeezes around him as he thrusts and holds, lingering inside her yoni as she sets their slow pace. As she releases he pulls slowly away. Her fingers again grip his rear and he glides ever so gently towards her, careful not to hurt her. Arching again, she releases to prepare to tighten around him again. Riordan slides back and slowly forward again, thrusting, burrowing deeper into her as she pulls him in, her tongue plunging deeper and swiping slowly to entangle with his. She moans breathlessly into him and feels he's already losing control. He realizes this is how she heals. How they will heal. Her sounds, her want for him, his heart beating for her, he feels completely vulnerable beneath her touch. She pulls him in again... and again...

38

Hers

Riordan

Riordan stretches, opening his eyes. He realizes she's not in his arms! He scans the bed, the room, the doors, no sign of her!! His heart beats faster, and he jumps up, throwing the sheets to the side and twisting to put his feet on the floor. He stands quickly, turning to try and find her. He rushes to the bathroom, she's not there. He grabs his jeans, quickly stepping into them, then reaching for his gun tucked down into his boot. He hears a noise out on the porch of the little beach villa; something fell and made a thud on the wood floor. Riordan runs to the window and sees her bending down. He exhales and opens the door and then the screen door. He peeks his head out, relieved to see her sitting back up and against the porch couch. She turns and smiles at him, raising a water bottle she dropped then shrugging. He puts the gun on the nearby table and steps out onto the porch.

"Hello. Everything okay?" His voice is gruff, his eyes puffy from a deep sleep. All they've been through finally hitting him. That coupled with her sexual prowess creates a need for intense rest. He feels he could go back to bed and sleep for days, he's just not willing to if she's awake.

Demi looks him up and down, admiring how masculine he looks barefoot, shirtless, and with his jeans unbuttoned. She pats the cushion next to her, inviting him to sit down, "Yes, baby, it seems my hands are still learning to hold things. I dropped my water...I'm sorry, did I wake you?"

Riordan sits next to her opening his chest and arm to her so she can lean in. He sits back, cradling her, and moves a strand of long hair away from her face. He thinks she's the most beautiful woman he's ever seen. He stretches a leg out and places it on the table, crosses it with his other. He tries to calm his racing heart, realizing he is particularly traumatized when he loses sight of her, "No, I woke looking for you and heard you out here."

"I didn't want to wake you. You were finally *really* sleeping. I figured I wore you out, and you might actually get a whole eight hours in." She chuckles softly, and he kisses her forehead. She's kind to him.

Whispering into her hair, "You did wear me out...in a beautiful, slow, and breathtakingly torturous way." He closes his eyes for a moment and feels a pulsing in his jeans at the memory of how they were the day earlier. He looks out to see where the sun is reflecting on the crashing waves and can tell it's about three o'clock in the afternoon. He's going to have to get her to eat something, so she doesn't get sick. It's been a few days of just water, nuts, and dates. The drugs should be detoxing from her system now.

"That was...incredible."

"Agreed." He sucks air through his teeth softly.

Demi smiles, proud of herself. She watches the waves for a moment and snuggles closer. "I don't know where in the world we are, or how you found *this*...this amazing little place, but I gotta tell ya, I don't think I want to leave here...ever."

Riordan exhales happy he's pleased her, "Good. We're going to need to stay here for some time Dem. To be safe and in the meantime heal."

Demi knows they have so much to talk about. She wants to take it slow, her fatigue is still heavy in her body, and she doesn't want to feel anything more then what she's feeling right now. Cortisol still so thick in her system. "I think that's best. As long as I have you, I'll stay anywhere you want."

Riordan caresses her hair and allows a tiny smile to graze his lips. His breathing finally eases because she calms him. He wants to tell her how much he loves her, how much what she just said meant the world to him, but he suppresses it. He feels he'd be taking from her in the moment. Deep down, he still feels tremendous guilt, and although confident in his abilities, he had a rude awakening at Teo's reach and ability to hurt him *by hurting her*. He knows they're hidden now, but that doesn't mean they're entirely safe. And there's the little issue of him killing a billionaire and making it look like Teo's men did it. Riordan squints his eyes, a slight headache lingering behind them. He can't believe how fucked up this job got. What a shit show. He inhales sharply and tries to push it all away, "I want you here with me safe."

"I'm feeling safe now. I needed to get myself together."

"It'll take quite some time…but you're the strongest woman I've ever known."

She looks at him, smiles, then kisses him. She rests her head on his chest grateful for the porch view out into the beach and waves.

"We've got to get some food at some point babe. You've got to get stronger." He pats her bottom, which he realizes is bare and sticking out of the bottom of his shirt she pulled on. He smiles and loves how free she is in spirit.

"Now, now, my love, don't get me fired up again. I may have to torture you some more, and we'll never get to eat." She's exhausted but playful, and her stomach is completely empty from days of little food and limited consciousness. She does remember him feeding her slices of some sort of sweet fruit, water and such in between passing out again. He's so caring with her. Her mind wanders to how violent he got, a cold, black look in his eyes after he killed Errol Adler. She squeezes her eyes shut, trying to erase the thought. If she could, she'd never think of that disgusting old man again…like he never existed. He brought out in Riordan something she's only read about in college. She knew of his business and his soldiering past from what he shared. Seeing it first hand and what it can do to such a lovely human, it leaves her speechless. She opens and closes her eyes again completely exhausted in his arms.

Two hours later, the sun has moved more into its evening position. Riordan's stomach growls, but he doesn't move so as not to wake her. Demi is curled up against him, her soft breaths resembling the purr of a sleeping kitten. For hours he's gone over so much in his mind. He doesn't care about the Passionista. He could care less about investigations or the authorities on the islands. He is concerned about Grant but trusts him to find them or somehow get in contact when it's safe. This island is defended well by the villagers and far enough away from the bigger ones where the Passionista might dock. He's just not entirely sure of how many of Teo's men might be looking for her and how far his money will reach despite his incarceration. He regrets not taking the bastard out the many times he could've. It would have looked like an accident. The simple fact is, he just doesn't enjoy death or killing. Justice is preferred, but it doesn't often stick. He knows he's going to have to find out who's running Teo's crew and put a stop to Demi being a target or a pawn in *his* being the target. He shakes his head in disgust at how money and revenge fuel Teo. The guy is such a covert narcissistic piece of shit. He looks down at her in his grasp and vows to never let her be hurt again. Ever-

Demi inhales and stretches, opening her eyes. She looks scared. She scans the porch, his legs, her bruised hands. Riordan hugs her and tenderly kisses the top of her head, "Ah, my queen awakens."

"Oh my gosh, I can't believe I fell asleep again!"

"You need the rest Dems, it's quite alright." He runs his hand down her back to settle her.

"I'm famished." She grabs her water.

Riordan plays with her hair, "Yes, we need to get some dinner. There's a market and small village through a path behind our cabin. We can eat and grab what you need-"

She saddens, "I don't have clothes."

He wants to laugh, but it feels foreign to express joy yet, "There are clothes inside in the drawers. Not as nice as your wardrobe, but it'll cover you. I've got to find something as well."

"You don't want this shirt back?" She giggles, and he huffs. The scent of her might drive him wild at dinner.

Riordan would prefer not to take her out, but he's got to give her the choice, "If you'd like, I can go get us something and bring it back. You're not 100% yet." Neither choice is his favorite. Leaving her in the cabin is a risk and taking her out is a risk.

"I don't want to be apart from you Rior, I'll try to keep up and not fall asleep again," she laughs, "these drugs have got to get out at some point."

"They will. You just had way more than you should've. Okay, babe, let's go find some threads to put on that sexy body." He knows the drugs aren't what's really getting her. Her body is strong. She was kidnapped and traumatized…all because of him. Her life is scarred. He stands and tries to push away his guilt. Reaching for her hand, he helps her stand. "Feeling okay?"

Demi stands and feels out her legs and feet, nods, "I think I can go a couple songs with you, wanna salsa?" She stares into his eyes and holds his hands…finally, a small smile appears on his lips. She tries out her legs and reaches up to him on tippy toes. He leans in and kisses her sweetly. He's the most beautiful man she's ever seen…and he's hers.

40

Fragile

Demi

Demi feels almost out of her body but, she walks alongside him, clutching his arm and looking around at all the people. Her heart is racing. There are islanders all around. Elderly sitting and staring, fanning themselves with homemade fans. Children run and play in between the chairs of adults around them. Riordan nods here and there to those making eye contact. His arm is tense, and she can feel his energy is uneasy. He's quiet. He caresses her hand and keeps her close to his side. The people seem to be very un-phased by their presence. Pleasantly accepting.

"Feeling okay?" He speaks to her without looking down at her as he doesn't dare take his eyes off their surroundings. Riordan had hold up on this lil island before between jobs or waiting out. He has no problem with the indigenous people it's Teo's idiots he's on the lookout for. He knows now he'll not hesitate when it come to Demi.

"Yep, I'm keeping up."

Riordan squeezes her hand, "You're doing great, babe. We're heading up a little farther to a pub called Anks. If you'd like, we can get dinner to go."

"Let's see how I do."

He nods. The streets are bustling as store owners sweep and bring their products in for the night. There are fruits and vegetables of vibrant colors, coconuts both green and brown piled up, waiting to be purchased. Demi wants to buy some, but she knows she can't carry them back just yet. Riordan seems preoccupied looking everywhere and in the faces of each person. There seems to be a few Americans peppered throughout, but mostly tanned, small is-landers are moving about. The wind blows beautifully through her legs, lifting the sundress. Demi presses it down to cover the small bandaged cut on the inside of her thigh. She gets a few stares and wonders if the bruises on her wrists make Riordan look like a beast instead of the hero he is. He towers over the crowd, which is helpful for whatever it is he's looking for. He gives her hand a light squeeze and nods towards a quaint little pub with a turquoise door.

Once inside, Demi feels a wall of heat and spices engulf her. Her heart begins to beat faster. She places her hand on her chest. She can't seem to pull it together. It's as if her body is separating from her mind. Riordan leans down and whispers, "Take out?"

"Okay." She huffs in gratitude. Her head nods before the word is completely out. She looks at her hands. They begin to shake.

"Dos platos de la cena por favor. Cuatro copas." Riordan asks the man at the counter.

The bar is full, and Demi can see many eyes upon them. She smiles and stares up at Riordan, admiring his Spanish. His voice calms her for a moment. The little man speaks back to Riordan, who then pulls out money and hands it to him.

"Would you like some port…wine, maybe? Something stronger?" He looks her in the eyes and can see fear. She's uneasy being out, and her body is shaking. He's saddened by her panic. He's seen this reaction before. Her body and her mind are working against her. He wants to get her back to the cabin.

"Sounds good, you pick." Demi tries to breathe slower, her chest pounding. Riordan eyes her realizing she may need to be carried after a shot, not to mention a few more weeks to heal. He'll carry her for sure. First he needs to help her calm.

He puts two fingers up, "Dos tragos de tequila por favor. Una botella de vino tinto para llevar." The man steps over and pours two shot glasses of tequila. Riordan hands him more money. He hands Demi her shot, "Here, baby, let's get your breathing under control, okay?"

Demi takes the glass without releasing her other hand from his arm. She takes the shot and hands him the glass. Riordan waits and watches to see if she needs his. Demi swallows, squints a second, then looks around and finds a bench in the entryway to sit and wait for the food. She tries to slow her breaths. Riordan joins her holding the shot, and watches her between glances at the patrons.

"How we doing?" He smoothes a strand of hair and pulls it behind her ear.

She tries to smile, "I'm trying to breathe normally. My heart seems to have other ideas."

"It's panic, baby, and trauma…basically PTSD. Your body seems to have a different idea than what your brain is telling it."

"Yes. I guess it was too soon to come out around people. I haven't had this, this bad before. I mean not even my divorce felt like this." She takes a deep breath and calms slightly. Riordan hands her the shot, and she takes it without hesitation.

The man behind the counter speaks to Riordan, and he stands to collect the food and wine. Demi stands to keep close with him trying to keep her legs moving. She smiles and nods, then waves and walks out with him. Riordan senses her tension.

"So where do you think we should enjoy this lovely meal, inside or outside?"

She smiles, "I guess that depends on the size of the mosquitos."

Riordan chuckles at her humor. He looks down at her just in time to catch her as she starts to go down. "Uh, okay baby girl, let me help you-" He picks her up, gently bringing her up over his shoulder. Demi goes out just as he gets her balanced. He walks faster, cursing himself for thinking she could handle the walk. She may be the strongest woman he knows but deep down she's fragile.

41

Ever

Riordan

He pours her a glass of wine and watches her look out of the window to the ocean in the dark. She awoke in time to see the moon illuminate the water. Riordan let her sleep. He has to be more careful. He doesn't want her to end up developing agoraphobia. He tries to stuff the feelings of guilt down again and feels a bit more at ease with the folks in town as only two in the pub could've been a threat. Easily taken out if need be, but a threat size-wise. He was careful not to be followed, still keeping a watchful eye out of their tiny secure cabin. If Demi knew of the arsenal beneath the floor, she may have another panic response. There's time to share that later.

Riordan has been concerned about Grant. He's usually in contact by now, it's been days, and he's hoping Grant isn't in jail or cleaning up the mess he left on the Passionista. He sighs, trying to imagine what Grant must have thought when he boarded the yacht and found the scene. He'll wait a few more days hoping Demi will be able to go into town with him. He needs to find a computer or phone to use. His wrist communication tore off in his altercation with henchmen #1. Hopefully, Grant found it before any authorities do.

"Penny for your thoughts?" Demi smiles at him and motions to their food to show him she's starving.

"Apologies, babe, please...please dig in."

"What's got you so far off Rior-"

He tilts his head, "Hey, I think you're feeling better...and you haven't even touched the wine yet."

"I am. I think the two shots just kicked in and relaxed me too much. Now this food should really help. Looks amazing!" Demi begins eating her first meal in days. She sees he's chewing and thinking, deep thinking. His face is beautiful. He's watching her realizing she doesn't know he carried her back. He's worried she's losing time when she faints.

She chews slowly, noticing every eyelash surrounding his dark eyes, almost as if he has a natural eyeliner. He's quite striking. The food begins to calm her, she motions for him to fill up her plastic cup with wine. She tries with him, "So..."

He looks at her while pouring, "Yes, my love."

"Let's talk. You've mentioned we need to talk...we have food and wine...let's talk."

Riordan's stomach churns, and he places his fork down, "Sure."

She notices his breathing change. He's been tormented, he cried. It pains her to see him struggling. She knows more than he thinks because Errol Adler babbled on and on as she faded in and out. She sees that Riordan thinks she'll stop loving him if he tells her his truths, which makes her love him even more. She's going to try to piece things together. She has an interest in healing whatever this PTSD crap is she's going through. She takes the lead, "So you put my ex in prison?"

Riordan looks at her. He realizes she heard more than he thought. "I own my own securities company. I was contracted over two years ago to work alongside the FBI to infiltrate a cartel ring. Teo Laczano's cartel. I worked undercover, well mostly surveillance, and sent much of my crew in to work the undercover."

"So you knew who I was when I walked into your office. That's why you and Errol Adler were arguing, right?" She's keeping her questions soft.

"Yes."

"You didn't want me on the Passionista?"

"I had already done enough to you..." He sits back against the chair. Defeat and guilt beginning to spike again.

She smiles, "To me?"

"To your life-"

"By putting my criminal husband away?" She cuts a small piece of chicken and chews it.

Riordan's watching her, "Yes, I took away the man you loved, your home, your possessions, your world...and I couldn't get you protection, like witness protection…and now we're fucking here!" He waves his hands in the air. He's getting angry.

"I'll admit I was a bit shocked at all Teo was involved with. I felt shame, sure but, love? What we had wasn't love, the home wasn't a home for me, and possessions? None of that made me truly happy. It was a lifestyle I had. As for witness protection, I think that would have been more of a prison for me. Have you considered for one moment Riordan that you may have set me free?"

His eyes glare at her. He did not think she'd react this way. "Demi-"

She cuts him off, "Did you watch me?"

His face saddens, and he looks down at his hands, "Yes."

"Really…watch me?"

"Yes, it was my job, Demi. I didn't start out-"

She leans in, "Then you really knew what I endured, yes?"

Riordan doesn't answer. He feels terrible at how she was abandoned and used, how she was kept in the dark and manipulated. He wanted to take her away from it…not destroy all she had. "In every case, there are those who-" He stops himself so as not to make her feel like an object.

"Did you fall for me?" Her voice is wanting and soft.

"I-"

"Riordan-"

"I-"

"Rior…"

He cuts her off, "I've loved you since the first time I heard your voice!" He places his elbows on the table and rests his chin in his hands. He looks out towards the ocean, unable to look in her eyes. He brings his head into his hands. His admission sounds like what they have now was all premeditated, like he selfishly put her in harms way for his heart and needs.

"That's why you treated me the way you did when I shook hands with you in your office. Why you were being distant…why I felt I've known you-" She stares at him, her mind racing with all the memories. He didn't want her to go off the yacht that first night and instead had dinner with her. He rejected her kissing him that first night. He tried to distance himself but, his love was stronge…

it's why he let her attack him that first time in his office. His love for her dictated all thats happened. He's failed her.

He exhales, "I can't be away from you, Demi…but, look at what happens to your life because of me." He pushes his chair out and slams his palm down on the table, making her jolt. He stands up and walks over to the side window, his hands on his hips.

She sees how hard he is on himself. Guilt has riddled his body, but fate and tantra have bonded them. He's at odds within himself. She gets up and briskly moves across the room to him. She hugs him from behind, feeling him surrender to her touch. "Because of you, I feel alive again, I can finally love. I GET TO LOVE YOU. Because of you, I am more safe than not. You risked your life and saved me! I love you, Riordan! I love you. Life doesn't go the way we think or how is SHOULD. Goddamn it! You've saved me more times than you'll ever know. I love you with my everything!"

He turns, and she lets go of him. He faces her and picks her up in a tender hug so she can feel his heart. Her words mean so much. She understands that beneath all his masculinity and honor, he's a boy who thinks his vulnerability is wrong…and that he feels he's not good enough. He whispers in her hair, "I've loved you for years, Demi. This thing with Adler was going to be my last job. I probably would have just watched you from a distance on that yacht, suffering in silence while I finished to my retirement. I would have gone on loving you as I had all that time before. I would have left you alone, I would have! I- I just couldn't believe you were in my arms when you…were. I couldn't believe how my heart was beating almost out of my chest. I wanted you. I wanted all of you. Gosh…that sounds awful."

"I don't think it's awful."

"And he brought you right to my doorstep…to *use* you, to get at me…I should have seen it Dems."

She smiles looking into his eyes, "These have been the best days of my life. I never want to go back to any other life. You are where I want to be. You think you ruined me, you think you took from me, you couldn't be more mistaken honey. You fuckin' saved me! Things just went in an odd way…but you saved me Rior."

Riordan closes his eyes and kisses her head again. "I've loved you for years, Demi. I never want to be without you…ever."

42

4 Taps
Demi

The sun begins to light up the morning sky. Demi looks down at Riordan sleeping in her lap. She's been up for quite a while, just listening to the waves in between his breaths. She runs her fingers through his thick hair, he's so beautiful, she could watch him all day. It's going to take time to get through the healing. He with his guilt and she with her trauma.

These days have passed lovingly. He gets her food, sometimes she goes with him. He makes love to her deeper, if thats even possible, and often. Yesterday she walked down to the water's edge and was able to sit on the sand with her feet in the ocean. Her hands only shook for a few minutes when she noticed a cruise liner way, way out, passing by the island. It was a tiny white speck, so far out, yet her body still responded. She squeezed her eyes shut to erase any pictures in her mind. She knows she must get farther and farther away from the fear.

Riordan inhales deep and stretches. He wraps one arm around her back and the other over her lap, his head laying on her stomach. She's noticed he's been clingy, protective clingy, and hopes his guilt dissipates more and more as time passes although she can't say she minds the clingy part. He really has no idea how he'd saved her life way before he actually *saved* her life. Demi looks down at him and plays with the curls around his temple. She watches as his shorter hairs make a circle and curl around her pinky. She smiles and thinks about how he must have been the most beautiful baby.

Tap...tap,tap,tap....TAP!

Demi's body stiffens at the sound! A muffled yelp escapes her lips as Riordan cradles her in his arms and heaves them both from the bed onto the floor, rolling with her! Protecting her.

"Shhh!"

She obeys, his body stiff. Demi's heart races, fear rushing into her veins. He's got her cradled within his frame, both of them on their sides with a clear line of view under the bed to the door.

Riordan whispers in her ear, *"Was it four knocks?"*

Demi huffs and nods, her body unable to let her speak. Riordan has a hand on his ankle gun, the other wiping her hair from her face, "Demi! Was it four knocks, in a rhythm, baby?" He has his mouth close to her. She inhales sharply.

TAP…tap,tap,tap….TAP!

Riordan exhales, relieved, and kisses her, "Stay."

Demi grabs at him, but he stands too quickly, he moves his pistol behind his back, and she only sees his jeans and bare chest as he smiles lovingly down at her. He walks around the bed and to the door. Demi grabs her fingers and holds them still trying desperately to stop the trembling.

43

Appreciate

Riordan

"Holy fuck! You're a sight for sore eyes." Riordan smiles at Grant and embraces him as he steps out onto the porch. With his shoes and socks off to the side and sand all over his feet, something tells Riordan he'd been on the porch for some time.

Grant huffs, "Brotha, you a hard coconut to find in the middle of all these islands!"

"I was going to give you a few more days. I lost all communications before I even got here. You okay? You need something to eat?" Riordan points to the cabin door.

"I'm doing all right. Please tell me you are? Demi?" Grant was genuinely worried, but the townsfolk told him that the giant man was with the pretty woman in the last villa on the beach. He was beyond relieved to not only find them but know they've been surviving without broken bones and gunshot wounds.

"Oh, I'll be right back!"

"Sorry if I interrupted..." Grant looks Riordan up and down, making it obvious, with his eyebrows raised, that Riordan is half-naked and barefoot with his gun in his hand, "I waited all night before tapping on the window."

Riordan chuckles, putting the gun in his waistband and half cursing himself for not knowing Grant was near. He did teach him everything he knows, so he's more proud than pissed. He rushes back through the screen door to find Demi and make sure she's all right.

"Riordan!?" Demi whispers, is still on the floor where he told her to stay, half of her body under the bed.

"Hey baby, it's Grant! He's okay!" Riordan reaches for her and picks her up and into his arms. He hugs her tight, "All right, all right,...you're all right now." He whispers into her hair, cradling her to stop her trembling. He hates that she was spooked again. He should have explained to her some of the code he and Grant use which may be helpful to her as well.

Demi sighs in relief, "I heard you talking…it sounded pleasant but, but…my, I-"

"I know. You're going to be fine. It's just going to take a couple more weeks."

"Weeks?"

Riordan gently pulls away to see her face, "Just a while longer. Hey, would you like me to draw you a bath? You wanna come out on the porch and talk, or do you feel like you need to lay down?"

"I'm okay. I'd like to talk with you guys if that's all right." She stares towards the door. Grant had not entered.

"Absolutely, just let me know if you start feeling like you need to rest, okay?"

"Thank you, babe. I didn't realize I had gotten so used to our solitude when I heard that knock…it jarred me a bit."

Riordan reached down and kissed her. He kissed her again. "I know it did baby, I'm very happy it was Grant. You're doing great."

She smiles, "So four taps, huh? Is that your bro code stuff?"

"Something like that." Riordan winks, realizing how well she is bouncing back after a fright. He's so happy Grant is alive too. He motions for her to go towards the door and keeps his hand placed on the small of her back so she feels secure.

Demi comes through the door and sees Grant stand his full height and walk slowly towards her. To her surprise, she embraces him without a second thought, elated that he is safe and uninjured. He hugs her back and winks at Riordan, envying him for not only keeping her safe but being the luckiest guy to ever be held up in a cabin…in hiding…with her.

"So glad you're here, Grant!" She lets go and takes a good look at him. He's uninjured. Not a scratch on him.

"Ugh, me as well. Here, sit down." He guides her to the sofa noticing faint pink wrists and ankles. He's worried about her since he saw the path of destruction his best friend left leading from the bondage rope and tape hanging above Errol Adler's lifeless body.

He's seen Riordan kill before, it's never something he's accepted or does easily, and he's incredibly good at it. Where most men would feel pride, Riordan feels remorse. He'll end you if he must, but he'll never like it.

Demi hops onto the couch, her legs curled under her, "Oh, don't fuss."

Grant looks wide-eyed at Riordan. She's obviously lost weight, her confidence hidden under trauma he hopes wasn't sexual. "You guys doing alright? It took me way longer than I thought to find you. Great lil' place you've got here." Grant cranes his neck to look around. "Is this the villa thing you'd used a time or two when on those other missions?"

Riordan nods, "We're holding up okay. Here, sit. You need a beer?" Riordan points at him before deciding to sit with Demi or go back inside to the fridge.

Grant walks back over to his chaise lounge and reaches down, picking up a half-empty bottle, "Already ahead of ya. You guys want one?" He points to a paper bag between the table and his chair.

Demi shakes her head, refusing but laughing. Riordan reaches for one and sits down on the couch, letting her snuggle under one arm. He sighs, "A hell of a breakfast…it's five o'clock somewhere, right?"

"That it is brother, that it is…" Grant takes a large sip, happy he's already on beer two since the conversation could get intense. Both he and Riordan look out at the ocean. Both thinking this job was up there with their other "cluster-fuck" awards. Demi notices the silence.

She decides to set the mood so they don't feel they can't talk around her, "So Grant, you said it took you quite a while to find this place?"

"Yeah, Rior and I usually have communications in some way. I knew we were fucked when I found your watch near "broken ribs" guy. Don't worry, I picked it up…and most of your *ahem*, items before the authorities boarded the Passionista." He pointed his bottle at Riordan.

Riordan nods, "I thank you deeply sir. I must have lost it in the tussle with cartel asshole number two."

Demi looked up at Riordan, hearing information he had not yet mentioned. She looks at Grant, "We're the passengers harmed at all?"

"No. When Riordan put out the evacuation code, I knew something was wrong. I had them stay on the island with my…with security so I could hustle back. I think I just missed you guys. I searched all the decks, so by the time I figured out to go to the engine rooms, I must have just missed you. I high-tailed it back to your quarters and tried to secure as much…uh, of the toys as I could carry."

Riordan's eyebrows went up, "Really? I thought for sure we'd lost most of our equipment to the local authorities."

"No, only what I couldn't carry, err…I don't believe they got any of it actually. I put what I could in one of the lifeboats. I was freaked because I saw you hadn't taken one. How the fuck did you get here, by the way? Swimming?" Grant waves his hand at the beach.

"Adler had some small fishing boat tied to the rear of the Passionista that he and his two side-kicks boarded from. Surprisingly it had enough motor to get us the hell out of there. I put Demi in it and gunned it while no one was onboard watching the cameras. I came around the opposite way, so the yacht blocked our direction from all you guys on the island. Not knowing who was involved, I didn't want anyone to follow us. I'm sorry, Grant, I had no time to leave you a sign or a text or…"

"Dude, no need to fucking apologize. Listen, you and I already know the deal with Adler. I figured out the rest when I saw his cowboy ass with a bullet between the eyes! I saw he used Demi as bait to get you where he wanted you. What I learned later was Adler's men were actually Loczano's cartel guys. Thats super confusing but I know you enlighten me yes?"

Riordan looks down at Demi to make sure she's all right. Her hands have stopped trembling and she nods letting him know she's fine. "Adler was in business with Teo Loczano. He owed Teo something, he mentioned me taking 51 million from them. FBI never caught on or gave us that intel, it may have been dealings they had after we put him away, I'm not clear on it yet. Somehow Loczano wanted me and wanted to use Demi to get to me."

"Whaaaaat? Wait, is that why Demi was on that yacht instead of her boss?"

She nods, "Yep. But I didn't mind." She looks up at Riordan with deep admiration.

"Demi, they baited him?"

Riordan kisses her then replies to Grant, "Adler says they bribed someone on the case." He frowns.

"Who Rior? Only you and I knew- Oh noooooo." Grant has a realization. "Was it one of ours? Who would've even known to use Demi against you? You didn't even tell me."

Riordan shrugs, "I didn't even admit it to myself until after the case was over and I missed her. He touches her face with the back of his hand and lovingly kisses her lips.

Grant runs his fingers through his hair, "Well, we'll find out! And where did they get that 51 million figure? Was that Laczano or Adler's?"

"I don't believe it was Adler's. And I don't remember that much money being seized actually. Makes me wonder what really went on in that case after we did our job."

"Right. So Adler somehow owed Taczano?"

"Apparently. Enough to come up with this whole bullshit stolen vials and jump drive case. When he was waving a gun at me he spewed some crap about getting Sagrid on the yacht and doing away with Lubna, getting his son on the yacht while taking care of his mother because Sagrid wanted her dead, getting me on the yacht then using Demi to force me to return 51 million. I'm not entirely sure who was behind all this but quite a few assholes were gonna win if Adler was successful."

Demi added, "I didn't realize Teo wanted me dead so much. It's not like I got much from him. I didn't want anything. Why he wanted me dead makes no sense. It's not like he even paid me alimony. He's in jail and nothing was in my name. All he left me was a mess to clean up."

Riordan caresses her hand nodding.

"Well, he was a sociopath. Narcissistic too. They're all about wins. He probably didn't like that the divorce was your idea…and he had no control in the outcome." Grant shrugs compassionately and sips his beer.

She agrees, "True. He was extremely controlling and I gave him no say in the divorce. Well, the judge ultimately gave him no say but he showed how I was his target…and the man I adore." She looks at Riordan like the god he is.

"Well, you both know more than anyone else."

Riordan frowns, "Really?"

"Yeah, the authorities are clueless. A lot of the Adler evidence, well your run in with him, is gone." Grant nods.

"Gone?" Riordan asks.

"It wasn't me T, I swear."

"What do you mean?"

"You guys didn't see the black smoke in the sky last week?"

Demi's voice cracks, "What do you mean?"

"I guess you can't see from here. You guys are a ways out, but uh…the Passionista was torched. Burned and sunk!"

"Oh my god! Were the couples on board?!!!" Demi puts her hand to her mouth.

Grant puts his hand up, "No, hon, I had them sent back home days before."

"Anyone hurt?" Riordan is visibly shocked.

"Not that I'm aware of. Not sure if it was Teo, Sagrid, or Adler's wife even. You know, for a cover-up, revenge, or insurance reasons. The investigation isn't over, so I have no idea what the outcome will be. I'm sorry, Rior, I wasn't able to gain access back on to get any of the uh…bigger stuff, or Demi's belongings. I took what I could that first day…then I had to disappear."

Demi exhales with relief. She puts her hand out to Grant to motion she's ready for a beer. He stands up and passes her one, "Breakfast of champions." She laughs.

She gulps, "I didn't have much of value on the yacht. What matters rescued me." She smiles at Riordan. "And all of my favorite people lived so…"

"And some not-so-favorites but…" Grant reminds them that Sagrid and Teo are still alive.

Riordan rubs her leg, "That's true. I guess we can appreciate this right here though. Everything else can be dealt with or replaced."

All three sip their breakfast beers and look towards the ocean.

44

Messages
Demi

Demi waits until Riordan goes inside the cabin then asks Grant questions she's compiled in her mind. She's feeling some fear over Teo's revengeful nature. "Grant, is there a way for you to find out if Riordan is still in danger?"

"I've got feelers out, Demi, don't worry. If it took me this long to find you guys, Riordan found a great spot. Those idiots will take a long time, if ever, to find us here. He's my hero. Nothing's going to get to him. I've known him since elementary school. That's one badass man you've got there." Grant stretches his toes in the ocean water alongside Demi, Riordan's empty chair on the other side of her.

"Thank you for all you do for him. I can tell you've both saved each other's lives multiple times."

"Yes, well…him more than me. I learned from the best."

Demi looks at the crashing waves and watches one come all the way in, to the tips of her toes, ocean suds sizzling before they retract, "I could stay here forever. I know at some point we should go back to our lives, but I can't really find a good enough reason why." She giggles, feeling her chest ease. It feels so good to dream.

Grant sips his beer and nods, "I hear ya. Without children, pets, a mortgage, or much family…I say the same each time Riordan and I are at the end of a job, especially when they're in parts of the world that are slower than the states. But, there's always another job to do."

"Do you love it?"

"Well, I love working with Riordan and our employees. I don't know how it's going to be now."

"Why?"

"Riordan said weeks back that this was his last job. Didn't he tell you?"

Demi shrugged, "We haven't gotten around to talking about that." She had no idea Riordan wanted to retire so seriously. He's very young but, she wouldn't mind knowing he'd be safe. She had no idea of the stress he's under. He certainly doesn't seem distracted while in bed. She's never met a man with more focus.

Grant nods, "Yep, and the way things are, it's probably best if you two stay put right here. It's going to take me time to get you both new passports, I.D.'s, cash, and an exit plan."

"Oh my, I didn't even think about that! All of our paperwork was on *Passionista*." She clenches her teeth and shrugs.

"It happens more than you think. Riordan's no problem, you...you'll take a little longer, so I hope you're okay with staying in your little sugar shack there." He jabs his thumb over his shoulder in the direction of their cute, romantic villa.

Riordan returns and slumps down in his beach chair. "Hey, I like our shack."

"I do, too, baby." Demi kisses him and runs her fingers through his hair. She recalls how short it was when first meeting him. He was dressed so professionally, looking every bit the military captain role, freshly cut and shaven. She remembers how her stomach swirled at the sight of him. And now, months later, with his hair so long the ends are beginning to curl, his beachy unshaven look is beyond sexy to her. She stares at how even more gorgeous he has become. Sun-kissed and wild. Her love for him has grown even deeper...despite the danger, mistakes, lies, and imperfections. She thinks about how she has loved others but nothing this unconditional. He's in her soul...

Grant continues, "Of course we could just get a nice motorized fishing boat, and I'll smuggle you guys back into New York in a few days."

"Ah, thanks for the offer but, I think I'll just take a secure laptop along with a secure phone-watch and hang out here until I can assure Demi is safe from Teo. I'm needing access to some funds, information, contacts, and supplies. I'll go back into the village soon and hope one of the locals will let me use their office. Dems and I have been making friends."

"I'm working on all the other stuff, boss." Grant points his beer towards Riordan.

"I know you are...and thank you."

Demi looks back and forth between the two. She admires their bond. Grant is attractive in a tall, babyface-thirty-something-year-old kind of way. She sees no ring and wonders if he's like Riordan in bed. Intense and deeply passionate? Perhaps a bit tantric in nature? She smiles slightly, wondering if such skill is talked about amongst friends. If they run in packs. Demi drags her big toe in the sand, huffing to herself, then asking, "Grant, are you married? Do you have family wondering where you're at?"

He smiles and shakes his head, "Naw, not yet. This job isn't conducive to the needs of a family. Besides, Riordan still has to teach me some things."

Demi looks over at Riordan and smiles, "What sorts of things can you teach Grant, sweetie?" Her eyes dance as she teases.

"He knows all he needs to. He just has to find the right woman…or wait for Jeanine to be free again." Riordan smirks toward Grant. He'd love to see Grant have a love like he has with Demi.

"Jeanine, Grant?" Demi sits back against the chair, her eyebrows raised.

"Yeah, I let "the one" get away…" Grant looks down, swirling his beer in the bottle.

"Oh no. The love of your life?"

Grant takes a sip, "Yep, I'm pretty sure. She's the only one that's never left my…uh mind."

"Well, you never know, right?" Demi tries to be encouraging and pushes his knee a bit with her foot.

"Sure. I'll never stop thinking of her…that I know for sure." A slight smile grazes his lips before it falls to sadness. He misses her so damn much. "I even tried to get a hold of her a few days ago. You know, in case this shit show takes another wrong turn. I just wanted to let her know some things."

Riordan stops before taking a sip of his beer, "You what?" He knows it's not like Grant to jeopardize any job by reaching out.

"I didn't compromise us. I just needed to leave her a message in case I don't make it through this one. After we talked about all the tantra stuff…"

"What do you mean?" Riordan is concerned. Grant's never mentioned a farewell to anyone before.

"I- I don't know, I feel like I need her to know some things. I want her to know the things I should have said years ago. If I had been more vulnerable with her, you know, just more forthcoming... sooner, she may have married me instead of that deadbeat." He shrugs slightly, a tear grazing inside one eye.

Demi leans forward, "She's married?"

"Years went by, Larry asked, Grant was on a lengthy mission, she said yes..." Riordan summed it up while Grant chugged his beer.

"Oh, Grant. I'm sorry, honey." Demi places her hand on Grant's arm then sits back, feeling sad for him.

Grant inhales and sits back, "Well, good ole' Larry isn't doing it for her, so..."

Demi looks at Riordan, who raises an eyebrow and smiles. He agrees but knows that brings only the slightest comfort to Grant.

"She's said that, Grant?" Demi is curious.

Riordan pipes up, "She hasn't needed to say it."

"Oh." Demi looks between the two of them, Riordan smirks, Grant smiles and finishes his beer. Demi catches on, "Ohh-hhhhh....."

"Yeah, sometimes we just can't..." Grant fades without words.

"Well, Grant, in my world, there's this crazy energetic thing called vibration...it's pretty serious stuff." Demi chortles.

"Oh, I totally agree. Riordan's explained a few things, and well...I can't really quit her, you know?"

Demi nods, "Oh, I totally know. So, have you told her how you feel? In the past?"

"Well, kind of. That was the whole contact part...but she, well, she wasn't there."

"What?" Demi looks concerned.

"I left a few lengthy messages."

45

Freeing

Riordan

Riordan slides his palm slowly up her ribs and cups her breast in his hand. The warmth in his touch makes her yoni pulse and ache for him. Demi moves her head back towards his chest. He reaches his mouth to her neck and suckles, sending delightful shivers throughout her body, causing her to arch into him, his lingam firm and feverish with want for her. He moans, feeling her plump tush gliding…slowly surrounding his cock with her slickness, moving at their own tantric pace. Breath slow, passion overtaking them.

She smiles, his moan igniting more fire within her. She's felt so much more aroused lately, if that's even possible. Riordan makes her almost crazy with his love-making. He's a god who's captured her heart, and she wants him daily, if not multiple times in a day. She moves her tush forward and back to the rhythm of their breathing, using her love-fluids to lubricate them both. She's safely engulfed in his embrace, his fingers of one hand gently caressing her nipple, the fingers of his other hand searching down her belly to the opening of her most consecrated area, the sacred place she's willingly given to him all these months. Running his mouth and teeth along her neck while softly pressing the pad of his finger down the fevered hood-skin of her clit, Demi shudders with aching pleasure. He follows her breathing, his body reacting to her arousal with his own. The connection is unmistakable. They're always in such beautiful vibrational alignment when their bodies are touching.

Demi reaches her arm back, grasping his buttock, bringing him closer, pulling him to her slick opening. Riordan's feeling his need for her become achy, he holds her earlobe within his teeth, trying to keep his composure. The way she moves with him, the way she sounds, breaths, and smells…she drives him wild, and he knows the pleasure that comes from withholding his gratification. He almost enters her, yet doesn't. Making love to Demi is always so much more. It's *always* so much more mind-blowing when he withholds until the right time. Lately, she's wanted him so much more, daily and multiple times, he's found that edging is best. But today, today is a day he can feel within that he must release. She's driving him mad.

"Sweeeeeeeeetieeee." Demi purrs in a whisper as she often does within the throws of their love.

He releases her earlobe from his mouth, kissing her lightly on the temple, "Hmmmm…" He can only muster a small, deep vocal note in response to her silky tush-play.

She smiles, curling her backside once again onto and around his shaft, excreting her warm sleekness for both their comfort, "Take me from behind baby, I need to feel you." Her hand grabs his rear, pulling him closer, the head of his lingam slipping into her entry mounds.

"Already, baby? I can continue what we're doing if you-" He whispers into her ear, a small chuckle following his question.

Demi whines, "I need you so bad. I'm aching with want for you inside me…" She moves forward slowly and then back again, teasing the head of his engorgement, letting it into her warm entry, clenching to tease and convince him.

"As you wish, my love." He moves his arms fully around her, pulling her in and down onto him, filling her fully with his large girth. He closes his eyes, the pleasure almost more than he can handle. Her moistness is accepting and engulfing around him, his eyes rolling slowly back as he feels her squeeze him tightly, a moan breathlessly escaping her. He begins a slow, sensual rhythm, he pressing into her holding at the top, she clutching and releasing him so he can keep on caressing her inside. The rapture almost unbearable, yet they don't want to stop. He adores the way her body suckles inside at his head!

Demi reaches her arm up, her palm finding his face, his cheek, then his hair. She runs her fingers through his silky curls then grasps tenderly. Riordan thrusts deeper, bringing his palm up her chest to the front of her neck, his fingers reaching her mouth. She suckles them, and he feels he might erupt as her tongue reminds him on his fingers what she also does when he's erect in her loving mouth.

He seizes, stopping his movements, groaning he says, "Deeeeeems…." He had to stop, so he didn't spill into her before she's ready.

She giggles breathlessly, "Yessssss…." She clenches him despite his stillness, his thrusts halted. She teases and taunts him, she wants him to have pleasure…*her* pleasure.

"I-." Before he can plead with her, she releases from him and slings forward. She makes it up from her side and on all fours. He looks up at her sleepily as she pushes him gently to his back and pulls his arms over his head. She's smiling and swings a leg over him straddling him. In one fell swoop, she comes down onto him, letting him slide into her filling her snuggly. They both gasp. Riordan surrenders to her, his teeth clenching, throwing his head back, his arms come forward to grasp her hips. He tries to slow her so he doesn't cum. She's thrusting slowly, rocking her hips, using her silky fluids to glide back….and forth…and back…and…

He grabs up around her waist, sucking air through his teeth. He's trying to slow her down. He's so close! Demi takes his hands again and places them back over his head, her lips grazing his as she reaches up, she releases her yoni from him. He relaxes, regaining his control. She's driving him wild with her slow, hedonistic body tantra, not to mention her energetic vibrational hold!

Demi exhales, kissing him deeply, her breasts trailing up his chest, he can feel her erect nipples fevered along his pecs. She releases from their kiss, lifting forward, placing her nipple between his lips. He takes her into his mouth, following her desire. She's so fucking sensual, he's enthralled. Gently she tugs, and he releases. She grasps his hands tighter, holding them to the bed in their little beach cabin. Moving her other ample breast to his mouth, he again tenderly suckles as she likes, feeling her warm plump nipple between his lips and tongue. Demi lets out a breath, his pleasure always so perfectly satisfying.

She moves down again to find his sensual mouth with her own, kissing him tantrically, deeply…down within his soul. She glides her velvety tongue into him, exploring him slowly and passionately. He reciprocates, kissing her as if it were the last time. He doesn't want this moment to end…as with all moments with Demi. He'll never tire of this.

Suddenly she releases his hands and sits up. He gazes up lovingly at her searching her leer for what she desires next. Her hair falls around her ravishing face and smile, and he wonders how the fuck he got so damn lucky to finally be able to love her after spending so many years longing for her. Reaching forward, he places his palm along her cheek, and she covers his hand with her own, clutching it to her face. She loves the way he touches her, always with such gentle fervency.

Demi moves her mouth to the side, taking his thumb into her mouth, suckling it until he groans. She feels him pulse beneath her. She lifts up, taking her other hand, wrapping it around his shaft. Riordan sucks air through his teeth at the delectation of her grasp. As she lowers down onto him, she guides him into her...but into her *tighter* of congenial entries. Riordan arches up his abs, scrunching, as his face does, grasping her hip as she opens to him, guiding him into her anally, *s...l...o...w...l...y...*. He can barely handle the delight of her tightness. She eases onto all of him. He leans back, remembering this exquisite fulfillment every time she does it. Demi is a goddess. He's wholly under her spell.

She's watching the gratification coursing through him and feeling all that he gives back. She releases his thumb, breathless. "Oh...uh...wow...soooo" She's gliding, building and constructing upon their erotic connection. He's so amazingly complete for her. She feels she's getting close. "Riordan...honey..."

He tries to focus on her face, "Ba...by..." She's with him so rhythmically perfect. Suddenly, she raises her arms up over her running her fingers through her own hair. He grasps her hips, following her slow rocking perfection. He's following her, and her breathing increases, her chakra energy rocking them. He increases his stride, trying too hard to hold on, guided by her lead.

"Ah...ah...ahhhhhhhhhhhhhhhhhhhh." Demi throws her head back, unable to hold on any longer, his rapture freeing her! Riordan hears her climax feeling her beginning to crash over what she can no longer hold. He lets go with her...liquid desire spilling into her, pumping, pulsing, feeling her draw his soul up and through her. A heightened delirium of sensation. *Freeing him...*

46

His

Demi

Demi steps into the claw-foot tub, careful not to slip or hurt him. He takes her tiny hand in his and guides her precious backside down into the water between his legs. She feels so soft, her skin cool against him in the hot lavender-scented water. She sinks in and leans back against the full chest she loves so much.

"There you go, my love, just stay right here." He half-whispers into the candle-lit bathroom. His melodious voice is lulling her heart to beat in unison with his.

Demi smiles, "This is exquisite…just like our evening." Riordan kisses her hair, inhaling her scent and nodding.

"It seems to be getting better and *better*. I don't know how. You're just so…" His breath hitches with the memory of their recent pleasure. He decides not to even try to put it into language.

Demi cradles his arms now wrapped around her, "I can't get enough of you, Captain Tate."

"You've been delightfully frisky as of late. I likeyyy…" He also very much likes that she seems to be farther and farther away from her panic attacks in the last few weeks.

"Well, you've helped me heal from all that stress. You do know that tantra is known to heal, right?" She turns her head toward the left, catching a glimpse of him in her peripheral.

He hugs her snugly, "I have experienced this, indeed."

They both quiet as they hear footsteps coming up the front porch of the cabin. A signature knock on the door eases both of them as they realize Grant has returned from the village. "Yo guys, just me. I'm gonna crash on the couch here again. Don't get up. I'm fuckin' tired as hell from all this sun. Night!"

"G-night!" Riordan returns the sentiment knowing his best friend is drained. He's not used to waiting around for weeks and weeks. Grant wants to work all the time but Riordan knows thats just to distract from Jeanine. He himself had done it for years. The right love can change that.

Demi whispers, "He doesn't want to come in and sleep on the couches in the cabin?"

"No. Grant is restless Dems. We're in a holding pattern job-wise. He's never been good with our down time even though he needs it."

"Aw. I love you guys."

"I love you." Riordan runs his fingers through her hair, reaching down and kissing her neck.

"Hmmmm…watch it, sir, I may have to turn around here in this little tub and have my way with you again." Demi purrs in a fun tone.

He smiles, "Oh, that's right, this little spot on your neck just starts all kinds of trouble."

"Sometimes." She reaches back with her hands, massaging up his quads, getting closer and closer to his groin.

Riordan moans at her touch. She's his perfect match. "Well, you only have to ask. I'm here to serve you, my queen."

"Oh, your bathing-talk is something I could get used to, Captain." She runs her hands forward, massaging his legs, and caressing his knees. Her mind wanders, "Hey, Rior?"

He lays his neck back against the tub letting his head fall back and stretch, "Yeah?"

"I think Grant and Jeanine really need each other. I could really feel how much he needs her. You know, with the way he talked of her when he first got here and then the little comments here and there."

"I've told him, baby. He does really love that woman."

Demi nods, leaning again against his chest, "He does, and for her to be visiting him through the years, despite her marriage.? I think she's drawn to him. Don't get me wrong, I wouldn't ever recommend infidelity. It's just…well, sometimes it's just not good to ignore what source pushes."

He runs the back of his fingers down her cheek and onto her chest, cupping her rotund breast, warming it from peeking out of the hot water. "Oh, for sure, I do believe in what you're saying. I tried to fight what should be…it doesn't work. In talking with him,

I sense he's leaning on faith now. He has patience I've not seen before. He's never felt with anyone what he has with Jeanine. You know they met in boot camp years ago…like way back."

"Really?"

"Oh yeah, Jeanine has skills. She went her way, and we went ours, but she's never lost touch with him. They can't seem to go too long without contact. I feel bad."

"Why?"

"Part of me feels like our work has kept him from her for too long. I think she married good ole' Lawrence because she couldn't find Grant for a while. Some of our missions took us away for months and months."

Demi covers his hand on her breast and squeezes. She likes how respectfully he touches her erotic zones and encourages him to continue caressing her while he's talking, "Kind of like Navy Seals…and their wives. No timeframe is known, no information is given."

"Yes, it's one thing to know someone will be away for so long, but when no information is allowed, the days can turn into weeks, months even. Emotions go up and down. I think the brain can eventually begin to move one or be convinced we aren't loved. Even if that's the furthest from the truth."

"I can understand that. Abandonment is still the most detrimental issue I see within my work. Especially when it begins in childhood." She switches it up, "Is that how it was with me? Did you convince yourself you'd never be loved?"

Riordan huffs, "Well, that was different. You didn't know me. I NEVER thought we'd be here. I was trying to persuade myself to just stop thinking of you hour by hour…then daily. I have a lot of guilt with all that, and I still struggle with deserving you."

Demi sits up, splashing some water. She turns around to face him, hooking her legs around him, looking deep into his eyes, "WE deserve each other, Riordan. This is everything I'd been manifesting.! You, although in a roundabout way, saved me from a life that would have destroyed me. I know you think you ruined my life, but that was a life I would have traded in at the drop of a hat if I'd known a love like this was waiting for me. After that ended, I dreamed, wished…prayed daily for you! I have proof putting out high vibration works. And I won't lie and say I hadn't started wanting you early in my marriage. If Teo weren't such an awful human I would never have known to want such a lovely one. I know now I loved you before I met you."

Riordan cups her face and pulls her close. He kisses her deep, long, and with love emanating out of him. All he has is his love and it's enough for her, *he* is enough for her. He loves her physical language, he loves her spoken language, most of all he loves her soul. She truly is **his.**

47

Leaving

Riordan

He looks across the room one last time at the beauty of her. The warm sun, peeking through the shades, dances upon her sleeping face. He didn't have the heart to wake her. Riordan hopes she'll not be angry. More so, he hopes he'll not trigger her panic, in the last month she's had no relapses. He hates departing like this, leaving her just a note. He has to do it this way because if he sees pain in her eyes, or if she begs him not to go, he knows he'll stay. The opportunity presented itself and it must be taken.

He steps back in the room one last time, walks to her, and lays a white island flower on the note. *God, she's alluring.* He clenches his fists. He doesn't want to leave her. They'd just talked of abandonment a few weeks previous in the bath. Bending to kiss her, the guilt rushes in! She begins to stir. He freezes patiently waiting for her breath to lull her back into her dreams. Riordan Tate exits the safety of their love nest, closing the door and peering out over the ocean praying she'll forgive him but, praying more that he'll return to his goddess.

Demi inhales, stretching her arms up, squinting from the bright afternoon sun. Suddenly, her stomach contents begin to creep up, and the morning nausea is back but fiercely! She throws the covers off and to the side, trying to be swift and not wake him! Sprinting across the cabin, Demi, fully naked, bounds into the bathroom to projectile vomit as she has on occasion in the last few weeks!

She makes it just in time, *again*. She's pretty positive she's carrying his child. Food and drink are fine until the mornings. She's not sure how far along she is and can't quite confirm the pregnancy since a test isn't exactly available. She decides it's time to talk with Riordan about it. Maybe they could walk to the village together and find the Shaman.

Demi washes up and brushes her teeth. Taking a good look at herself in the mirror, she turns sideways to check out her belly. Nothing yet, flat. She slides her hands over her taut, mocha colored tummy. A smile creasing at the corners of her mouth, she can't think of anything more divine than having Riordan's baby. She's been wanting him more and more too! In every way…her appetite for him insatiable. As for her last cycle, it must have been months ago, and yet there was that brief spotting weeks back which she brushed off as a result of a panic attack.

Her muscles sore from heaving she bends down to pull on her bikini bottoms and looks around for her top. Nothing. She must've left it out on the chair last night when Riordan so easily helped her out of it. Maybe he'll want to swim in the ocean with her! She thinks he may already be out there with Grant as she doesn't remember jumping over him to run to the bathroom. Despite puking, she's feeling better, quite hungry surprisingly. Running her fingers through her hair, she bounces out of the bathroom to go find a way to cover her nipples and join her lover for some lunch.

Demi turns the corner into the cabin, her smile fading, her body freezing!

"Who…the fuck are you?" The female voice sends an inconceivable chill through Demi.

48

Blue for Boy

Demi

Demi's legs almost go out from under her. Pointed at her throat from across the room is an angel blue Walther P22 barrel wrapped in long, feminine fingers. One finger is very much on the trigger. Demi locks her knees, breasts exposed, arms up.

"I *said*, who the fuck are you?" The strikingly attractive red-head is resting comfortably in the corner chair, her legs crossed, one hand resting under her ear, the other holding the tiny gun at Demi.

"Demi."

"Demi? Is there a last name Demi?" Her voice is low, calm, and even. As if she's a professional at pointing guns at people.

"Greer. Uh, Demi Greer…"

Her eyes glance down over Demi's breasts, her stomach, legs, and back up to her deep, scared blue eyes. "Well, Demi Greer, I'm going to ask you a few questions. I'd like you to answer them truthfully, or I'm going to put a 22 in your cheek and let it bounce around your pretty little head until you puddle onto the floor, then I'll have to put one in your heart."

Demi stares at the stranger then darts her eyes around the room. Fear washes over her whole body and she fights back nausea. Riordan is not in the room. *He could be hurt! Has Teo found us!!* A wave of familiar terror courses through her. She'd been healing, and now her body was headed into fight-flight-freeze mode again. She half-whispers, "All right."

"How long have you known him?"

Demi frowns, not sure who her red-headed terrorist is referring to. She tries to speak, "Wh-"

"You look confused! Shall I repeat myself?"

"I-" Demi's hands begin to tremble.

"Grant! How long?"

Demi doesn't know whether to feel relief, "I met him the first day of the Passionista cruise. A few months back."

"This latest job?"

"Yes." Demi tries to lower her arms and cover her chest.

"No, no, noooo. Keep those hands in the air."

Footsteps come abruptly up the porch steps. The redhead reaches for a second gun tucked along the chair, this one black.

A rushed knock precedes the door flying open! Grant barges in, calling for Demi, his breath ceased at seeing her half-naked, arms raised in surrender. He lowers his eyes, jumping aside when he catches a glimpse of the two guns pointed towards each of them. "Jeanine!???" He instinctively raises his hands towards the barrels to block her aim at Demi. "What the fuck!" He moves his body fully blocking her. "Wha-".

Jeanine Barrjiano doesn't flinch. She stays seated, one pretty tiffany-colored gun pointed at Demi, another plain black Walther 380 pointed at the love of her life. Demi realizes how bad this looks and feels slightly exposed now that Riordan's best friend has just seen her tits. "Hello, Grant. You're not so easy to track down."

Grant moves his hands higher, "Jeanine, put the guns down?"

"No."

"Please." He turns to look at Demi behind him making sure she's all right. She's covering herself now with her arms but they're trembling uncontrollably.

Jeanine waves one weapon in her direction, "Ms. Demi Greer and I were just discussing how long she's known you."

"How long wh-…no, no, *noooooo* sweetie. I'm not here with Demi. Demi is with Riordan!"

Jeanine looks up at Grant, her eyes soften. "Riordan?"

"Yes, baby. Please. Please put the guns down."

She cocks her head slightly sideways, deciding if he's telling her the truth, "Where is he?"

"He left."

Demi looks from the guns to Grant, "*Left?* What do you mean he left?"

Grant turns around and steps towards Demi, not taking his eyes entirely off of Jeanine. He can't believe she's here. "Yes,. I was coming here to tell you. Did you receive a note?" Grant is still not looking at Demi. Out of respect, he's got his eyes averted from her perfectly ample breasts, grateful she has bikini bottoms on. He knew she was gorgeous, but her nakedness is a whole other level.

Demi looks around and catches sight of a white corner to note paper sticking out of the covers she threw off her when she ran to the bathroom. Her heart sinks. Riordan writes her notes often but the last time he wrote one and wasn't around she was kidnapped. Another wave of nausea hits her, she dry-heaves. Her arm comes up to hold her mouth shut, the other crossed her chest. Both Grant and Jeanine glance at her. Jeanine lowers her guns, and Demi sprints to the bathroom!

Grant looks over at Jeanine then to the bikini top draped on the lampshade. He steps, grabs the top, caresses Jeanine's cheek, then rushes to the bathroom, looking away but tossing Demi her top. Demi is throwing up with very little coming out. He waits until there's a pause. "Dems, I've got to talk to you when you get a chance. It's about Rior-"

Demi nods, waving him away. He turns the corner and rushes to Jeanine, who's put her guns away. He wants to be mad at her, but he can't. She's a wild one and was probably pissed thinking he was there with Demi. She's never been jealous before and she knows damn well he sometimes has to play the part of a doting companion while undercover. She stands as he reaches her, and suddenly a seven-month pregnancy belly emerges from the sundress she has on! His hand slides to her cheek, but his eyes evert down to see the protruding stomach between them.

Unclear as to what to do, he steps back to search her face, "Jeanine?"

She smirks. "I uh…"

He takes a second step back, a look of fear on his face. He about died inside when he heard she married fucking *Larry*. He doesn't think he can handle this. She's pregnant!? He'd been hoping they could go forward…not lose her again to Lawrence the broke broker!

Demi comes around the corner, a napkin pressed against her lips, her bikini top fully intact. She grabs a sarong and shakily tries tying it around her waist. She's watching them, trying to compose herself. She realizes this is THE Jeanine they were speaking of on the beach the day prior.

Grant's hand drops from Jeanine's face. He stares at her as if waiting for her to break his heart. Demi stares, not sure what she's witnessing...not sure if her body can take much more.

"I came to find you. It took me a few days to track you. You had called. As usual, I never know where you are, but you called, and I called in a favor to track you, uh here. Well, actually, I tracked you to an island nearby and tried to think where you would be after the authorities told me the ship had burned. Do you know what it's like to wonder where the fuck you are, Grant?"

He's staring at her, shocked that she tracked him, more jarred that she's standing in front of him seven months pregnant! "I-." He doesn't know what to feel.

Jeanine looks up at him. She's never seen Grant like this. She's got to tell him. This whole situation has not gone the way she'd planned. She's made a fool of herself but she must tell him. "He's yours, Grant."

Grant steps closer, unsure of what he's hearing. His eyes search her face.

Jeanine reaches up, caressing his face. Demi's shoulders release, she steps towards her bed and grabs the note and flower from under the blanket, shakily tiptoeing out onto the porch so she can give them their private moment. She's trying to breath, terrified of whats in the note, half alive from the fright of having a gun pointed at her. *Please be okay, please be okay. Riordan pleaaaaseee.*

Jeanine is staring into Grant's eyes, "Sweetheart, did you hear me?"

"What do you mean?" Grants hands come forward, instinctively toward her protruding belly. He looks down at the bump beneath the flowered material of her sundress. He touches her and looks up into her tear-filled eyes. Water begins to well up in his.

Jeanine smiles and exhales at his reaction. She's so relieved. "I mean, he's yours. The baby. He's your son Grant." She places her hand further up his cheek and the other on top of his on her belly. "I'm carrying *your* son."

49

Gone

Riordan

I'm sorry. I've got to start with that. Demi, I'm sorry. I didn't want to wake you, but more importantly, honey, I didn't want you to persuade me to stay when I've got to do this. Now that Grant is here to protect you, I can go make sure we are safe. It's how I work. I have to do this even though being away from you kills me. I'll be back as soon as I can, baby, please try not to worry. I'm not leaving you. I'm just gone for a little while until I can ensure our safety and future freedom.

I love you, Demi-

Always,

R-

Demi exhales, tears rolling down her cheeks. She folds the tiny note back to the way he had it and smells the wildflower he left her. Looking out at the ocean, she regrets not telling him what Jeanine was just able to tell Grant. Maybe he wouldn't have gone if he knew. What will he do? What will happen with Teo? What if he doesn't return? She puts her hand on her tummy. She's definitely had the *worst* morning. She looks down at the note in her other hand; she's shaking, the paper moving in her grasp. It's been so long since she's felt this, but it's right back at the same level. When he's not around, it's the same...the same as when Errol Adler took her from him. Her chest feels heavy.

She takes in a deep breath and sends loving vibes to the baby she feels is there. She shakes her head and inhales deep into her lungs, deciding she must be strong! *Be strong now.* If he's going to sacrifice his safety to try and make their future safe, the least she can do is stay calm and love their baby. No more panic. *No!*

Demi stands and places the note and flower on the end table. She walks tottery down the porch steps feeling the beach sand softly mold under the bottoms of her feet. Ahead, out by the waves, are chairs. She can feel the exhaustion coursing through her, and her eyes grow heavy. Despite waking only a sort while ago, she feels the need to rest again. The adrenaline from morning sickness, then Jeanine pointing a gun at her, and Riordan gone…it's all so, so much. Just too much. *Rest.*

Demi sinks into the sand, one foot after the other, sluggishly making her way out to a chaise lounge. She's already breathless when she reaches it and unties her sarong spreading it on the chair. Slumping down gently, she spreads out on her tummy, their beautiful baby snuggled safely inside her. She…is…so sleepy…weary-

50

A Son

Grant

Grant closes the bathroom door and locks it. He spins around and holds Jeanine by her hips, gently picking her up. She smiles and wraps her arms around his neck, pulling his mouth down onto hers as he walks her to the sink counter. He lifts her dress and places her down on the largest section of the wood counter. She kisses him deeper, passionately, his cheeks damp from crying in her arms. She parts his lips farther, exploring his mouth with her tongue, reaching down to unfasten his shorts. Kicking off his flip flops he finds the lace sides of her underwear. He realizes he's moving too fast as they often do when they've missed each other for months. Consciously slowing his touch he lovingly caresses her skin along the sides of her panties and to the gorgeous plump belly she's grown. He wants to enjoy this, every minute it of it.

Already rock hard, he feels his chest well up with pride... she's carrying his baby, *HIS son!* It arouses him in almost animalistic ways. He stops and gently pulls away from her. Gazing down at her dark green eyes, he's still convincing himself she's really here! Placing his palms on either side of her face, pushing her hair away to see deep within her features. *God how he's missed her.*

Jeanine looks at him and smiles wide he, beginning to tear up again. She likes this sensitive side of him, "Grant? What is it, baby?"

He stares, the words caught in his throat. *You're actually carrying my son...* His mind trying to reconcile it all.

"Grant?" She tilts her head, reaching up to stroke his hair. Her other hand is trailing down into the front of his shorts, caressing his tight, muscular thigh then around towards his erect head.

"Seriously, J? You and Larry are done? Are you really here? This is *my* baby?" He whispers, needing her to say it all again. She's never lied to him before, and he truly doesn't want to insult her. He's just so overwhelmed with elation.

Jeanine slides down, reaching further along his shaft to find his fevered, wanting scrotum. Her hands gentle and caressing. She stares into his eyes while gently stroking him lovingly along one side and then to the other, feeling how rock hard he is for her already.

"Seriously. Larry can't have kids, Grant. It's you. It's always been you, just...things have changed now. I can't be second anymore. I won't be left again. I fucked up once before thinking you didn't want me. I married the wrong guy, and you still came around, always there for me...yet, *not*. I could never get you out of me. I can't be without you, Grant, and now there's two of us that need you. I need you to hear me. I need you to consider family first now. I know you love your work but in all seriousness, I need you to love he and I more."

Grant closes his eyes and slowly throws his head back, not only from her magnetic manual pleasure but because he knows Riordan is right about all this. The tantra thing, the connection...creating life. He and Jeanine have an unmistakable bond. Nothing has been able to keep them from each other. No matter the hurdle, the time spent away, other relationships, the years... They've always found each other again, and again, and again. Forgiveness always came around, and love grew.

He inhales and looks down at her, "I need you both so much too. Jeanine, I've been in love with you since that first moment I laid eyes on you in boot camp all those years ago. You walked past me, and I've never been the same. It was as if you wrapped me in your spell. I tried to let you go, give you space, but I just couldn't stay away from you. I don't want to be without you anymore." He leans in, his lips on hers. He wants to be hers, worshipping her, as she deserves, his one truth. His own goddess.

Jeanine soothes and sinks into the kiss with how his words make her feel. She moves closer to the edge of the counter, guiding his head into the entry of her swollen, eager wetness. He follows, seeking her love and the pleasure that solidifies it. She reaches around his waist to pull him into her, he thrusts long and languidly and they both moan at the sheer pleasure of feeling each other again. So perfect. Familiar. He pulls her towards him and buries himself into her deeper...and *deeper*. She feels so damn good. They begin their rhythm, more leisurely, ploddingly, with perfect, impassioned thrusts...

Jeanine trails kisses down his neck, lingering and suckling at the end of each connection, knowing it drives him wild. He continues to burrow into her deeper and deeper, his excitement coursing through his veins. His heart beating almost out of his chest. He brings his head up and catches a glimpse of himself in the mirror behind her. *We're amazing together!* He suddenly slows...then stops. Jeanine looks up at him, wondering what's going on. He tenderly cups her face, staring down into her. He stills all except for a gradual pump inside her every few seconds to circulate their tantric bond and keep their coupling.

"I want to make love to you." He looks from her eyes to her lips...and back to her eyes. He reaches down to suck lovingly on her bottom lip then releases it.

"We are, honey." She's breathless her pregnant appetite for him ravenous. Any way that Grant devours her body has always been resplendent! He's the best lover she's ever had, absolutely incredible stamina with a natural compassion not even he realizes. A perfect match.

Grant smiles because how they do things is *always* intense, "Slowly, I mean. I've missed you so much. I want this to prolong. I need to really *feel* you. Your pleasure. This moment, this day...I'll never forget it."

Jeanine smiles. He's excitingly vulnerable, his tenderness even more appealing and arousing, "Hmmm, I wouldn't mind slower...I want to feel you."

Grant picks her up under her arms as she clings to him. He walks across the bathroom, her legs wrapped snuggly around his waist, she loves their connection. He kicks off his shorts and underwear with each step and makes his way to a large chair in the far corner of the bathroom. He's aroused and excited to enjoy their reunion. Admittedly, their indiscretions were more often from losing control...not seeing each other in months, trying to live in separate lives, *trying* to be faithful to relationships that just didn't have the depth or connection they do. He'd often have to be near drunk in order to deal with the guilt of rapturing another man's wife...and then the trauma of leaving her, or rather giving her back to a man who didn't deserve her. It's been hell until now. *This*...feels so right! To him, *she* is his, and that's *his* baby. Everything feels right finally!

Jeanine sits comfortably on top of Grant, gradually she begins rocking back and forth to match his newly slowed, *glorious* rhythm. He's guiding her with his palms upon her hips, his long thumbs caressing the sides of her beautiful belly. He looks into her eyes, their breathing beginning to comfortably sync. He smiles feeling exhilaration...ultimate happiness. He can't believe she's here, in his arms, riding him again with her slow, pulsating love ensemble. She's carrying his son! He begins longer, stronger thrusts and pulsing. The pleasure is maddening for them both. So much more is felt with their breath cadence. He remembers how they were like this, just like this, once about seven months back. How they were at his place, and she spent the entire weekend. He looks into her face and remembers suddenly, the exact *moment* they conceived their baby!

51

Regret

Demi

Demi's stomach growls tumultuously, waking her from a deep, *deep* sleep. She feels slightly sour inside and knows food, or at least some bread, would help greatly. Her eyes flutter awake. She remembers and immediately feels pain within. His energy gone. He's not there. She reminds herself Riordan feels he must make things right and safe, but something inside her knows he wouldn't have gone if he knew they were going to be a family, or...would he do something even more? She feels a pang of regret. Regret that they even have to consider Teo! *Ugh, fucking malignant narcissists!* Even in prison, his reach is as intrusive as his personality disorder was for all those years. She regrets ever even believing in him, meeting him even. He's a fraud. A false being!

She squints, trying to squeeze the thoughts of Teo from her mind. She never wants her anger for him to touch what she's found, and she refuses to allow her unborn to marinate in anything but his father's love. She turns on her side and looks through half-open eyes out into the palm tree brush of the small island. The breeze blows the fans of the palms, and she blinks slowly, hoping they lull her back to sleep. Movement causes her to stir. She focuses and sees an old man. He is an islander, his beautiful wrinkled skin sun-kissed and bronze. His attire is minimal, and he is with a young boy who resembles him but a much younger version, hair long, eye-brows thick. Demi watches as the elder is teaching the boy. Pointing and touching the large tree leaves. He tassels the boy's hair, and they laugh together. Demi smiles. Just then, she sees them look over toward the cabin. She lifts her head and watches Grant come down the porch steps toward them. The old man waves in a kind gesture, Grant waves relaxed in return, a smile shared between the three. The boy runs to Grant, meeting and walking with him towards the large fallen tree trunk the elder now sits on. Demi lays her head back down to pretend she is sleeping. She doesn't want to pry. The island people have been so welcoming and kind; she thinks they are beautiful. She sees that Grant has made friends with the two.

The boy opens his waist pouch and retrieves something for Grant. He nods and puts it to his ear. It's a cell phone! Demi sits up abruptly. Could it be…Riordan! Suddenly feeling dizzy from sitting too quickly, she takes a deep breath and places her hand on her abdomen. She wants to run to Grant. She wants to demand to know if Riordan is on the phone. He's been gone so many hours already. The entire day! Grant turns and scans the beach. His head stops when he sees her, nodding, and a serious look. He places his free hand on his hip and nods more as if he is taking instructions. She tries to stand, determined to walk towards all three but loses her balance and sits again. The sand is so pure and soft.

The elder stands from his tree trunk, his walking stick perched in his left hand, his gaze upon her. She knows if she shows any weakness, the man will come towards her. She never wants to be a bother, just something within her is making her desperate to talk with Riordan. Will Grant tell him of her morning sickness? Her nakedness? The gun fiasco with Jeanine…her trembling? Demi relents. She doesn't want to deal with any of it. Should he find out this way, from his best friend who's been tasked to keep her safe, over a cell phone call? *So exhausted…*

The boy now steps around Grant and peers at her, as does his elder family member. All three gaze at her, so all she can think to do is smile and raise her hand, waving assuredly.

52

Tell Her

Riordan

Riordan turns one last time and shakes the hands of both, Doug "Dugger" Cantrell and Rich Leyner in gratitude for the lift. The blades of the helicopter make the men's farewell more about nods and thumbs-ups than words, due to obvious sound and suction dangers. Riordan doesn't ever call in favors, especially when it concerns personal matters, but today he did. Dugger and Leyner were right on schedule as promised. Once he saw their ladder lowering down to his dingy Riordan knew he was back on mission! This time it's personal. His old Delta buddies didn't hesitate. Everyone owes Riordan Tate. Most owe him their lives.

He runs swiftly along the tarmac and out of sight so they can depart just as swiftly without eyes on them. The bird lifts off and disappears, as does Riordan behind a storage container hidden within thousands on the warehouse dock. He'll be sure to compensate his friends for their time even though they'll try to turn it away. They're good guys.

Looking and scanning his surroundings, Riordan confirms he hasn't been seen yet. With his back against the storage container, he stops at a long vertical seem and knocks four times with the back of his knuckles. The door opens, he locks eyes with Constantine Levy, nods, and enters, shutting the door swiftly. She hands him the phone, takes his wet clothes and bug-out bag to free his hands, then leads him to the waiting armored Range Rover at the far end of the container. Riordan jumps in the back.

"How is she?" Riordan's voice is low in the quiet of the backseat. Levy starts the engine. With the push of a button, an electric door opens on the other end of the container, and she guns it driving them both full tilt.

Grant is calm, "We're good to go. You safe?"

"Affirmative. She angry?"

"Sad."

Riordan's heart hurts, "Oh." *Shit.*

"No worries, R. Just do what you've got to do and get back." Grant looks over at Demi, who's staring at him.

"Should I talk with her...tell her I..."

"Riordan, she's in good hands." Grant knows Riordan needs his focus. "Don't worry brotha, I got you."

Riordan exhales, "I know, man. Much appreciated. I'm headed to the L2, then to the Warden."

"Good luck with her. I'm glad you're safe. I've got to dispose of this burner." Grant doesn't want to compromise any of them.

"Yep. All right...Grant? Tell her, well..."

"She loves you, man,...and I will. Be safe."

Riordan feels guilt deep within his core, "Thanks.

"Of course. Out-"

The phone goes dead. Grant hands it to Rashi then fist-pumps his grandson in appreciation for their help. He bids them farewell and backs away. Renyai takes his grandfather's walking stick and uses the spear end to destroy the cell phone he's just thrown to the ground. They both bend down to pick up the pieces and then disappear silently into the thick palm tree brush. Grant smiles and walks towards Demi's chaise lounge in the sun.

53

Loves You

Demi

"Feeling okay, Demi?" Grant eases into the question with a softness in his voice so as not to jolt her awake. He notices her eyes opening slowly.

Demi still feels sad. She knows he'd been talking with Riordan, and she wasn't included. Her heart is heavy as she is worried about him, "I'm alright, a little queasy."

"He loves you, Demi."

"Oh."

"He does."

"Thank you."

Grant can tell she's not happy. "He's doing well, Riordan always does. He was extracted from a small boat he snuck out on, with that elder you just saw talking with me. His Delta buddies picked him up and took him safely to where he needed to be."

"Grant, what if I never see him again? What if he does something to Teo and it ruins us?" Demi's voice is low. It's not like her to lose faith.

Grant understands her angst. "Demi, this is how Rior is. He's the best at what he does, and he has to do it in his time, *his way*. He didn't discuss it with you. Hell, he didn't even tell me until he was leaving. Riordan isn't one to upset others or ask permission. He hates for others to suffer. He'll tell you what you ask...but only after, and only if you really want to know. He's never been one to stress others. It's actually a blessing if you think about it. It's his way. Soldiers do the behind-the-scenes work so others don't have to."

"I believe you. I guess I'm just feeling like my ex has ruined enough. I don't want him being able to hurt my family...my new family. I'm scared, Grant."

Grant bends down to be more eye-level with her, "Demi, Riordan felt so much guilt putting Teo in jail and ruining your life.

He was torn for so long. He hated traumatizing you. Now, he needs to put closure to it and ensure your safety. He feels responsible for so much."

Demi places her hand on Grant's forearm, "He's saved me more times than he'll ever know, Grant…and now, now he's given me the greatest gift." She instinctively cradles her abdomen with one hand. "I didn't even have a chance to tell him." Tears form in her eyes.

Grant cants his head and smiles wide. He completely understands her fear now. Touching her hand on him he nods in congratulations. Hiding his own elation he explains. "Demi, when he finds out you're carrying his child, you'll have cured him, and all this sacrifice will be worth it. I can't think of anything better. You're giving him the greatest gift. I couldn't be happier for you both."

She finally finds a small smile, "Thank…thank you." Her voice is cracking.

"Listen, Riordan is an expert at what he does! He'll be back before you know it."

"You're right." Demi huffs an unconvincing assurance, retracting her hand then pushing his chest a bit and changing the subject, "And YOU? How about that! We were discussing your love for Jeanine weeks back and now look, she's here with even more love yes?"

Grant falls back gently into the sand, a look of awe glowing in his face, "Dems, I- I honestly just have no words for how this day has changed my entire world."

"Right? What a fucking day."

Grant laughs dusting sand off his shorts, "I'm so happy. I can't even begin to tell you how happy I am.

"Who knew you and your best friend would become daddies in the same year."

"I think this is so cool. We are celebrating when he gets his butt back here!" He points a finger at her. "We have so much to be grateful for…oh, and Dems?"

She's smiling for the first time all day, "Yeah?"

"I'm real sorry about the gun stuff in there. Jeanine is real good at finding me but not so good at accepting all the areas of my work. It was okay when she was married but now with the pregnancy and being separated."

Demi huffs and small laugh, "I understand. It was a bit scary at first but luckily she's calm and took the time to hear you." She shrugs her shoulders hoping the fright in her body dissipated while sleeping all afternoon.

Grant knows she's trying to downplay it, "But really, we're both really sorry. After all you've been through."

"I'm stronger than I look Grant."

"That's the truth!"

Grant stands, "Okay, what do you say we get some nourishment? I know you're feeling queasy, but there's got to be something my niece or nephew can eat, right?"

Demi laughs, nodding and raising her hand to him so he can help her up.

54

Volcov

Riordan

Riordan keeps the top two buttons of his dress shirt open and slides the suit jacket up onto his broad shoulders. He has just enough cologne to entice, his hair long to his neck but his beard newly tapered to his strong jawline. Valentina Volcov is not his favorite contact, admittedly, and her reign as warden at Teo's penitentiary is proving to be the corruption he'd foreseen. He takes the tiny recording device and presses it behind his left lapel. Valentina is not a favor he could call in, she does nothing for others, and this could be tricky. Luckily, he knows enough about her profile to test her. He'll do anything it takes to keep Demi safe…*anything.*

Riordan parks the Audi far from the cameras, but he knows she can already see him. He makes sure to leave his weapon secured in the car and walks himself into camera view. He's played this game many times before. He knows how to give just enough to use later in court.

He wasn't asked to sign in. He wasn't even asked who he was visiting. Riordan would have much preferred to arrive through the underground tunnels, but he needed the employee witnesses and the camera proof of his visit. He's escorted, by a pudgy middle-aged corrections officer, to the top floor and brought to a set of very large gray doors that resemble something more of a penthouse entrance, than that of a warden's office. The officer opens the door for him but does not step in, he doesn't even make eye contact. Riordan is sure to catch the name on the round ginger's name-tag. Gerritz is engraved on the brass magnet. He'll be sure to add him to the report file.

Riordan steps into a quiet, ridiculously large office suite and catches the sound of her high heels coming towards him along marbled flooring. She appears in front of him, the low lighting almost erasing the age upon her fifty-something physique. Slender and almost beautiful, Valentina Volcov was what most men would call "exotic". Without a word, she locks eyes with Riordan, comes right up to him, her hands spread running inappropriately up his large chest, her lips meetings his, licking his clenched teeth before pulling away to look him up and down.

"Oooooh Riordan darling, I don't think I've ever seen you looking so…what is dis, alive?" Valentina turns to croon and shakes her rump seductively as she walks towards the couches, waving a hand to invite him to sit.

"Thank you, Volcov." He follows her lead and chooses a seat close but not too close.

She smirks, moving to a chair closer, so she's within reach of his knee, "Valentina, please, Riordan. We are friends, no?" She attempts a smile reminding him of Cruela Deville minus the Dalmatian fur coat and irradiate driving.

Riordan sits back against the couch, adjusting his belt while scanning the room to see where her hidden cameras are. "Of course, Valentina then."

"So out of all the inmates you've graced me with, let me guess who you're here to see…" She searches his face inquisitively.

Riordan knows her game. She's already aware of why he's come. He's sure of it. He just needs to figure out her angle. Valentina has always been a game player, not a team player. He gets to the point, "I need to know why you've let Teo Laczano have such a permissive reach here under your command."

"Surely I don't know what you mean, Tate the Great…" She purrs and smirks attempting to downplay his question with her dismissive manipulation.

Riordan disguises his agitation behind an expressionless gaze. He knows now that Teo has her on his payroll. *Fuck.* This guy's money is everywhere. No matter how much the feds take from him, he finds ways to make more, even from his jail cell. Riordan hates to do it, but he's going to have to play her game. He's certain Teo wants him dead for putting him in jail, giving all his secrets to the feds, and now taking his ex-wife into his bed. He failed with Errol Adler so now he's using Valentina for something…but what?

She leans in, "I think we should get to know each other a bit more, don't you? Perhaps I could help you with whatever troubles you have." She reaches towards Riordan's leg, her warm hand gliding along his jeans towards his inner thigh.

Riordan doesn't flinch, "Oh? What did you have in mind?" His training has taught him that when an older, experienced woman in power uses her prowess and suggests a prolonged connection, she's either lost her power or needs to secure her safety.

"Well, I've got to run…meetings, but I'd like to get together while you're in town. Maybe I could help you with your current case. Are you free, say tonight?" She tilts her head and looks at him through squinted, overly done up eyes. She's testing him.

Riordan knows the game and is already prepared to play. She's not going to give him anything unless she secures what she wants first. Seductively he says, "I'll make time. Where and when?" Looking at her as if he would take her right on the couch.

Valentina Volcov feels a win already! Uncrossing her legs and standing to her full height, she tries to entice him with her figure. Riordan looks up her body, all the way to her waiting eyes. "I'll find you. We'll share some vodka, no?"

"As you wish."

"Hmmm, yes." She looks down at his chest, his tight stomach, and rests upon the front of his jeans. A smile graces her thin lips, which she slowly licks. Lifting her gaze to meet his, she lingers, then turns and walks away. "Let yourself out, darling. I must go."

Riordan watches her disappear, and the sound of her heels on the floor gets farther and farther away. He knows what he has to do. He loathes it, but he'll do anything now. He stands, buttons his jacket, and exits with Demi heavy on his mind, pain in his heart.

Riordan leaves the way he was shown in. He doesn't see any inmates. There is one he could visit who owes him a favor but the guy is a tad psycho. Riordan can't have contact with anyone who might be a loose cannon and take Teo out.

He makes sure he's on camera exiting, his keys in hand. After signing out, making sure to say goodbye to the correctional guards, especially Harry Turner, his veteran buddy with white hair, he departs, making his way to his vehicle. He calls Constance Levy to be sure she booked him a room at the usual swanky posh hotel in town, so Valentina can find him easily and set him up. He knows how she operates. He'd almost bet she's already in Teo's cell. He's got to be careful to be touchable but not enough to be compromised. His next call is to his team. He knows they've listened in on the quick meeting with Valentina and he needs a few extra agents placed within the hotel bar and around the property. The advantage is he's given very little time for Teo to do much. Coming into sight so quickly creates chaos and some danger and with Teo wanting to know where Demi is so badly, he'll make mistakes while still keeping Riordan alive until he gets her. He'll use Voscov like he used Errol Adler…because narcissists always think they are one devious step ahead of the world. Teo's inflated ego is actually very helpful. Kidnapping Demi means he wants her more than he wants to be intelligent. Teo is about power and possessions. If he hated her, he would have just had Adler put a bullet in her. Instead, he tried to take her. Riordan knows he wants *him* dead, but Demi…Demi is a trophy he wants *forever*. Even if he can be with her. Sociopaths like Teo don't want others to have more than them. He *can't* forget her. He feels Riordan took her, ruined him, and locked him away.

He needs Riordan. He needs him to be weak like he is. He thinks Valentina is just the woman to get him whatever he wants. Teo knows nothing of a real man…or the love he and Demi share. He thinks all men can be seduced or paid off. Riordan is not *all* men.

Riordan finishes the last call with his contact in Mexico and starts the engine. He puts the vehicle in drive and pulls out of the penitentiary parking lot, positive he's being watched. He accelerates down the road and gazes at the massive prison he's helped fill. There's no hope of rehabilitation. Not with the level of criminal he'd put there. Satisfied with doing his part in society, first protecting freedoms as a soldier, and then protecting all humans as a contractor, he nods. He's done. He's ready. For the first time in his life he doesn't need to know everything about the future…he just needs her.

Riordan exhales and thinks of his beloved. He sometimes wishes he could reconcile with murderer. This would all be so much easier if he had no regard for life. A bullet to Teo's temple, while out in the prison yard, would take care of all of this *today*.

He rubs his forehead, trying to ease the fatigue behind his eyes. Demi is there in his mind. She's always there. His chest is tight with worry for her. He knows now he never wants to be apart from her ever again. He feels such a deep connection with her; it's now almost physically painful to be away. Everything in him says to just take Teo out, even in the next hour, take him out and get the hell out of dodge. He's only ever killed in self-defense, and at that, it haunts him. The military, in other countries, on missions, it was all kill or be killed. He hates to take life...he would do anything for Demi, though. *Anything*. Errol Adler knows that wherever his bastard soul is.

55

Tiny Island

Riordan

Riordan looks down at his shot glass, his back to the door, which he never, EVER does, but he has to appear off his game, like he's too relaxed and needing her. A hand is suddenly warm on the back of his neck. Riordan uses everything in him not to react. Valentina swings around him, her lips upon his, her tongue forcefully in his mouth. He accepts her gently until she releases. *Whore.*

Valentina Volcov is every bit the wolf her name implies. She croons, "Oh my, Tate the Great is just that aren't you." She slumps down on the barstool next to him. Riordan allows a small smile to appear and looks over at her. "You've started without me...I taste." She reaches her lanky fingers towards his mouth wiping away her lipstick.

Riordan summons his undercover agent, also their bartender, over with two fingers up, "Martini?" Valentina smiles, obviously pleased he not only asked but also suggested the most expensive drink. She likes that he views her as a classy, powerful alpha female.

"Dah, you are lovely." She rubs her hand along his large back and down his suit jacket, snuggling closer to him.

The bartender reaches them, and Riordan speaks assertively, "Manhattan, two olives." The bartender nods and saunters off. Riordan relaxes his gait and turns his body towards her on the stool.

Valentina is trying to be seductive, leaning in, kissing both his cheeks as if to complete her greeting. She inhales his scent then leans back and bit to look him over, "You look tired, Tate. What can I do to help? What's this case about?"

"I am tired, *very* tired Valentina. Like I mentioned before, I need to know why Loczano has...privileges. Why is he able to reach into my work while he's locked up in your house?" He watches her, wondering if she'll turn.

She moves closer, looking at his gorgeous face. His skin, his eyes, the beautiful cheek bones and delectable lips. She wants those lips on her. Valentina Volcov has dreamt of Riordan between her thighs for years. She's determined to get him there this time. Her long witchy fingers reach up and run through his sun-bleached curls, "I like this look, Tate. The longer hair, the closely trimmed beard, the muscles beneath such impressive fabric. Retirement…or this what is it? Vacationing?…it looks good on you."

Riordan chortles, "I guess." He hadn't really let anyone know he was retiring, so she is definitely in and versed on the Teo-Errol Adler thing. He looks at her, wondering if she knows he killed Adler. She retracts her hand as they're approached. She stiffens and sits back. Just as he thought, she's ready to make a scene. He puts his hand out, and Jeremy places the paperwork in it. "Mr. Seikie."

"Tate." The well-built thirty-something is Grant's new trainee, and right on time.

"How we looking?"

"Seven point one, as you offered. Eight bedrooms. The keys will be ready tomorrow after your final signature here."

Riordan takes a pen from inside his jacket and leans into Valentina, whose mouth has dropped open at what she's hearing. "Apologies, my dear, just tying up a few loose ends while I'm in town."

The bartender brings their drinks, and she remains quiet. Riordan knows she now wishes she was playing for the right team. 7.1 million is a whole hell of a lot more than what Teo Loczano could give her. The way she's gulping down her Manhattan, he knows it won't be long before they can head up to his room…well, his fake room. He motions for a second martini.

He signs the papers, happy with himself that he could get this taken care of for him and Demi in a few short hours…and use it to manipulate the wolf sitting next to him. Despite Valentina not giving him shit yet, he did see in one of the papers within the pile the confirmation from his team that she's accepted large sums of cash from an unknown source and is attempting to hide it in an off-shore account. Riordan feels quite sorry for her. Beauty and status got boring, and she succumbed to thinking money would bring her power. He signs the last paper, clicks the pen, and gives everything back to Seikie. "Thank you, sir. I appreciate you coming out on such short notice this evening."

"Sure thing, Mr. Tate, always a pleasure doing business with you." He turns and exits. Valentina watches him leave as she is not one to miss the pleasures of a good looking man. She stares then at Riordan, who finally sips his drink...*3*...*2*...*1*...

"Tate darling, I think we should take our drinks and well... head up to a more comfortable spot. You know, something quieter where we can talk?"

Riordan turns in her direction, looking her deep in the eyes. He can see that she wants to fuck him in a way that leaves her screaming her own Russian father's name while cumming. She's that twisted. It's time. He's tired of the game already. He'll have her rolling over on Teo in less than an hour. "As you wish, Ms. Volcov."

She picks up her clutch and slides down the barstool onto wobbly five-inch heels. Straightening her dress quickly, she gives a quick glance to whoever is her meathead bodyguard in the room then reaches for her second martini. Riordan takes her free hand as if to assist her and downs his drink so as not to have to carry it in the elevator. It was only water, but she doesn't need to know that. He notices she has the dumbest look on her face, and he almost feels sorry for what he's going to do to her. She winks, thinking he doesn't take notice, a tell for her bodyguard to stay put so she can go get laid. Riordan hates this part of the job. He's wondering if she'll bend in the elevator or stick to her guns until after. Her desperation is such a turnoff, almost as much as her dishonesty. He suddenly thinks of Demi, and his heart hurts in his chest. He misses her so much. He just wants this over...there's just that one last piece he hopes comes through. He wants to get the hell out of here and back into her arms.

Valentina walks along swiftly with him, chugging the second martini and placing the glass on a shelf near the elevators. Riordan smirks at her attempt for liquid courage. He can see she's happy with herself. She not only came to get railed by him, a notion he'll never understand for her, but now she's thinking she's going to make bank if she can get him to offer her enough bribe money. She's. A high priced whore. He looks down and over at her profile, her mind going a mile-a-minute with how much of a win she feels she has. He smiles at her sweetly, despising everything that she is, and feels sorry for whatever childhood trauma and daddy issues brought on such self-hatred. He's seen it so many times before and knows all too well he can't fix character; he won't even try. Riordan lifts his large hand and uses his index finger to move the hair away from her eye. She thinks it's endearing. He's just making sure her face is in full view of the cameras.

The elevator doors open, and he lets her step in ahead of him. He gives a quick glance out the door to his east end guy and flicks two fingers down by his side to signal that he wants no more than twenty minutes with the wolf. The doors close, and she launches herself at him locking her lips on his as if she's desperate for his tongue. Riordan plays along and places his free hand gently on the small of her back, pressing her into him. He knows there is no way he can get hard for this woman, but he can at least pretend it's starting. She jabs her tongue in his mouth, and he hears her clutch fall to the floor. Her hands come up and slide along his beard and then to his neck, where she grasps him fiercely so he can't get away. He slows his breathing, but hers only gets more erratic. He can tell she's a horrible lay. He thinks of Demi and how she's ruined him with all others women because of her loving goddess magic...he also hopes she won't hate him for this.

Riordan finds the zipper around the neck area in the back of Valentina's dress and slowly begins to click each tooth slowly, *slowly* down. Valentina moans a bit, letting him know she's pleased with his moves. She's kissing him deeper...he's yielding things wishing the damn elevator would reach his floor.

She moves her right hand from his beard, and he knows exactly where she headed with it, right to his crotch. Every girl who learns to fuck from porn has the same moves. She reaches down and cups him, then squeezes. He takes note of her cold, rigid Russian way yet moans softly anyway. He knows she's wondering why her tongue-judo and dildo grip aren't helping him get stiff. She's probably used to little "fuck-boys" as Demi would say.

The elevator dings twice, and the doors open. She releases from him and swings around, bending over to pick up her clutch bag while resting her tush in his crotch. He hears her giggle and fights the urge to bounce her out and right on her neck, snapping it and making the night a short one. He'd never hurt a woman, but he sure wouldn't mind seeing those like Valentina get their karma. She's been a part of so many getting hurt in all this, a money whore for Teo Loczano instead of an upstanding warden who runs a tight ship. Riordan wonders if she enjoyed her last day at her job.

She finally stands tall and begins to walk. He guides her towards his penthouse suite as he looks into the camera knowing the team is probably getting a kick out of the hot mess "Volcov the Wolf" turns into when she's all hot-n-bothered.

Riordan lets them in, and Valentina kicks off both her heels sending them across the room. She's got her zipper all the way down so he can see the top of her black laced thong peeking out of the low back open area of her dress. The lights are low, and he's happy about that. Judges need to hear audio with these types of cases, not see nakedness in their courtroom. Riordan doubts this will ever have to be seen in a courtroom but just as a precaution he's videoing every moment. He does enjoy rules, so he begins.

"So Ms. Volcov, here we are. Why don't w-" Riordan see her pivot and come at him, her eyes squinted, her body heaving onto him so he has to catch her. Again, she assaults him with her seventh-grade level kissing, and he's unable to finish his sentence.

Valentina wraps her lanky legs around his waist and squeezes uncomfortably, thinking this is what he wants like any other guy, but he is not like any other guy. Her lips continue to slobber all over him, her fingers fumbling at his shirt buttons. Like a rabid animal riddled with attention deficit disorder, she switches to his suit jacket and tries to push it inside out over his large biceps. Pushing his arms away, she soon realizes his grasp on her is gone! She slides down him and has to land with her feet on the floor. Riordan is relieved because she has to take her fish lips with her. She giggles at her faux pas and begins yanking on his coat. Why some women tried to *aggressively* take his clothes off, over the years, always baffled him. It's actually a running joke within his teams, who've had the pleasure of watching him on camera or undercover because he's rather large and clothing does not simply come off. They all think it's hilarious that he has to have most of his clothing custom sew to accommodate for his overbuilt thighs and biceps. Watching audacious women try their power moves on him is quite entertaining for his coworkers.

He takes the opportunity to speak as she's yanking and pulling, "So, Valentina…"

"Yes."

"Yes?"

"Dah. I will help you."

"Uh-"

She finally gets his coat to the floor and finishes the buttons of his shirt. "You want Loczano, you got him….but it's going to cost you."

And there it is, exactly what he needed her to say. "Name your price."

She flings his shirt open and stops to gaze at his tan chest, her eyebrows raising and her face reminding him of the Grinch when he takes presents from under the tree. "Well,… first we need to see how well we uh…work together?" She looks up at him as sultry as she can and lowers to run her lips up his stomach and to his pec. Her touch is disgusting, her energy a black hole.

He cringes and knows his crew is laughing their asses off, "Well, we aren't doing such bad work right now, Dah?" He makes fun of her.

Valentina giggles and take his nipple into her stiff, emotionless mouth. "You are funny AND sexy, aren't you, Tate?"

"I guess I am." Knowing he's getting close to the twenty minutes mark before his men arrive and knowing she's going to get quite annoyed when she learns none of this is getting him hard, he tries again, "So are we talking about 3.5 million kinds of working together…or say four…?" He needs her to god-damn agree to a price on audio.

He stops her assault on his poor nipple, fairly sure Demi would not appreciate seeing Valentina's teen level evidence on him. She looks up into his eyes. She is enamored with his numbers. She smiles and inhales, pinching his other nipple between her fingers making him want to heave her lanky witch body across his penthouse suite. "Well, I think four would be a good start, dahling no?"

And there it is, just what he needed. "Four million then?"

"Four million." Valentina Volcov just agreed to take a bribe in exchange for being a narc against Teo Loczano. Riordan couldn't be happier. Step one is done. He can now focus on the next phase and stopping her degenerate mauling of him. Like clockwork, he can hear the keycard slide in the door and his crew come busting into the suite. Valentina yelps something in her Russian tongue, reactively covering herself with her hands despite not being fully undressed. Riordan reaches down to begin buttoning his shirt, thankful he can soon feel the shower back at his real hotel room and shower her drool off.

"Ma'am, turn around and place your hand at the back of your neck." Agent Constantine Levy is more than happy to do a female pat-down and take Valentina "the wolf" Voscov into custody. She looks as if she's waited all day for this.

Valentina is appalled. She looks at Riordan as she turns, "Grebanyy Mudak!"

"Spasibo." He steps away and lets his employees do their job, bending over to pick up his suit jacket. He smiles, sending gratitude out for his good luck. He smiles thinking of Demi in his arms by tomorrow.

"Valentina Volcov, you have the right to remain silent. Anything you say-" Constantine is beaming as she recites Valentina's fifth amendment Miranda rights. Valentina is furiously resisting while speaking in very fast Russian, only what Riordan could recognize as the foulest words he's ever heard in such a beautiful language. She is livid and rightfully so. He set her up the same way she allowed Teo to set up Demi with Errol Adler. She let Loczano have reach out of the prison walls Riordan put him behind to protect *everyone*, especially Demi. Now she'll pay the price and be behind bars herself.

Riordan looks up and sees Dean Lowren standing by the door. His gray hair is totally white now. He nods at Riordan and steps out. Riordan steps around Valentina, who is trying to spit on him with that wretched mouth of hers. He follows and meets Dean waiting out in the hall.

Dean Lowren, a long time friend and confidant, waits for Riordan, his hand out with a smile. Riordan shakes his hand, "Dean."

"Tate, I'm glad you called."

"I appreciate the short notice work. Time is of the essence with Loczano."

"Oh, I know. He's a bastard that one."

Riordan turns his suit jacket sleeves right-side-in and put it back on, "So Mexico then?"

"Yep, he's shipping out within the hour to one Felix Pedro, Warden to 2700 of the world's finest in Apodaca Prison, Mexico. He's eagerly awaiting Loczano's arrival. Maximum security now, and let me tell you, that man is none too happy that Teo Loczano got away with killing his whole family in that minivan ambush. You know that bastard hung all five of them from the bridge in Uruapan?"

Riordan runs his fingers through his hair to fix it, "Yeah, that was a tragedy, Dean."

"Kids, wife, even the grandmother. I don't give Loczano a week."

Riordan nods, "I'm out of this mess now. I just purchased a small island with a beautiful home out where none of this can reach me anymore. I'm out."

"Retirement Tate?" Dean chortles.

"Yep."

Dean's eyebrow lift, "I can't imagine he'll last long. If Pedro don't get him, the Zetas will. He can just drop him in gen pop and nature will take its course." He shrugs his shoulders.

Riordan huffs, "Nature. Yeah…I guess that is nature." He laughs and presents his hand, "Hey Dean, I owe ya, man, thank you so much for doing this. I gotta get back to my lady and surprise her with her own tiny island."

"My pleasure Tate, I'm glad you called. I owed you. Hey, take care of yourselves wherever in the world you go. I'm just a phone call away if you or Grant ever need anything." He shakes Riordan's hand and walks towards the elevators.

56

Return

Demi

Demi can feel the heat of the sun streak coming through the tiny cabin window. It warms one eyelid, the ray glistening down her cheek, neck, and right breast. She realizes she's naked in the room but, she doesn't care. It takes a lot of strength to care about anything now that he's gone. It's been days...

She stretches and rolls over, letting the sheet fall the rest of the way off, her hand reaching over to his side of the bed, then under his pillow. She dreamt that he was there, yet her hands find no warmth. She negotiates to go back to sleep, so she can avoid the emptiness of his absence for awhile longer. Her stomach growls, but surprisingly the morning sickness is not taking over just yet. She snuggles down, inhaling deep, she can smell him, his musk, his skin...his essence. It soothes. She aches inside for him. Her love is ever deeper.

The aroma of strong coffee permeates her nostrils, it smells glorious, she pauses, not knowing if it's a phantom scent or somehow real...and if "Baby Bean" is going to let her enjoy coffee today. She rolls over, realizing she's waking, whether she likes it or not. Suddenly she thinks of Grant and Jeanine. Perhaps the coffee smell is coming from them out on the porch!

"Shit-" Demi whispers and feels around for the sheets to cover herself. Her eyes open then, and there, above her, are the same monotonous palm leaf shaped ceiling fan arms swaying around and around. She rests her forearm on her forehead, trying to determine if it's another morning of tears or just agitation. The hormones are not very nice, and she rests her eyes taking a deep inhale.

A bag crinkles. He places his takeout coffee cup down and rises from the chair he's watched her from for three hours. He so grateful she's awake. He's missed her so, so much.

Demi sees his silhouette, "Riordan!" She sits up abruptly, launching at him, and he catches her in his arms.

"Hey, baby." He falls with her to his side of the bed and kisses her deeply. There are no words to describe how good it feels to hold her.

Demi grabs his face in her hands, pulls away to look at him, then continues to kiss him like it was their first time again. He looks beautiful! He smells amazing! She wants all of him!

Riordan cradles her head in his hand. He feels the need to be extra gentle with her. He's wounded her, he left. That's not something he feels good about, but he does feel good about both Teo Loczano and Valentina Volcov disappearing from their lives for good. He turns his head to kiss her deeper.

Demi can't express what's going on inside her body. His energy is igniting every cell within her, just knowing she's carrying his child, that he is the father, that *they* together created life from their beautiful connection. No one can ever take this...

Riordan senses a hunger within her, an intensity he's familiar with and honored to be the recipient of. He presses into her, and an uncontrollable throaty moan escapes her. He drags his warm palm down her back all the way to her perfect cleft. Pulling her in, he presses again, knowing he's awakened her goddess energy. Demi moans again but deep in *his* throat, kissing more aggressively now her arousal building.

She releases her hips and grinds into him again, tantrically squeezing her inner energy up and through her chakras to meet his. She feels she may explode if she doesn't feel him inside her soon. It's as if her being has been taken over by his spell, his energy, her most favorite in the world. She feels him trace down her tush and along her thigh, so she lifts her leg up and over his hip. Riordan caresses the back of her knee pit ever so lightly, then pulls her leg in more so he can press into her as they breathe. His passion is infectious, and she's ready to meet it. Their love is undeniable. She knows for sure she's exactly where she's meant to be...in his arms.

Riordan's jeans are soft, and she can feel his warmth and want for her beneath them. Reaching down, she finds his prefect manhood already engorged, yearning for her touch. She gently squeezes, his own deep moan escaping. She reaches down with the other hand and unfastens and unzips all that is in the way of their fire fully igniting. She frees him from his underwear and slows her touch along his long smooth shaft. He's so fevered with want for her, she's unsure if she wants him inside her mouth first or her womb. God, she loves his body, he's such an Adonis, and he's all hers. Demi moves from his lips and suckles down his neck unbuttoning his shirt. The smell of hotel shampoo mixed with his faint musky cologne makes her tingle inside as she continues her trail of oral pleasure down his chest...stomach...and waist sliding his shorts down. Riordan's breath hitches in his throat as she engulfs him swiftly in her mouth, taking him all the way in. She loosens her mouth to caress and cradle him within it, her fevered moistness at the same time gently cupping his well-endowed scrotum; caressing and embracing him. She suckles lovingly taking him a bit deeper. Riordan inhales through clenched teeth and grabs the sheets in response to her tender oral rapture. She knows how to render him resistless in a matter of moments.

"Dem...I'm-"

Sensing his tension, she releases her mouth and climbs up his massive frame. His hands come up to find her waist, but before he can catch his breath, Demi slides her glistening slickness over and down liesurely onto his rock hard shaft. Both of them exhale in sheer pleasure, and she begins a rhythm not quite as slow as they're used to. Rocking, her want and desire have taken over, and she takes all of him. Riordan tries to grasp at her hips for fear that if he doesn't, he may explode. Her beautiful, slick warmth nestles and suckles at him. He fights to remain with her splendacious pleasuring. Demi leans back, her arms raising up and running through her own hair, her yoni taking over and lulling him into her spell. Riordan lifts and sits upright, hugging her to him to tame her wildness with his grasp. His mouth meets hers, and he explores her with his tongue. She's all his, and he loves her so much.

Realizing he's still clothed and she fully naked, he turns her and places her onto her back releasing from her a moment to compose himself and disrobe. He's getting too close, and he doesn't want their pleasure to end too soon. She looks gorgeous, breathing erratically with want for him. He pulls his shift off and onto the floor. Next is his shorts and boxer briefs. He looks down at her as if she's his everything, and he's about to show her. Demi grabs for him, her body writhing and pulsing for him. He slides down, his arms coming up under her rump, his tongue supple, finding her clit with perfection. Demi calls out some form of a word not quite in their language and runs her fingers through his hair as she arches up towards his suckling mouth. She can't take his oral hedonism and begins climaxing unexpectedly! She moans languidly, he recognizes his name within her breathless prayer. His cock responds to her pleasure sounds, and he feels himself pulse against the bedsheets. God, she can really affect him. He loves every inch of this woman.

Knowing she's crashing down and will be intensely sensitive, Riordan releases his suckling and trails kisses along her hip and up her tummy. He notices she's been incredibly orgasmic lately, an insatiable hunger that appeals. He slides his palm up and onto her abdomen to ease her yoni convulsions. He loves what all happens within her, she's truly a miracle, and he has so much respect now for her goddess energy.

Demi grabs his hand and brings it to her lips, panting. She puts her face in his palm and closes her eyes. She can't express how grateful she is that he's returned. The not knowing and not hearing his voice or knowing he was safe was *killing* her. She pulls at his hand, signaling for him to come to her. He complies, his body still fully responding to her every breath. He moves up, and she looks into his eyes with more love than he could ever ask for. Demi reaches up under his arms and pulls him into her body, her legs open, enticing him into her sacredness. He slides into her, filling her, groaning into her neck at the contentment of her. She wraps around him snug never wanting to let him go.

Riordan balances on his forearms, her body accepting and taking him deep. He moans, his deep voice breathless in her ear. She's already turned on again as the girth of him fills her completely. She begins her tantric squeeze at the end of each of his deep thrusts and breathes with him through each loving, energetic exchange. This time the movement is slow and labored. He moves his hand around to the back of her neck to cradle her, kissing her souly…making her feel safe. Making *them* feel safe. He is every bit their protector, and she feels there is no better man. She couldn't ask for a better father for their child. She can feel him getting close, and she wants this reuniting of their souls to be bliss.

"Riordan baby…" She's now breathless in his ear, only the two of them able to hear the whisper.

Riordan tries to look at her, his body trying to take over, "Yes- my love?" He thrusts deeper, she accepting then squeezing him.

"I have to tell you a secret."

"Anything, baby." He moves closer with his ear to her mouth, her hot breath teasing his climax.

Demi whispers to his soul, "We created life, my love…we're going to have a baby. I'm having your child, *Riordan*………"

Heaven rushes through them, surging through them as heaven will, in the world of a tantric…

in *a soul of a tantric-*

DEZI GOLDEN is an American Author from

Burlington, New Jersey. This is her fifth novel. Dezi lives with her family in Las Cruces, New Mexico.

Find Dezi online or write her at dezigolden@gmail.com.

Acknowledgments:

The author would like to acknowledge:

That tantra, neo-tantra, erotica, sex, or intimacy in this novel is fictitious. It is not to offend anyone or their personal preferences, culture, or history.

I am grateful to those who shared their experiences and time with me as I was researching my story's characters, scenarios, plot, and careers. Your generosity and friendship is so appreciated.

My proofreader, Domonique Penci, who followed this story through its many chapters, THANK YOU. Your extraordinary focus is contagious.

My family members who read my books, my friends who support me, my fans who are dedicated and leave such loving reviews I APPRECIATE you. Thank you for being in my world.

And lastly, to those relationships, tantric and otherwise, that nurtured me into loving love and forever wanting to write about it. I need you always. Thank you.

Praise for novels of Author Dezi Golden

Soul of a Tantric

"Lose yourself in this remarkable story!"

-Miami Herald

"This author has successful invented a new genre. Tantric Erotic is my new favorite."

— ethos.com

"Human sexuality is varied, complex. Thank you for reminding all of us that turn-ons ands kinks originate from love not man-made porn." **newyou.org**

"I've never read a more sex positive novel. Admittedly, I read it at least once a month!"

- D. Penci, Fivr.com

"Tantra enhances my senses of the spiritual in the sexual. Thank you Dezi Golden!" - **Biva Lyant, Sacramenti Book Review**

"The language of sex had yet to be invented. The language of senses explored. Dezi did it. I'm a fan forever!"

-D. Freedah, Amazon Germany

Golden has written another amazing book. She expresses with words the stories our bodies want to tell!"

bestsellr.com

"She gives readers insight as to the love they deserve and should seek. This is every bit the satisfying novel, and exactly what I look for."   - Jeremy Ward, Erotie Book Review

Thank you for purchasing this book published by Author, Dezi Golden.

To receive an autographed copy for your collection. Contact the author at dezigolden.com or dezigolden@gmail.com.

www.ingramcontent.com/pod-product-compliance
Lightning Source LLC
Chambersburg PA
CBHW051532020726
47506CB00007B/1050